the puppet king

and other atonements

justin a. burnett

ISBN: 978-1-68510-047-6 (sc)
ISBN: 978-1-68510-048-3 (ebook)

First printing edition: May 20, 2022
Printed by Trepidatio Publishing in the United States of America.
Cover Design by Justin A. Burnett
Cover Layout by Don Noble
Edited by Sean Leonard
Proofreading and Interior Layout by Scarlett R. Algee

Trepidatio Publishing, an imprint of JournalStone Publishing
3205 Sassafras Trail
Carbondale, Illinois 62901

Trepidatio books may be ordered through booksellers or by contacting:
JournalStone | www.journalstone.com

TREPIDATIO
PUBLISHING

praise for
the puppet king
and other atonements

"An inheritor to the mantles of Ligotti and Langan, Justin Burnett writes bleak, unrelenting and philosophically challenging horror that chills every dimension of its reader—mind, body, and spirit. Through lush prose, his debut collection, *The Puppet King and Other Atonements*, unravels the fabric of reality to explore the deepest trenches of loss, self, and human experience that lie beneath its frayed surface. Burnett is an exciting new writer to watch and *The Puppet King* is well worth your attention." —Kurt Fawver, author of WE ARE HAPPY, WE ARE DOOMED

"With grippingly beautiful prose, Justin Burnett weaves a tapestry of philosophical and existential nightmares that speak to grief, love, identity, and the human condition. These tales have weight and immediacy; they give us glimpses of the dark, unfathomable edges of the world, pulling back just enough to leave a lasting impact that had me still chewing over the stories long after reading, savoring each one. There are flashes of Ligotti, Langan, Barron, and Padgett, yet make no mistake: this is a wholly original collection that ought to cement Burnett as a must-read new author. He has crafted some of the most compelling horror I've read in recent memory, and I can't wait to see what Burnett has in store for us next. Do yourself a favor: read this one with the lights on!" —Jo Kaplan, author of IT WILL JUST BE US

"A collection brimming with sublime torments. Burnett masterfully grasps the transcendent grotesque, weaving tales charged with cosmic danger. A refreshing and powerful new voice in contemporary dread." —Rebecca Gransden, author of SEA OF GLASS

"Burnett takes you through a journey of contrasts. At once delicate and painfully intimate, yet vast, reverberant and strange, *The Puppet King and Other Atonements* draws the reader deep into the primordial to the very edge of the stars. Highly recommended." —Emma J. Gibbon, author of DARK BLOOD COMES FROM THE FEET

"Burnett weaves a surreal web of horror that is familiar, uncomfortable, and beautiful. Many images from *The Puppet King* are going to haunt me for a long time." —Vincenzo Bilof, author of THE PROFANE

contents

introduction

TO BEGIN WITH a disclaimer, Justin A. Burnett has become a friend of mine.

We share an uncommon amount in common. We are both fans of horror, and both have a voracious appetite for trying to keep in touch with new and emerging forces in the broad "indie horror" scene. We both have a fascinating with fear across media, and have bonded over not only short stories and novels, but comics and video games as well. Most importantly, we are both Texans.

Texans, as anyone who has ever had the fortune/misfortune of knowing one will tell you, inherit a sort of "bigness" from our state. We tend to have large personalities, outsized egos, and loud voices. I don't know if it's something in the culture, the water, or both, but there's a mix of obnoxiousness and charm that characterizes most Texans when they travel "abroad" (i.e., anywhere outside of Texas). Justin and I both, however, have a complicated relationship with home, although he is far more upfront about this in his fiction than I am.

In particular, the Texas panhandle looms large in Burnett's fiction. At the risk of offending anyone from the panhandle, I am in the habit of apologizing to anyone who tells me they've driven through it. As the unnamed narrator of "The Golden Thread," explains:

> "I'm sure you noticed how derelict the panhandle is. Like someone bought the whole goddamned state in an auction and promptly died heirless."

There is an emptiness in the Texas panhandle unlike anywhere in the world. Burnett touches on this in "The Golden Thread," creating a story that echoes Algernon Blackwood's "The Willows" in its evocation of mesquite trees:

> "It wouldn't strain most people's imagination to describe this area as 'treeless' — in truth you're standing in one of the thickest forests in the nation. These knobbed little freaks are trees, same as any other."

One can't help, for a moment, to accept Burnett's love for the panhandle, a part of the country with all the hallmarks of rural America (inexplicably still-standing gas stations turned churches, vague warnings about the return of Christ plastered across peeling wooden walls, and an uncertain mix of the friendliest people you've ever met and those who don't take kindly to outsiders) but harsher, vaster and more enduring. Maybe the next time I have to drive through the panhandle, God help me, I'll be less impatient to leave.

But though Justin is my friend, and though we're both Texans, I would not be writing this if I did not believe that what you have before you is an exciting debut collection. When introducing a "new writer" (I say "new" even though Justin Burnett has been writing and publishing since 2016), there is an immediate impulse to try and place their work in dialogue with more established voices. Reading Justin Burnett, there are inevitable comparisons to other writers. One identifies equal parts Ligotti, Slatsky and Padgett in the introductory story, "The Toy Shop," which establishes the mood and reoccurring themes of the collection. "m.Other" invokes Gemma Files, Jonathan Raab, and other writers who use descriptions of other media to further the telling of their stories. But that's just it. At the end of the day, these are clearly *not* anyone's stories but Burnett's.

And that is a very good thing.

Central to many of the following stories is a sense of dread and loss, particularly how losses haunt entire families. It would be easy to get lost in the many simultaneous stories of "The Toy Shop," which includes an apocalypse, a strange doll, and a family feud. But the anchor of the story is a woman's grief over the death of her son, and the inability to cultivate a relationship with him. Something similar may be said of "Endemic," which centers on the disappearance of a mother and the strained (though not unloving) relationship between a father and daughter. The theme of family, and of loss in family, comes up once more in "m.Other," which is one of my favorite stories in this collection. The nexus of relationships between husbands, wives, jobs, and mothers contribute the uneasiness of "She," a story which would be creepy enough even without a shambling, faceless mannequin accompanying a serial killer. "Our Endeavors" is another story of desperation and family loss, though the witness to this story is themselves something of a cosmic horror.

But then, there are the ideas, the philosophies of these stories, too. The best writers to whom I could compare Burnett take a risk in engaging things like capitalism critically, and it is always a gamble. This is the nature of this collection's titular story, "The Puppet King," told through a lecture complete with citations and philosophic allusions that would make any Borges reader giddy. Luckily, Burnett's characters are intelligent, but they do not talk past the readers. Nor is it the case that one need approach Burnett as they do Borges, with an encyclopedia next to them just in case they need to reference some obscure historical moment. We are instead taken through the locales and themes slowly, introduced to the mythologies of black metal, of the barren and long patch of earth that is the Texan panhandle, and even outer space. Indeed, though set in space (and thus regrettably not a "horror" story), "ABDN-1" centers on Burnett's interest in religion, or rather religiosity, which characterizes his magazine, *Mysterium Tremendum*.

I often joke: "Texas is barely big enough for two Texans."

However, it is my pleasure and honor to introduce you to Justin Burnett. I believe that you will, as I have, find yourself thinking about these stories long after you put them down. But be careful, lest you dwell on them for too long. The shadows outside, knobbed little freaks though they are, are trees just like any other, and just as good for disappearing into than any other forest.

—S L. Edwards

the puppet king
and other atonements

the toy shop

ON THE MORNING I discovered the doll, I wondered what Braxon's rain had been like. The one I walked through was a listless drizzle conjuring a cold mist from the sidewalk, the kind one might abstractly describe as romantic but find oppressive in reality. Was Braxon's uncomfortable? I hope it wasn't. It *had* rained on the day in question—whether it was light or heavy, sagged in curtains or whipped to an angle, no one could say. There was rain, however. He wouldn't have seen the sun. It's impossible not to think about that.

Over the months, I collected this information from the Internet, a single day exploded into a spectrum of useless details—it was a Sunday, appropriately enough, Sunday having always been the dreariest of days; there was the rain, and an electronic candle left aglow on the nightstand with a plastic flame that bobbed back and forth in a convincing play of reality (This detail is from memory, and I'm tempted to wonder if he had watched it while...But no, that's too far). It was the day of a shooting in Pittsburgh, an Evangelical church blown to pieces by an angry young man in military fatigues. In the early morning, a fishing boat had departed from Boston only to be lost in some unknown disturbance at sea. It was a day set aside for evil, an attack on the dreams we conjure to help us believe that our lives follow rational paths to quiet, honest deaths.

Was Braxon's death quiet? Was it honest? A woman I once thought of as a friend back in days of Colorado City sent me a message on social media asking permission to present Braxon's "situation" to her congregation. "We believe in God's power to bring your boy to repentance. Through the Almighty, all things are possible." I blocked her without answering.

Who can say how quiet an overdose is? Is it like falling asleep? Is there pain when the heart fails to force life into the brain? I do feel that it was honest—perhaps more so than dying in a hospital bed surrounded by friends and family, the very people most eager to begin the process of forgetting.

No, Braxon has no need for repentance. It's God who owes the apology. Or at least a fucking explanation.

As I walked through the rain on the morning I discovered the doll, these were the shades that filled my mind. I write this with confidence since there has long been little else to think about. Some events become details of a memory, vignettes in a larger story that masters them into a sense of meaning. With Braxon's death, I discovered another, rarer type of event, one of infinite hunger that swallows the rest, a bottomless grave waiting for everything before and after.

The store was on the corner of one of the many forgotten streets winding away from the courthouse like the broken fingers of a web. The row of nearly identical shops passed on one side, mirrored by the vastness of the city on the other, hidden behind the mist. I walked every morning in those days, careful to avoid retracing my steps, unmoored in a place faintly unreal next to the gleaming radiation of my son's suicide.

I would have missed the display window if not for the way it briefly caught and intensified the diffuse glow of the fog. Dusted with grime like the others, what lay behind it was nearly invisible: faint slopes of tiny shoulders nestled between featureless heads as small as fists. It was a toy shop, I realized with astonishment as I neared the door. Not a comic book store filled with plastic monsters from adult video games and busts of superheroes designed for display, but a living anachronism of figures made for children in an age where children learn to use a touchscreen before they walk.

I've never been much of a shopper, and the general waning of desire following Braxon's death had only increased my aversion to crowded spaces. But I suddenly felt an affinity for things left to gather dust on high shelves, sympathy for obsolete objects made without the practical world in mind, things trapped midway between death and life in their fertile uselessness. Like them, I wanted to recede from being without ceasing to be.

I stepped inside, startling the thin, bespectacled man behind the counter.

"Good evening, ma'am," he said.

I nodded and quickly vanished in the maze of shelves. It was surprisingly hot inside the cramped shop. A heater hummed somewhere, generating excessive humidity that didn't seem conducive to the preservation of plastic merchandise.

Porcelain dolls with tiny hands and faces gray with age filled one shelf; wooden tops, their strings hopelessly tangled in pale masses crowded another. I bent down to peer into a knee-high basket packed with faded toy cars, jagged angles of broken doors and fragments of shattered plastic windows jutting dangerously from the indistinct mess.

The cars began to stir some of the pain I doubtlessly sought. Memories of the strange, distant boy I lost flickered to life somewhere in the depths before winking out like a dream. I breathed deeply, savoring the sting, happy that the pain had become a bridge, however insufficient.

I waded through a toy kitchen. A tiny plastic oven was stuffed with a horde of plush rabbits, their faces crammed and distorted against the glass door. A stack of miniature pans tilted dangerously from a sink, and the smell of food and rust was real. Plastic dinosaurs shared the cupboard with teacups—a thin film of sour condensation seemed to cover everything.

And there he was again, just a glimpse: a boy with a shock of gold hair kneeling shirtless on the carpet surrounded by a waning moon of dinosaurs. When he turned, the brilliance of his blue eyes made me smile. I held the smile, remembering the forgotten act of smiling, intent on savoring the recognition and smiling like an idiot in the empty shop that reeked of dust and mildew.

I selected a few of the dinosaurs from the cupboard, one bipedal with teeth and small, ineffectual arms, and another with a neck like a giraffe's. Braxon would know what to call these things. He would've known their diet, what geological period they inhabited, and where their bones were discovered. I held them together, the one with teeth facing the one with the neck, posed for a battle to the death. It was exactly how Braxon would've held them. I kept the pose, mimicking the thing I wanted to drag back across the border, letting the uselessness of the gesture warm me with sorrow. Tears didn't fill my eyes, though I was no longer afraid of weeping. I had stopped crying months ago, as if the well inside me had been emptied and all that was left was a cavernous tunnel humming sadly in the wind.

I don't remember how long I stood there. When I was finished, I took the plastic dinosaurs and turned toward what I believed to be the exit, but the aisles of toys were now unfamiliar. Games packaged in cardboard boxes worn featureless with age, decks of cards warped at the corners by handling, miniature instruments, keyboards, guitars, and violins, snapped in various places to expose strings or wires meant to remain hidden.

I rounded a corner, barely noticing the unfamiliar rows of objects before rounding another, winding, as it seemed, deeper and deeper into the toy store's heart. The heat was pulsing now; a finger of cold sweat traced the lower curve of my spine.

Then I found the dolls.

The shelves were filled with them: ventriloquist dummies in various states of decay, Barbies with absentee patches of hair, plastic infants missing fingers and eyes. I recognized Punch and Judy's exaggerated features, outlines of TV characters hidden beneath layers of gray dust. And somewhere beneath it all, a giggle, a smell; Braxon's bright little presence before the later years could desecrate it, the thumping of tiny feet on the carpet, a sound sealed safely from the man who would grow up to murder himself.

I stopped. "Braxon?" I said aloud in the alley of uncanny grins half-hidden by shadows.

Something had changed.

The Braxon I heard then wasn't summoned from the mists of imagination. The edge of his voice wasn't soured by my own unhappiness. It was bright as water, sharp as sunlight. His steps resounded on the physical panels of the wooden floor, somehow, impossibly, escaped from the imaginal hell I'd made for us both.

I reached into the tangle of dolls, inexplicably guided by him, as if his real presence were condensed to a point somewhere beneath the heaps of discarded toys. Yet he was all around me too—for the briefest moment, he was everywhere, nowhere, and in one gleaming star like a teardrop at the bottom of a cardboard box.

I dug deeper. My hand closed around a small limb and I felt a connection, a key turning in a lock, the wet dog smell of my child's hair after an afternoon outside. The months of mourning welled up then, trembling to burst in a new flood of horrific joy.

Then he was gone. I stared dumbly at the doll in my hand, an unremarkable, androgynous wooden figure of unmistakable antiquity. It possessed a humanoid form and nothing else, a small mannequin without a face. I tucked it between the plastic dinosaurs I cradled and hurried on, wondering if I had genuinely crossed paths with some spectral presence of my son. The more likely explanation—that I was losing my mind—occurred to me only in passing.

To my surprise, the front counter and the frail man hunched behind it appeared around the next corner. "Have you found everything you were looking for?" he asked, eyeing me suspiciously above his glasses.

I placed the items carefully on the counter.

He picked up the dinosaurs and inspected every inch of them, looking, presumably, for a price tag. Finding none, he grunted and turned to the doll. Something indefinite passed over his features. At the moment, I didn't care to know what it was.

"No children, I hope?"

I didn't answer—the oddity of the question somehow failed to surprise me.

"Many of these things," the man said, gesturing to the shelves behind me, "have retired from the cruel ontological experiments of children. It is with them that humans first discover the malleability of the world. It's against these unfortunates that mankind first tests the boundaries of creation."

He placed the faceless doll on the pitted counter before me and typed a prohibitive price into the register.

"'There is in a great toy store an extraordinary gaiety which makes it preferable to the finest bourgeois apartment. Is not the whole of life to be found there in miniature, and in forms far more colorful, pristine, and polished than the real thing?' Baudelaire wrote that. One often wonders," the man said, grinning with satisfaction, "if the damned were better left with their caretakers."

The look of shock on the gnomish creature's face when I silently produced my credit card and paid the outrageous fee would've greatly amused me in another time. Muttering incoherently, the defeated old man carefully stacked the toys in a paper bag. Without looking back, I marched to the door, back into my own hell, leaving the old man to swelter in the steam of his.

‡‡

On the night of the supernova, I remember waking suddenly. I waited, as usual, for Conrad, waited to see if his weight would shift the mattress beneath me or if I'd feel a sleep-blind hand clumsily navigating in the dark. What would happen, I often wonder, if he *did* appear? Could I bear that any easier than his absence? Not that we didn't get along—it was marriage number two for both of us, and our expectations were thoroughly realistic. Nevertheless, there are days when I imagine I see him hunched over the computer in the study and I bend down to whisper something stupid and playful into his ear—I see it clearly, though colorless, a memory muted with disuse. I see the coast and a lighthouse jutting obscenely from a knot of rock offshore—he's in the foreground of this image, lank and bearded and smiling contentedly despite the cold wind screaming from the waves. This one's shamelessly picturesque, as if it were invented by nostalgia. At least in that moment, we were just a little too perfect—too carefree to ever last.

Finally, I was satisfied that he wasn't there. I didn't blame him and I wouldn't have it differently. Braxon wasn't *his*, after all, and despite the impressive effort at sympathy, I eventually forced him to the conclusion that I didn't *want* to heal. He framed it like an accusation and apologized for it later, as if it were a flaw of mine he had purposely exaggerated—I assured him it was simply the truth.

I rose and staggered sleepily through what I mistook for spare rays of dawn stabbing through cracks in the curtains. The mosaic tiles beneath my feet—patterns of brown and dark green I had once hated before I lost the will to feel one way or another about them—were colder than usual. I sank into the chair before the desk and clicked on the computer. I failed to notice that three hours had passed rather than the usual seven. On the night of the supernova—the first occurrence in a series that would reset the indifferent continuum of existence outside the walls that immured me—I indulged my obsession with the same bland desperation that had become my peculiar *élan vital,* a force that gave and consumed in equal proportions.

Mark, the man who had purchased by auction the contents of Braxon's apartment during my grief-stricken paralysis, informed me that the sofa and coffee table were still in his possession, and just *how much* did I say I'd be willing to pay for them? I'd never been rich, even with Conrad, and the inevitably of losing the new car I never drove, followed, eventually, by the house, loomed ever closer. Money, I'd learned, is nothing if not a tool to accumulate needed objects. It wasn't that money was less important after Braxon's suicide—my needs had simply shifted.

Needs: this heap of unwashed clothes in the middle of the mosaic tile still smelling of cigarettes, sweat, and the muted tang of things left too long undisturbed; stacks of Braxon's records, their covers slathered in pastel colors and Chinese characters—something called "vaporwave," the Internet explained—the office chair with the busted adjustment lever; a pile of broken glass resting in the corner from back when things first became too unreal, a metaphysical experiment of my own that reminded me then of the shopkeeper's lament from the evening before. Nothing has been touched, even the glass—these were no longer objects but evidence that reality extends beyond the limits of verifiability. Sadness, pain, and terror unlocked an introspective depth that does not rudely declare its boundaries in a moment of impact. The crash of dinner plates against a wall was a cry of impotence, and things of the depths responded to the echoes. *"Needs"* seems an absurd way to describe them: they had become so many shrouds of Turin, little corpses of Saint Xavier, shining points of recognition in a constellation of black stars.

When the phone rang, I turned to the window. How late *is* it, I wondered? Elizabeth's "wellness" calls were infrequent, increasingly tinged with frustration, and emanating from a reluctant sense of familial duty—all that, but *never* early. The light behind the blinds was bright and possessed an alien quality I hadn't recognized until then. Too pale, too somber; not the bleary confidence of the sun.

"Are you seeing this?" my sister asked.

I drew opened the blinds. Behind a fistula of clouds, rays of cold blue light.

"What is it?" I asked.

"A star. That's what the news says. Oh, Braelynn, I'm scared."

I placed the phone on a stack of records and opened the window. A new Janus moon appeared, lit on one half by the sun, the other by the new light. A no man's land of darkness separated the two warring realms. I could hear Elizabeth's tinny voice chattering away on the phone, but for a moment the night was silent. Then, as if summoned by an invisible sign, voices: the sound of windows screeching along their unused tracks, men and women babbling in wonder or shouting in something closer to terror in the new, ghastly dawn. *Welcome to the new world,* I thought, as if the ordeal wasn't as much a surprise to me as to them.

I reached down for the phone, but what I found in my fingers was the doll. I held it to the sky, the crevices in the face without features deeper now in the searing, icy light. And then, the movement beneath my fingers. A warmth. The child-no-longer's laughter all over again. I looked at the star. "Is that you?" I whispered.

‡‡

"A supernova," Elizabeth explained, filling the space between the term and its wasted definition with a long draw from her overpriced coffee, "is an exploding star, cosmic fireworks. When a star gets too old, it just goes *poof.*" It's clear that she's trying too hard, a sign that she's still frightened, even though it's difficult to read it behind the dark sunglasses. I nod, feigning interest halfheartedly, permitting her little victory. *Please, tell your clueless sister about the situation, Liz. Comfort her so you don't have to acknowledge the indignity of needing comfort yourself.*

We had picked a spot under the awning, even though Elizabeth always insisted on basking directly in the sun. "Sunlight is good for depression," she'd tell me, as if the loss of my son were a condition that could be eradicated with a handful of wisely selected home remedies. Today, the light from the supernova combined with the sunlight, producing an intense glare that no one seemed to trust. She had leered suspiciously at the way the brilliant light sparkled against the angles of the metal tables and chairs before retreating wordlessly to the shade. She still insisted on a patio table, my ever so stubborn sister.

"Did you ever connect with what's-his-name, that administrator you know? Did you uncover any leads about work?"

A sloughing of immense energy, the collapse of a god into something even stranger, a transformation rippling through time. Cosmic rays—protons and atomic nuclei blasting through space near the speed of light—bleeding in every direction. Toward us? They say it's unlikely to reach so far—and we'd know by now if it wasn't.

"No, Liz. I haven't."

But isn't it nice to dream?

"Braelynn, you've got to do something about this."

Something inside me curled into a fist. *Do something? For whom? What do I owe you?* I wanted to scream, but I recognized the uselessness of protest. It was harder with Elizabeth than it had been with Conrad. A lover of experience is always primed for the end, waiting for the transience of all passions to resound with the spent solemnity of a bell. Convincing a sister that you no longer need them, that living now means something different than the useless accumulation of company, is one thing I've never accomplished. So on we went, trading injuries in our desperation to communicate.

The sky seemed to crackle with energy behind her, erasing the sharp contours of her profile. I waited for her to take another drink before exacting my petty revenge. I half wished she would choke.

"How's Hank?"

I watched in delight as her eyebrows formed an angry little arrow that she desperately tried to wrestle into a look of confidence.

"Oh, good, good! Things are going great, thanks for asking. You know, I don't think there's anything we can't solve, Brae. That's one great thing about marriage. There's always Something Higher helping things along."

"With God all things are possible," I said, preempting her usual response.

"Even you," she said, smiling lightly, "aren't a lost cause to Him."

‡‡

The EMP pulse followed late that night. I knew because I was watching the newsfeed online, holding the wooden doll in one hand and listening to a popular scientist reassure his viewers of the benignity of the cosmic event. Conspiracy theories had already begun to proliferate. One group of self-designated "free thinkers" posited a UFO origin and corresponding federal cover up. Some Christians took it for a sign of the apocalypse; others recalled the story of Bethlehem's star and interpreted it more charitably. One particularly strange suggestion, entailing a terrible disaster in a secret space station serving as a remote weapons research center, had already gained surprising traction.

When the feed froze moments before the screen went black entirely, I wasn't surprised.

Or afraid. Or any of the other things we were all supposed to be that night. It was all fitting—almost pleasing. It was like stepping into a dream you've always imagined but never dreamed, stumbling across a dark alleyway that has always haunted you without becoming real. The sensation of weird gears snapping properly into place.

The lights went out with a soft click. I closed my eyes, doubling the darkness while the smell of damaged electrical equipment slowly filled the air. I remember feeling relief at the loss of the laptop. Even then I sensed the finality of the event and tossed it into the pile of glass. The reddest sin against Braxon's memory was distraction. Now I could finally drown in him. Swallow the red.

I picked up the figure and carried it to the window. Such a dull, rough thing, a veteran of untold ages so marked by time as to be rendered featureless and empty.

I sensed a fullness in the extremities of emptiness.

I suddenly remembered a passage from an essay long forgotten. I left the window to search for the book, leaving the doll perched on a stack of records, protected by a brilliant white beam of light from the dead star. I located the volume quickly, despite the unprecedented aversion I'd developed to reading. A slim, dark book with copper lettering on the coverless, cloth face. The passage, as I suspected, was Rilke's, from "On the Wax Dolls of Lotte Pritzel." I returned to the figure and whispered the words: "we have to conclude from their appearance that there are no children in their lives, that the precondition for their origin would be that the world of childhood is past."

I stared again into the rough, blank gaze. It was on this point that we converged, I realized. We both were annihilated by the loss of childhood. Rilke's seraphim then filled my mind, fire bellowing from their eyeless sockets. I remembered then that annihilation is another way of being born.

‡‡

The screaming began late in the night. It began in the distance, like a faint siren. I opened my eyes and listened to it crescendo out there in the temporary daylight. Somewhere an explosion rippled through the earth, rattling the windows and avalanching a stack of records in the living room. The musty tang of smoke followed a few minutes later. The screams continued.

I imagined a whirlwind of souls pulled from their bodies, draining into the sky like a great, translucent maelstrom. The screaming was the sound of its wind.

There *was* something inhuman about it, something I still can't account for. It was the first event since the toy store that chilled me, that requiem of wails echoing across a space too vast for this planet alone. I thought I was still dreaming, and for a moment I did drift off again. I was in the ocean, floating on my back toward a red light that scanned the night. From the corner of my eyes, a lighthouse bobbed into view, covered in bloody organic tissue. Pressed against the glass was a figure looking down at me. I couldn't make out his features. He was just a shadow, palms spread before him, breath fogging the gore-drenched glass. I kept floating. Still the screaming never stopped.

When I awoke again, something felt different. I lifted myself from bed and came to the window. Outside, a fog blindingly dispersed the blue light of the supernova. Not fog. Smoke. *Where are the sirens?* I wondered. Then I remembered the EMP blast and opened the window, letting the smoke fill the room. The screams were louder still, twisting through the false daylight like tentacles. Maimed, wild, inhuman. *Can this be real?* I thought, trying not to guess how many murders, rapes, and mutilations it would take to erect such a pillar of wails.

Then something shifted in the kitchen. It wasn't much, just an adjustment of weight, but significant enough to be unmistakable. Still, I couldn't rip my eyes from the glowing smoke stretching fingers to the long-dead star, anointing it with a bleary halo.

A heavy footstep, certainly male, followed by another, brutal weight shifting from the wooden kitchen floor to the tiles in the living room. I closed my eyes. Perhaps it would be quick. Perhaps there wouldn't be more pain than necessary. Perhaps.

And then it stopped.

I turned, stared cautiously into the shadowed corridor between my bedroom and the living room. The light outside failed to penetrate the heavy darkness draping the hallway. I lit a candle at my bedside and carried it with me, taking a moment to examine my emotions. There wasn't fear, nor was there ease. There was nothing but a half-giddy expectation for the worst. I didn't own guns, but I wonder now if I would've bothered to take one if I had. *Soon enough, son,* I said to myself, without the true hope of meeting him again in some gilded paradise. To share the same darkness...that would have to be enough.

But there was nothing. The light spilled over the records, and I could see the kitchen window beyond, a luminescent rectangle revealing undisturbed dishes scattered across the counter. Every object quiet and empty, sated by the lack of human attention.

I almost went back to bed when the pounding on the door began. I sighed—*why not?* The sensation of menace had gone, replaced by a sudden weariness. I walked through the cluttered house, realizing that the wailing outside had ceased. All had settled into an uneasy silence. All but the sharp, entitled knock at the door. *Elizabeth,* I realized before opening it.

"Hey," she said.

"What is it?" I asked, harsher than I meant to.

"Can I come in?" I stepped aside, letting her brush past me. "It's fucking Hank," she said, throwing her purse and jacket onto the couch as I locked the door. "The bastard. The motherfucker. The electricity goes off, the whole city's thrown into chaos, and the first thing he says is, 'I've got to see her.' I ask him why and he says it's because she has two kids. *She* can't defend herself, poor cunt. God, I could tear his fucking eyes out."

"Well..." I said slowly, considered something, then thought better of it. "If you sleep on the couch, you might want to keep a candle on hand. There's a prowler around."

I couldn't suppress the electric tingle of glee when her eyes widened.

"What do you mean?"

"Someone...moving around. They must've been looking into the windows."

"Jesus Christ," she said, rubbing her eyes. "I can't fucking deal with this right now." She looked older then, drawn in on herself, far from the pretty but arrogant little girl I had shared my childhood with. I noted this, but without any warmth or compassion. Everything was gone. Everything's been long gone. I am much closer to a thing than a human.

"You'll manage," I said, and turned to the bedroom. As I walked, I could hear my sister's quiet sobs fading behind me. I reached the stack of records where I'd left the doll. It was gone.

‡‡

"I see you," I said to the figure on the other side of the window. Deep shadows hid the face pressed in the space between his open palms as his breath fogged the glass. Between the deep ridges carved into his flesh and the bright light behind him, I couldn't make out his features.

"I see you," I said again.

That heavy breathing.

"You know, I've always wondered why we didn't get along better. It was difficult, feeling like I never connected with my own child. You reach down into that hollow inside and realize that he lies sprawled and broken at the bottom of a pit deeper than your arms, like a well so deep you can see the stars through the daylight at the bottom. Is that true?"

Still the breathing. The breathing and the light and the inhuman wailing streaming from the glowing smoke beyond.

"I tried to dig—dug until my nails were filled with blood and dirt; you know that. Something in that vast emptiness called to me. Was it you? Or was there something in there with you, a loss you didn't even know how to articulate? I felt that if I found it, I could dig it out, remove the tumor and absorb it in myself and you would heal. I thought if you could begin to heal, then you'd be closer to the surface. Close enough for me to cut you out."

The thing stood perfectly still—didn't shift its weight like a human would, standing so long. Did it see me? *Could* it see anything? Or was it still in darkness, wandering blind in this newly old land, this home away from home?

"They tell me not to blame myself. I truly don't. Never did, really. You were buried too deep for me. You always were. God knows I tried what I knew. But the bare fact of your isolation, that the universe could throw a being so helpless and lost into life...that there *are* things like you, empty and impossible to fill, all housed in such a beautiful little prison of flesh...that's...enough."

I waited for tears to sting my eyes. They didn't. They never did. Not anymore.

"What did Rilke call it, Brax? Tell me. 'That hollowness in our feelings, that heart-pause which could spell death.' Is that what this is? Talk to me, son. Talk to me or kill me, goddammit. I've waited for you long enough."

"Braelynn?"

I whipped around. Elizabeth was at my bedroom door, face twisted in confusion.

"Are you...talking to someone?"

I turned back to the window. There was nothing but the smoke, frozen in the cruel light.

"I'm fine, Elizabeth."

"Look," she said, "I know things have to be tough on you right now, but we *have* to start thinking about survival. I'm not going back to Hank. We must *pull it together.* There's no choice now. What are we going to do for food? How are we going to protect ourselves?"

My mind went white with anger. I grabbed my purse from the nightstand and shouldered by her into the hallway. I didn't bother to change out of the men's shorts and filthy t-shirt I had been wearing now for days.

"Where are you going?" she screamed behind me. "You can't keep running away and hiding from everything, you know!"

"Like hell I can't. Watch me," I called back to her, regretting it as soon as I did. It would've been so much better to say nothing at all.

I don't remember how long I walked that night. There wasn't much less light than there was during the day, but the change was enough to coax the city to disintegration. Fires belched from shop windows; people huddled under blankets in dark alleyways; a well-dressed man pulled the purse directly from my arm. I didn't even stop to watch him disappear. Women with children in tow climbed over broken glass to breach the grocery store down the street and came back with TVs, video game consoles, microwaves, and various kitchen devices I'd seen featured on paid ads over the years. It didn't seem to matter that the EMP burst had destroyed all electronics—the symbols of status were still in place, although in a weird, hellish parody of themselves. In every face I sought the scarred, empty visage of Braxon, the living embodiment of the missing doll. Even as I watched for his brutal, inhuman features, I feared finding them.

I came across the toy store. It was gutted, its contents spewed out into the street in an indistinguishable tangle of plastic, metal, and wood. I sifted through the ruins, crawled through the busted windows and into the hopeless jumble of ruined shelves. The bespectacled man was gone.

And on the night wound without thought or care, simply the hunger for a face that wasn't a face, a boy who wasn't a boy inside a body that wasn't a body. At least not of flesh.

I didn't have time to wonder if I had gone mad. It no longer mattered then. It doesn't matter now.

When I found my way home, the door had been wrenched from its hinges. I followed a smear of bloody pulp to the couch where hair and bits of bone were mixed into the loose stuffing. The blood went all the way up to the ceiling, smears here and there, circling a giant handprint that wasn't my sister's.

It led out the door and into the opposite direction from which I came. I followed it, the smear like the trail of a giant slug, stinking like copper and still steaming in the night. There were large, gelatinous heaps along the way, like something had torn her to pieces while dragging her, a long, gruesome tire track marked by the remains of an animal.

Footprints straddled the trail made by enormous, impossible feet. I followed them as the spaces between them became wider and wider. Then, in the middle of the road, they stopped.

I looked into the sky, listening for the screams once more, but the night was silent. Up in the immensity of night, across a distance the dead starlight had traveled for eons, the pinpoint of alien light gleamed. I shielded my eyes, watching for movement in the depths of blackness. Suddenly, the light winked out.

‡‡

It was over. The End, and free to go on, to barter a new existence from the aftermath. I imagined for a while, as I sat reading Rilke through the long day and the return of true night, that Braxon had intended it all as a gift, a foreclosure and new lease that those in mourning never receive. Perhaps.

I found myself thinking as frequently of the old wooden doll as the golden-haired boy with his plastic dinosaurs. The scarred, faceless creature outside the window carried over into an endless stream of restless dreams. I even dreamed of my sister between hours of sleeplessness during which I marveled at the inability of a dying star to influence the endless tolling of loss. Even God finds Himself spent and useless before the rot that accompanies birth, the inevitable return to the blackness after the false light fails.

Still, I tried to live on.

And couldn't.

One day the electricity will return and a representative of the bank will make their way to this house. By then, the stench will be terrible, despite the air fresheners I've hung everywhere. If it is easier for the authorities, let them blame me for the disappearance of Elizabeth. I tried to preserve what I could of her, but there's no ice, you see, and the animals got to most of her before I could. You'll find some of her remains buried next to the bird bath out back. Let them do with my things what they will.

But you, whoever you are, I want you to look.

Look at the bloated corpse before you, barely recognizable as a woman—look at the distended flesh and lolling, swollen tongue. *My* flesh. *My* tongue. Know that this is inevitable. Know that we can't even hope to join each other in mutual darkness, for I am there now and have found nothing. Above all, know that there is nothing.

sister

YOU ARE WONDERING who I am. You have known me for some time, but familiarity is the most thorough of all erasures. Nothing is more invisible than the trail burned across the sky by the sun. You see these hands? You know them, but you're blinded by the fact that you're unfamiliar with your current surroundings. This is to be expected.

Begin with what you last remember. Not the knives entering your body, not the taste of blood that began like ice at the base of your tongue. Forget the pain—nothing but electrical impulses tracing the crude map of your biology. Reach back further. You must find something simple. center the weight of your being against an empty detail. It is *those* things that make you who you are. Your identity was always carved against the rough edges of the profane. Now that you are lost, you must find it once more. How can you comprehend what I am if you don't fortify the distinctions between us? You are like a darkened lighthouse in a raging sea, but your power is still there: a chaos of undifferentiated phenomena roiling beneath the stars. Reach out and ignite the beam.

You have found something. Good. Feel it in your hands, slick, cold, and filling you with a sickening expectancy you've come to enjoy despite the bitter shame. Your commingling of hate and love is dreamlike, but you'll find that all your life has been like this.

The glass is not warm, but it wants to be—the sweet, ammoniac smell fills the room, and your jaw tenses in anticipation.

In the corner, you see two men. You know them both—have slept with them, in fact, although you don't often dwell on that. What you contemplate instead is the strange fact that both are soggy sacks of flesh stretched over organs quite comparable to yours. Sweat, stains, the sour stench of filth lodged in crevices difficult to reach when the mind is preoccupied with the horrific ecstasy that has made a wound in your existence—you share these things with them, with *all* beings. The great miracle of biology.

"The whole song, man. You played the wrong fucking riff through the whole song."

"Good thing it's under a fucking minute long, yeah?"

They're arguing, as usual. You watch the smaller man heat the glass pipe in his hand and you sigh, lovesick. This is not the locus of your guilt: all pleasure is chemical, after all. To draw the line here strikes you as arbitrary now that you've crossed it.

"It doesn't matter. *You played the wrong riff.* Can we even say that we've played that song tonight? You violated its essence."

"Fuck your essences," the smaller man says to the large one. "Grind is about intensity. It has nothing to do with your riff. The crowd moshed just like they would to anything else, didn't they?"

"Wrong. Essence is everything. We're all about *authenticity,* man. That's what separates us from the rest of them. That's why we can still draw a crowd even after the greats have fallen off. That's why we've outlasted the heyday."

Draw a crowd, you think, *if by "crowd" you count the two dozen locals clustered around the pool tables in the corners.*

You have accepted your fate. You're in your thirties, addicted to methamphetamines, and dating a bassist in a band named Devoured by Darkness. He makes $150 a set on a good night, and most nights there's no set so every cent goes to ice, board, and gas. There's no longer room for delusions of grandeur.

"Authenticity my ass." Gene says this, the skinny one whose name you now remember. "Don't give me that shit. How do you define authenticity? Is there, like, some inner gauge that aligns the band to some higher purpose? How would we find it if there was? 'Authenticity' is just a fancy word you drag out to justify your egotistical misconception of what we do here. There's nothing but the music and the people who pay to hear it. We're salesmen, just like everyone else on this fucking planet."

And now you remember that this is how things began. Or ended. "Began to end" seems closest, although everything has long felt to you like a series of beginnings of endings. Why does this one deserve special notice? You've already answered: it doesn't. See? Your sense of self is stronger now. You hardly need me at all.

Pytor, the big, loud man of essences, throws a bottle of Bud Light across the room. It crashes against a half-stack, tearing a hole in a speaker that'll take months to pay for.

"The fuck?" screams Gene, but Pytor has already stormed out of the insufficient backstage storage area and into the bar beyond. Someone greets him loudly by name, and another crash alerts you that he's still not in the fucking mood.

"Big fucking child," Gene mutters. You get up and cross the room to him. His glazed eyes finally register you, and something like the memory of a smile stretches across the shrunken valley of his malnourished cheeks. You lean in, make him think you're going in for a kiss, but you grab the lighter instead. The small deception goes unnoticed.

‡‡

You're taken with your new duties, since they distantly remind you of who you are. Or who you were. It strikes you as almost worth asking if there's a difference between the two, but of course it isn't. There are simply the trees, knobby live oaks growing out of the pocked limestone and shielding you from most of the sky as you haul the doll further and further into the woods.

The trees remind you, predictably, of your childhood, for when is there ever time for nature now that you've outgrown that perpetual enthusiasm? The person you are now would rather focus on locating a mattress under shelter—any fucking shelter—with a pipe and a solid supply and a new cell phone. Nevertheless, you're glad that you're here, even if the ghosts that follow you have already swarmed to fill the new shadows in your peripheral vision. You willfully concentrate on the whispering leaves and pretend you don't hear the manic articulations of language beneath the disguise. You try to remember a time when sunlight didn't taste like a threat and the snapping of underbrush simply meant squirrels or dogs and nothing more. You resist imagining the park filled with bodies: bloated, inert masses of flesh sharing the mossy damp with the limestone.

The doll is heavier, its plastic head knocking softly against each root protruding through the deer path. You've been told to dispose of it, and it's difficult to remember why. Was that shame in Pytor's eyes, or the same welling blackness that's always been there? It's just a prop, you tell yourself, even when you suspect it's a proxy for something far worse. The things they did during the show—the blows, the spit, the boundless acts of malice—are difficult for you to understand. It's best not to dwell on them, even though something tells you not to return, to dissolve into these woods, without regard for the possibility of winding up among the small cities of tents forever accumulating and dispersing again under the overpasses. You're always only a step away from that existence, but you take pride in the fact that you've never fully succumbed to it. There's always been some place to hole up, a bed to share, other people just as fiercely sad and desperate to latch onto. There's never any reason to be alone so long as you aren't too picky.

As you near your destination, cardinals burst from the thick like a heady rush of blood. They disorient you in their brilliant swell, making you imagine that you are somewhere else—giddy, you see yourself beneath the gleam of a familiar light you cannot place, an indoor gleam from somewhere long ago. A man's there, your parents too, and it's not excitement you feel but confusion, panic, the urge to run, but now the cardinals are gone and the woods are still and empty except for the flutter of ghosts.

It's before you, the place you were told to find. A pyramid of old iron bars protrudes from the space between two large stones. You set the doll— your double—aside, leaving the blank, sightless eyes to focus on an empty space in the canopy of leaves. Exhaustion spreads through your muscles, but the anticipation of crystal drives you on, your reward for a job well done.

On your knees, you examine the iron grate and the darkness beyond. The holes in the limestone are stained black with guano along the short stretch of cave wall lit by the sun. You have long lost much of your sense of smell, but you inhale anyway, catching sour glimpses of the tomblike depth. The bones of a small animal rest on the ledge below, covered with a fungus you can't identify. You grip the handle of the rusted hatch and pull, and it opens just like it's supposed to—the clipped padlock loses its grip and clatters against stones you can't see in the ink of shadows.

The next part isn't as easy as it should be. You look over your shoulders, immerse yourself in your surroundings, encouraging the paranoia that is so often a ceaseless torment. The well-worn trails are far behind you, servicing the easy pace of families and young couples. Out here, there's only the deer paths and the heaps of faded, multicolored fibers remaining from long-abandoned tents. *You're* here, nevertheless—that means others could be too, and the thing you must do feels oddly like a crime, even if the body beneath your hands is made of inert plastic.

You look into its eyes, only one still adorned with the faded black stab of paint representing a pupil. "Where did they find you?" you finally ask out loud, and the sound of your own voice startles you. Something that feels like a mixture of electricity and ice makes its way down your spine as you realize how useless the question of origin is. A sex shop, filched from a clothing store, a model left in the dumpster outside of the art department of some college—does it matter where if looking at it makes you feel like you're staring into a mirror that isn't there?

The ruined visage stares back at you as you maneuver it into the opening. You have to force it through at the waist, but soon it falls into the blackness with barely a sound.

‡‡

"Have you heard?" Gene, your partner, asks. You can barely make out what he says against the white noise of the band onstage, another grind act, named after an obscure method of Japanese torture.

You glance around the room, seeking your ground. You don't know where you are, what day it is, or if you're still in Austin. Pytor lurks in the corner of the room, holding a beer. He's staring directly at you, dead eyes unwavering through the shapeless swirl of the small crowd separating you. The stench of weed stings your eyes in waves and makes them moisten. You can't tell how many people in the room are real and how many are products of what Gene calls "meth psychosis."

"Have you heard?" he asks again, and you turn away from Pytor's gaze, shrugging.

"We've made it onto a label. This time it's a pretty big deal. They like what we've done, and Pytor seems happy with the new stage act, so that's a plus. What do you think?"

Gene's face is shallow and sad, but something like excitement creases the corners of his eyes. You don't remember him looking much different, but you like the way he lifts you onto the side of the bed when he's high enough to fuck. You smile and shrug once more, wishing the music would stop and that there wasn't a spiral of inarticulate voices waiting beneath it.

"We could maybe try again. We'll have money," he says, and reaches down to touch your stomach over your shirt. You pull away, overcome by something you can't quite put to words: an antiseptic smell, the flurry of bodies around you, pain.

He leans in to kiss you on the cheek, and the sourness of beer and sweat reaches you distantly, like a red flare dangling above an empty sea. "I love you," he says into your ear.

You squeeze his hand and guide it back to your belly. "I love you too," you say, and suddenly you don't want to let go, as if the words and his touch are buoys saving you from sinking into the frozen depths of a star-flecked blackness. Somewhere far away a voice introduces the band, multiplying across the speakers lining the room and pulling you back to its ghost-filled center. Gene is already receding, settling back into his place in the world like a peg in the maw of a blood-drenched machine.

"I've got to go," he says. You search the room again. The corner table where Pytor sat is now empty.

‡‡

All things evolve. You aren't the person you once were and you will never again be the person you are now. Each new thing you find to grind your corners against changes you—tiny, minute alterations that accumulate over time. If you were to grasp for the thread that unifies your development, could you? What is there to hold on to? A physical characteristic? Your almond eyes, once-blonde hair going brown and gray? Teeth never aligned perfectly and worsening, your crooked smile a victim of the body's insatiable demand for sustenance? Are these things enough to sew you together?

Or are you a story? Stories are the only things that can be said to have a purpose. It's a nice thought: Life is a story. Life is *something*.

And then you realize that the images from the preceding evenings intermingling with glimpses of the present in your head are a narrative: evolution striving blindly for a story, manufactured meaning, a house-plant variety of essence.

There are more dolls now, an assortment of plastic humanoids subject to the vicious interiority behind Pytor's dead eyes. His movements ape an artist's between songs—he goes from doll to doll, arranging them carefully as feedback hums from the amps, shifting one closer to another in the strange half-circle they form, placing one's hand on the other before removing it again. Every night is different, but you sense that he's groping for a specific configuration that doesn't easily translate back into the world of objects.

Later into the set, they choose one. The criteria of the choice is unclear; irrelevant, perhaps, but a choice is made. It's always Pytor's.

It's difficult to think about what happens next. It's easier to empathize with the commingled disgust and awe of the growing crowd—they've forgotten the music for a moment and watch the knives enter the plastic body. The absence of fake blood only makes the event more repulsive. The ritual's artificiality is brought sharply into focus, a lie oozing from the mimetic violence and consuming the world around it. Soon, the crowd is also plastic, the stage a formal structure suggesting nothing beyond its own function, Pytor's pupils two dabs of paint adorning twin plastic globes.

You look at your hands, the edges of your thumbs burned yellow from the lighter. They tremble, but not with the pain of transformation—they are yours still, biological, still full of blood.

For how long?

‡‡

The trunk cracks open and he wrestles a black plastic bag from its interior. It lands on the concrete far too heavily.

"There," he says.

"What is it?" you ask.

The silence that is never really silence stirs restlessly through the trees. In the pockets of sunlight, you see dozens of oak leaf rollers dangling from their webs.

He digs through his pockets and produces a small baggie. He holds it up so you can see the crystalline chunks inside.

"No different than the others." Irritation paints his voice fiery red.

You've worn this route so thoroughly you wonder if its finally more yours than the deer's. You take the corner of the bag in your hands, but the bulk resists. There's a new inertia, one of tissue that isn't full of air, gravity's grip on all things wet.

"It's not the same," you say without daring to say more.

The smell begins to wind through your dulled senses, the carrion stench of shit and blood.

"Close enough. Do what you're told if you want your ice."

You'll do it, of course. You'll do what you have to, no matter how much the indignity of it stings. Your shame appears to you like a blue teardrop, vibrating with cold. In your mind, it fits in the palm of one hand. You let it thrash against you, let it demonstrate its insubstantiality before allowing it to return to the undifferentiated sea of shades.

Sure, you'll do it: forget the smell, the way one appendage bends stiffly to the side, the way something sloshes thickly in the bottom of the bag, the way the flies have already sought you out.

‡‡

Gene grips your hand beneath the table. The light here is too bright. You count the napkin dispensers—you can tell there should be one per table, but some tables have been pushed together, doubling the dispensers. You count again, pretending you don't see the smoky outlines of people sitting at the empty ones. Your jaw works ceaselessly against the boundless energy pulsing through your body, but the pleasure has already begun to fade. You squeeze Gene's hand back, and he recoils.

A door opens somewhere, and you hear Pytor's booming voice. Soon, he sits across from you and Gene, accompanied by a young man you don't recognize.

"See the way they're looking at us?" Pytor asks, indicating a table you can't see.

"Who's this?" Gene asks, ignoring him.

"This is Gerard. A fan."

Pytor turns to signal a waitress. She approaches the table cautiously, eyeing the men with something approximating fear. You look at them yourself, trying to see them through her eyes: unwashed males with long, unkempt hair wearing shirts with illegible band names splayed across their fronts. But it's you her gaze avoids—*your* hair, *your* haunted eyes and wasting smile, you realize. You hear someone laugh as Pytor orders coffee for himself and Gerard, but when you turn to the table it came from, its chairs are empty.

"It isn't often," Gerard says, "particularly in this day and age, that the performative aspect of music is given its due. Streaming is all the rage, and there's little to impel the artist onto the stage with any sort of creative impetus beyond the drab boundaries of the given. To adopt a theme—a theme, especially, with formal resonances within the fine arts—in today's cultural landscape is most admirable. I applaud you for it."

You turn, impelled by the sensation of being watched from behind. You find that the murmurs are divorced from any basis in reality; the multiplied gaze between your shoulders exists somewhere else, in a time long removed from your own, if it exists at all.

"The puppet," Girard continues, "is not merely the *most* human of inanimate objects. It's *more* human than humans themselves. If the deepest human trauma is the trauma of birth, then the puppet surpasses us in its suffering. It isn't born, but stillborn, arrested in nonbeing. It lives vicariously, as we do, the externalized gaze of the audience bringing it to life much in the way our externalized gaze—our self-perception—dreams us into reality."

Gene lights a cigarette and you can't remember if smoking inside is legal. You look back at him a moment later and his hands are empty.

"The puppet is a dream of the audience's—conversely, the audience is the puppet's dream. Half-formed, it can only yearn for the temporary nature of humanity. Instead, it is locked into our form but emptied of death. The puppet *is* death, the ultimate alterity. As such, it is God-like. It is our double—the dead version of the self, radically externalized."

"Like you," Gene says, looking at you.

"What?" you hear yourself ask from a vast distance. Somehow, the restaurant's lights are wrong—too dark and too bright all at once, tinged with a color far too theatrical for practical purposes.

"Remember?"

The antiseptic smell—hands that aren't your own or Gene's. Your parents are by your side for the first time in years. A splash of blood across the front of your nightgown like a sudden eruption of cardinals.

"Remember your *own* double?"

The dead version of the self, radically externalized. The thing you held in your hand, its own little fisted hands, the plump flesh already cold in the pool of your palms.

Pytor's eyes shift to you. There's something there now: alive, inhuman, and terrible.

‡‡

"What about thoughts of self-harm?" the woman in scrubs asks. You shake your head.

"Any voices?" You have to concentrate over the endless susurrus to understand her.

"How are the hallucinations? Do you remember why you're here? Any side effects from the medications?"

Lies, lies, lies. You lie about everything, just like they expect you to. Still, you tolerate their procedure. You nod agreeably during your daily session, forcing your hands to stay still at your sides while the doctor's disinterested gaze makes you feel like a carcass after an autopsy. You make sure not to raise your head at the orderly's flashlight, even though you don't sleep thanks to the endless whisper of shadows the night can't seem to still. It is simply a matter of endurance. You're good at endurance.

"My husband left me," a woman says during a mandatory AA meeting in the small, plain room at the back of the unit. "Oh God, I didn't know I could feel this awful. I took a whole bottle of Prozac when I realized what was happening. I didn't realize it would make me feel worse. I thought maybe I'd go to sleep, you know? Just close my eyes and never wake up. I had no way of knowing it wouldn't work."

When it's your turn to speak, you stick to what you've learned works best: *My DOC is meth. Life was good before. Now I'm ready for A Higher Power to restore me to sanity, whatever the price.* But this time you add something new: "I was originally a twin," you listen to yourself say. "I didn't know this until I lost the baby and they told me I had two uteruses. It was a weird feeling, like a redundant sort of grief. There was the loss of my baby, then the loss of my sister all at once. I have four kidneys too. An extra set of lungs half developed under my own. I had forgotten all of this. I must have swallowed her before I was born. I wish I hadn't. I wish she was here."

Everyone in the group looks at you strangely and you wonder why you said it. You've done this often enough to know you didn't have to give them anything real. These places have ways of pulling things out of you.

During a session, the doctor looks at you directly and asks you why you're here. "You've indicated the same superficial desire to quit using that you always do," he says. "Is it addiction that *really* brings you back to us or is it something else? I ask this with perfect sincerity. A lot of patients simply want hot water, electricity, and warm blankets for a few days. I encourage you to speak plainly with me."

You nearly tell him everything: the heavy bags you drag through the woods, Pytor's dark and terrible eyes, the metallic scent all over everything in the back of the car that meets you in the park, the bewildering talk of transformation... or is it *translation, transposition*? Even though he calls you—the nurse at the front shouts your name above the din of TVs and hands you a phone attached by a cord to some receiver behind the desk— even though there's true concern in his voice—*Why did you do it? If you want to quit that bad, we can just talk about it*—Gene always comes back to the music, if music's what you want to call it, the sounds that act as a backdrop to the fierce and unimaginable malice of the men in your life.

You *nearly* tell him, but you don't.

It would be hard for them to see, in retrospect, that you wanted saving. But I know you better than them. *I understand.* After all, what can anyone really do about living other than simply endure?

Through the bars in the window above your cot, the moon is wrapped by the torn edges of low, unsettled clouds. They move quickly, teasing the chalky light into faint vectors across the black sky. Somewhere between sleep and wakefulness, Gene comes to you. He's wrong, somehow, made up of material that isn't flesh. His eyes are filled with fear that threatens to spread to you. He's holding something in his hands, something rubbery and emitting a stench that makes your dream far too real. He struggles against the stiffness of his joints in order to bring the thing closer to you. He wants you to look, even though everything in you screams not to. There's a soft dripping as liquid leaks between his fingers and hits the floor.

You must look into its face. You don't want to, but you do it anyway.

‡‡

The music is more ambient now, favoring hollow electronic textures rather than fierce bursts of noise. You try your best to vanish into the audience as the lights dim near the end of the set. For a moment, the universe has turned against you. You sense a vast canvas of eyes beyond the chaos of metal beams supporting the roof of the venue. Eyes that are a part of a machine, a machine connected to God, a God linked back to a darkness so thick and vacuous nothing can traverse it. Its malicious rays, the opposite of sunlight, reach down to you like strings, finding your thoughts beneath the cover of the crowd and linking them to the vast, hungry pit beyond creation.

Stars wink into existence in the deepening shadows above the stage. You can't tell if they're part of the set or creations of your mind. The lights continue to dim and more stars appear. The music has calmed to a low, wind-like drone. The band members disperse to the corners of the stage, vanishing with their instruments in the darkness with the uncanny seamlessness of the figures you're used to seeing in the shadows. And the stars continue to increase in brilliance, whiter and whiter against the rich, matte emptiness.

The audience dissolves, the backs of heads becoming mossy rocks scattered through an ancient landscape. Voices transform into the unquiet energies of a midnight breeze until they're nothing at all, a current beneath the great, empty-earth hum that seems, somehow, to come from the sky. For a while, there is nothing but the curious stars, brilliant streaks of white with a life of their own, flickering and pulsing in the distance. Your sense of confinement falls away, and you are no longer asleep in the realm of artifice but awakened to the unimaginable vastness beyond.

Then something shifts. You think for a moment the movement is an illusion, furtive as it is against the immensity it foregrounds. It recurs, a massive transformation of shadows where shadows shouldn't be. You try to explain it away, but can't. You're forced to acknowledge that something enormous looms against the stars, momentarily shattering the sensation of limitless space.

The humanoid figure approaches the center of the firmament. The stars, you notice, are familiar enough. Polaris shimmers at the tip of Ursa Minor, and its sister, the Great Bear, peeks tentatively over the invisible horizon. But something is wrong, as if everything is refracted through a prism.

The shadow obscures a set of stars somewhere to the west, nearing but never quite reaching the middle of the stage. It stops, waiting while the stars take turns blinking serenely out of existence, obscured by momentary disturbances in the atmosphere before resuming their roles in the soundless orchestra of the night. You almost forget the giant while waiting for something to happen, succumbing to the urge toward inertness that oppresses all beings in the absence of light. For a moment, you even forget yourself—you are no longer an individual watching an audience watch a stage. You are travelers in the mute currents of stillness, dreamers lapsed into the early moments of wakefulness in which the wild and fiery carnivals of sleep are burned into the undersides of your eyelids.

But then something rustles in the night, the soft whisper of moving fabric. Slowly, a smaller figure rises from a heap on the floor. Its hands appear first, visible above their sleeves in the glow of an intrinsic luminescence. It continues to rise to its full height, filling out the empty folds of its pale covering until it occupies center stage.

It's a man, thin and wiry beneath an excessive robe of torn cloth. The blankness of his face when he turns to you is startling. You remember distantly that you are watching a performance; the faint outline of a human being behind the glowing puppet is something of a relief, even if you can't identify if it's Pytor or Gene or someone else.

The puppet surveys the darkness, faces the sky, turning its back to the audience. It doesn't seem to notice the giant towering against the night. A second thing rises from the folds of its robes gathered on the floor: a woman, adorned in finer, more colorful cloth. Like her partner, her face lacks features excepting a full head of hair. She turns too, surveying the audience that appears to have vanished—a trick of the light, you decide—before linking her skeletal arms with the man's and matching his abstracted stare into the distance.

And when they stop moving, your peace is shattered. Something terrible infuses with the scene onstage, a visceral immediacy that violates the distance art maintains from its audience. You remember your first time dropping acid. Your sudden realization then—that things were *too real*, that any movie you watched while tripping became indistinguishable from reality—is a rudimentary version of the unveiling you're in the grip of now.

Your head throbs viciously and you want nothing more than to leave. You can't, of course, because your feet are nowhere near the ground. You can't look to confirm this, but somehow you know it to be the case.

Another figure rises from the collective folds gathered at the male and female puppets' feet. This one lacks the grace of the others. No shadow is there to guide it along strings from within the concealment of darkness.

The way she thrashes against the stage makes you sick. Her screams are far too naked under the relentless light of the vast, silent auditorium. The animal panic in her eyes, the way she pleads to the audience, and the way her suffering is met with utter silence—it is too much to bear. Suffering like this has a way of emptying all that is extraneous, and the suction of the void that's left behind makes you shiver. Even *you* have always been insulated by safety compared to this. You want a hit of ice like never before, a yearning so intense it hurts, but your body isn't yours right now. It's busy receding as your last line of defense, a dissociation from things too horrific to imagine. You know you'll have to wait until what is happening stops happening, but you also know it'll be too late by then.

Below you, the naked woman trembles with sobs. Defeated, she pivots away from the audience until she faces the simulated sky. You hear her gasp all the way from your vantage point near the gutted ceiling where great strips of insulation hang like stalactites. You don't have to follow her gaze to know it's locked on the massive figure.

You watch the panic force her to breathe faster. You watch her flesh go pale and glisten with sweat. You want desperately to save her from what happens next.

Maybe it's because she looks familiar to you: freckled skin, thin, sunken frame, eyes like drowned almonds above the wasted hollows of cheekbones.

The puppet man and woman turn to her, hook her arms in theirs, and begin walking. If you could scream you would, but that's something else that has been taken from you, the last in a long series of thefts that will never be restored. They walk toward the horizon, the confines of the stage somehow falling away to make room for the new world that has been summoned to replace it. The woman below who is your double screams, struggles against her wooden captors as the impassive outline in the sky looks on. A faintly glowing mist drifts into view, and they vanish behind it.

And now you know what happens next. You see it all before you pass out: she will emerge changed, this double of yours. Her panic gone, movements hollowed out by an artificial grace. Pytor's shadow will crouch next to her, guiding her every movement. With wooden eyes, she will no longer see the black figure towering against the stars.

‡‡

You still see them, the stars, even though they disappear sometimes, just long enough for Gene to reach over and shake you awake again.

"I'm sorry, I'm sorry," he says over and over. You know that he means it. You can tell by the way he's choking back tears, which you've never heard him do before. "I should've never let this happen," he says, eyes trained on the road, the truck going so fast it feels like you're flying.

You're propped up on something soft, even though you shouldn't be. Gene doesn't realize the blood drains faster this way. Best to keep it pooled around the heart, but it's already everywhere, so much of it that you distantly realize it's too late.

"I'm sorry," he says again. You want to smile, tell him to just keep driving into the dark, but your face is frozen.

Judging by the lack of light, you are heading away from Austin. But that doesn't make sense because the hospitals are clustered within the city.

The headlights illuminate the patch of road ahead as Gene twists further and further into the lonely labyrinth of asphalt. There should be bushes, trees, the occasional house or gas station. There isn't.

You look up and the being's still there, her vast features nearly imperceptible against the darkness. You hear something as well, a low hum behind the roar of the engine and Gene's crying. The road falls away too, along with Gene and the coldness that you can't seem to shake from your extremities. By the time it reaches your heart, you see me, sister, and it all snaps into place, like a bone that was broken but never set correctly.

Maybe most lives lack a stable essence. Ours is different, isn't it? I've always been here, sunk just below your line of vision.

When your world goes out like a red flare sinking into a black ocean, it makes it easier to see mine.

devourer

"WHEN YOU SAID you were out in the middle of nowhere," I said to the sketch of a man seated across the table, "you weren't kidding " I gestured vaguely to the window and the wall of looming pines encircling the clearing beyond. I smiled, trying to show that I meant no harm while hiding my own discomfort. I'm not sure he even heard me.

My notes describe his trailer as "dilapidated," and "straight out of *Silent Hill*." Of course, none of that made it into the published version. Not that anything was meant with malice or derision on my part—more than anything, I was simply surprised that the legendary Mike 'Devourer" Lowry lived in a mobile home bloody with rust in the middle of the woods. On the drive over, I half-expected to find a secluded mansion.

"So," I said to the gaunt, crouched figure igniting a foul Astra Filter, "you don't mind if we start this thing, do you?" Again he didn't answer, so I went on: "You're known in the black metal circle for maintaining a pretty impressive collection of memorabilia. Legend has it you own a load of original demos from most of the classic albums: *Panzerfaust, Apocalyptic Raids, To Mega Therion,* and the like. There's also word that you have the original photo of Dead's suicide famously used as the cover of *Dawn of the Black Hearts,* and let's not forget the signed guitars from legends like Zoltan Bathory. Can we see any of these gems?" I forced a smile despite the realization that the scripted question seemed absurd given his impoverished living conditions.

Devourer stared at me with empty, bottomless eyes as smoke danced softly around the edge of his beard. I fought the urge to glance away, held the smile as long as I could. By that time in my career, I had already found myself in contact with more than one fiercely antisocial musician. The popular assumption that extreme metal is filled with violent psychopaths isn't entirely off base, even if the ratio of monsters to normies in the corporate world is likely worse. The best thing to do, I knew, was to get through the damned thing without getting rattled. Returning Devourer's stare, I felt I was facing down a wild animal.

Finally, he sighed, turning his gaze to the pines outside. "All that's gone," he said in a voice gone gravelly with smoke and disuse.

"What happened to it?"

He took his time answering. "It all just...disappeared...lost down the k-hole of the Internet. It costs money to survive, man."

"I understand," I said, resisting the urge to cough. Within the rancid cloud of smoke, something rotten emanated from the kitchen. Shadows concealed clothes, books, magazines, and unidentifiable objects heaped in the corners of the cramped living room. If he had electricity, I couldn't tell—not even the window unit was on, despite the heat. I couldn't help but wonder how one of the biggest names in black metal found himself in such conditions.

I gathered my composure for what had to come next. Maybe it was because I was uneasy, but it was suddenly important to show that I wasn't afraid to express disappointment. "Okay, well, I had planned on doing the photo shoots with a few items of your collection. I guess we'll have to settle for some shots in the woods."

"No pictures."

The way he said it shattered some of my courage. I swallowed hard, conscious that I couldn't give in so easily. "But, Mr. Lowry, we need *something* to go with the interview. There's absolutely no way we can go without an image."

"Album covers."

"Those would have to come from the record label—it could delay publication."

"No fucking pictures."

"Okay, fine. I guess I'll have to take it up with my editor."

"You do that," he said, stabbing the horrible cigarette out on the surface of the table. "I'm gonna take a break." I watched as he got up and vanished into the impenetrable dark at the far end of the hallway. I hadn't even made it to my second question.

I stepped outside to call Lucy while Mike was doing God knows what in the back of the trailer.

"No photos? Are you fucking kidding me?"

"Not at all," I said in a low voice, conscious that Devourer could likely hear through the paper-thin walls.

"Well, the asshole could've mentioned that beforehand—how the fuck can we print a cover feature with no photos? There's no social media we can pull. Every pic online is linked to another media outlet or record label. This could be a legal nightmare."

The air was windless and silent, and I remember thinking that my voice violated something dark and sacred in the quiet immensity of the trees. Suddenly, I wished Lucy would tell me to pack up and head home, that I could put this perfect backdrop to some backwoods horror flick firmly behind me. Of course, I got the opposite of what I wanted.

"Dig your heels in," she hissed, "soften him up or take advantage of a moment of carelessness. Get him drunk. You know how much I hate relying on a piece that isn't in hand yet, but we're depending on this interview big time. All's quiet on the western front aside from Devourer's new album, so you're out of options." With that, the call went fuzzy and dropped.

"Goddamned woods," I muttered aloud. I redialed Lucy's cell and got nothing, the reception having suddenly dwindled to zero. I'd have to try again later. With one last look at the labyrinth of pines, I turned back to the trailer. I wondered what it would be like to get lost in there, how quickly the trunks of trees would begin to look the same in the darkness shielded forever from the sun. How soon before you died of thirst? How long before something hungry found you?

‡‡

Devourer was waiting at the table, another rancid Astra burning between his fingers. I looked into the serene black pools of his eyes and smiled. "Everything's cool," I said as I sank into the fold-out chair.

He said nothing, waiting for me to get comfortable before pushing a wooden bowl across the table. It was filled with what looked like muddy water.

"What's this?"

"Kava tea," he said without inflection, lifting the cigarette to his lips.

"Thanks, but I'm not thirsty," I said, pushing the bowl back across the table.

"This has nothing to do with thirst. *Piper methysticum.* You can type that into your smartphone there if you don't trust me. It's a root that Austronesian peoples have chewed for centuries as a useful way to facilitate conversation. Completely legal and mildly sedative, nothing more—way less so than a joint."

"Look," I said, making an effort to choose my words carefully, "I don't mean any disrespect by this, but I think I'll pass, Mr. Lowry."

Devourer sighed. "I guarantee I'm the most sober man you know," he said, bending his wiry frame across the table. "You drink alcohol, don't you? I'd offer that instead, but I don't keep poison in this house." He lifted the bowl to his mouth and drank, his gray-ringed eyes watching me coolly over the rim. When he finished, he wiped his mouth on the sleeve of his flannel and pushed the bowl back to me. "You want an interview, yes? This is the only way you'll get one out of me."

I stared into the muddy water gathered at the bottom, trying to remind myself of the many interviews I'd conducted over a beer or a gram of good hydro. *This isn't any different,* I told myself, swishing around the pond water in the bowl. *Like hell.*

Before I could change my mind, I lifted it to my mouth and drank. The taste was earthy, but not as bad as I expected. As I finished, a tingling numbness spread from my teeth to my throat.

What ensued over the next couple of days was not one, but two interviews, the first of which was later published in the magazine. The second is the reason I'm writing this account. It's been hidden for a while now, a pile of handwritten notes and recordings long ago transferred to thumb drives tucked away in a box at the back of my closet. There's also a photo that I never shared, a glimpse of a tree line at dusk that you don't want to look at too closely. An image I still see in my dreams, associated with the snapping of branches I sometimes hear outside the bedroom window late at night. Something I want to explain away, find an answer for in this new arrangement of the evidence.

To help the presentation, I've included the published portion of the interview in bold font. Nothing else, for one reason or another, made it to print.

Me: So, let's go ahead and begin with the reason we're here. *Mysterium Tremendum* releases in a month—it's a heady mix of what I'll call "classical" themes and black metal quite different than anything you've done before. What brought about this stylistic shift?

Devourer: Well, that album arose from a lot of hard work from a lot of people, least of all me. **The E_____ Philharmonic Choir really shines there, thanks to a certain uncredited composer with a lifetime study of Arvo Pärt under her belt.** I barely had anything to do with the fucking thing. Just some tremolo picking in the background, vocals, and a few of the thick drone textures to give the album a pass in the world of dark music. It's in the past now. Been recorded for two years. Dead and gone.

Me: Well, like I said, it's quite unlike anything I've heard in black metal before. I'm sure fans would love to know the influences you drew on for this release.

Devourer: If you haven't heard anything like it, then you haven't been paying attention. I don't know if you're aware, but there's a war going on. Absurd, Nokturnal Mortum, Peste Noire, and the rest of the Nazi scum are out there trying to keep music tied to communal boundaries. Exclusion, racism, all that shit that makes the world we live in a vile place. The world's changing—we're transcending, man, and listeners are looking for a place to upload. **Liturgy, Batushka, at least before Krzysztof got fucked in the ass by his label, and an artist going by the name Lingua Ignota** are trying to give fans a real place to plug in. They **are the forepersons of *Mysterium Tremendum*. I wanted a similar juxtaposition of the**

sacred and the profane. **Transcendental black metal is what I'd call it, a communion with the other world, or at least an attempt.** That was the idea. That was before I realized how useless the whole enterprise was.

Me: How do you feel about the reception of the album?

Devourer: I couldn't give a shit less, to tell you the truth. The label's making money, I've got enough to stay alive, so fuck it.

Me: So, you don't want to say a word about the resistance of some fans to elements of your music that aren't traditional? Isn't there a second war in black metal, one between fans of the lo-fi elements of the first wave and those in favor of experimentation?

Devourer: Jesus, man, you really need an update. You feel anything yet?

Me: No, not really.

Devourer: I'm not entirely surprised. Kava has what's called an inverse tolerance. The more you have in your system, the better it hits.

Me: Too bad, I guess. What about my question?
Devourer: Look, man, you aren't here for the reasons you think. *Mysterium Tremendum* isn't the cutting-edge album you feel compelled to make it out to be. People have been crying "sellout" ever since Emperor threw keyboards into the mix on *Nightside Eclipse*. It's a bit too late into the 21st century to get excited about juxtaposition.

Me: Well, why *should* anyone be excited about your work, then?

I hit stop on the recording app and waited for an answer. On top of the heat, isolation, and filth, what I then perceived as Devourer's disdain for his fans was simply too much. Back then, I prided myself on my thick skin, but nothing got on my nerves more than the sense of entitlement the music industry tends to generate in successful artists.

"Why should anyone give a fuck?" I repeated. For the first time, something like a smile was winding its way into Devourer's features, a smile every bit as thin and hollow as the black stars of his eyes. He thumped another cigarette from the pack and lit it with the smoldering butt of the last one.

"I should apologize." His voice betrayed a distant amusement. "I'm not used to conversing with anyone—I'm a bit out of the way out here—but I've found that apologies don't add up to shit. Words are like money; the more of them you waste, the less you're worth."

"Then I find it telling that you're willing to spend so many of those words dismissing the opinion of the fans you rely on for your elevated status as a metal legend." I crossed my arms, waiting for the punch to stir something beneath that listless pool of his face. It didn't.

"You don't get it—gratitude has nothing to do with it. I'm thankful for the money—every cent of it has gone back into production. It's just that this isn't important—*what's next* is important. *All I care about is the future,* and if you've seen what I've seen, you'd feel the same way."

"You mean your next album? I'm sure it's great, but I'm here because you're Devourer, onetime front man of Pestilent Christ, mastermind behind the undisputed classic album *Saviour Disease.* You are a phenomenon of historical relevance, like it or not. Without the past—particularly your past albums and performances—you're nothing, just Mike Lowry, hermit living out in the middle of bumfuck nowhere. You can't simply dismiss your album, especially after agreeing to do an interview promoting it with one of the biggest black metal publications on the planet."

Devourer sighed, blasting a stream of thin, blue smoke across the table to me. "Look," he said, voice steady and without the slightest hint of anger, "I know you have a job to do. I don't plan on making it difficult. Fact is, you have another purpose here that you don't realize yet, but you'll find that soon enough. If I answer your last question by saying something like, 'I'm thrilled with the response; fans have really turned out for *Mysterium Tremendum,* and it's amazing to me that people are more accepting than ever of innovation and experimentation,' would you feel better?"

"I just want to quit wasting time."

He laughed then, a metallic, lifeless noise that sent chills down my spine.

"You and me both, friend," he said.

As the sun sank behind the trees, he offered me the couch for the night. I didn't have to take a second glance at the stained, tattered wreck to decide. I told him the magazine had reserved a room in the city. It was a lie, but I had the company credit card, and Lucy never complained so long as I stuck to Motel Six. I assured him I'd be back in the early morning to wrap things up. As I pulled out of the bed of dead grass that served as a driveway, I saw his tall, lanky form vanish into the overgrown field littered with junk behind the trailer.

The old dirt trail seemed to wind forever through the pine forest, taking twists and turns that I hadn't recalled in the light of day. It gave me plenty of time to think about Devourer—something bothered me, something more than his eyes and living condition. I couldn't put my finger on it until I had left the forest behind for sky dusted with the lights of the distant city. *He was totally sure of himself,* I realized. He was unmarked by the anger and insecurity that typically characterizes the misanthrope. He had an unshakable sense of purpose, the grim resolve of a soldier who's been emptied out by the horror of his mission. The thought made the forest and his solitude somehow all the more terrible. Throughout the night, I focused on the sounds of the street on the other side of the motel walls, trying to eclipse the image of the clearing in the middle of the woods and the way it seemed wholly untouched by time.

When I finally drifted off on the hard mattress, I had a dream that I must add to this account: I saw Devourer, thin but muscular, a body familiar with hard work and hunger, drifting into the woods. A cold fog thickened around him as he faded into shadows—I followed him, repeatedly asking a question that I only remember was crucial, urgent even. He kept moving until I could no longer see the cabin behind me. When he turned, the sockets of his eyes were empty, an intense blackness shining through the fog. "From here, you can hear the planets sing," he said, pointing to the sky. I looked up. There was Jupiter, its stormy rings impossibly visible against the empty backdrop of night. And he was right. I could hear a low rumble pulsing through the air, vaguely shimmering with discordant harmonies.

‡‡

The second bowl of kava was either much more potent or the reverse tolerance was kicking in. Within a quarter of an hour, while I waited for Devourer to draw water from the well out back and rip open a fresh pack of Astras, I was already looser, more relaxed, as if I just popped a Clonazepam. The effect was welcome since the prospect of returning to the shack in the clearing had put me on edge all through the long drive out.

"A few more seconds," he said when he saw me settling back into yesterday's chair. "I need to make sure the generator's online." He disappeared out the screen door and into a maze of rusted machine parts. So, there *was* power. Then why no light, or at least some goddamned AC in the trailer? I soaked in the stillness left in the sudden absence of his unhurried movements. I busied myself by reading the spines of technical manuals and music theory texts in the stack closest to me, trying to ignore the oppressive absence of sound. There were no birds, no rustling in the underbrush, no breeze—as if the forest had been brutally stripped of life. As if the clearing radiated a perpetual state of death.

"We're set," he said, shuffling through the screen door and fishing an Astra from his pocket.

"My mother died that way," I said.

He looked at me evenly as he lifted the cigarette to his lips. "Cancer?" he asked.

"Yeah."

"Sorry for your loss."

"It was a long, drawn-out deal. Chemo and all that. She suffered a lot toward the end."

"The way of all flesh," he said, lighting the Astra.

"It doesn't bother you, the prospect of dying?"

He smiled softly before answering. "One way of looking at it is that you live to die, that life is the thing deserving of fear, and death is nothing at all, the throbbing heartbeat of existence."

"I remember her choking as she lay there, drowning in her own cells."

"That's not death. Cancer itself is a superabundance of existence. The latter part of *living* was pain for her—death was a step outside. A breath of pure, limpid darkness."

Something like anger flickered inside me—who was *he* to say what my mother's death was? But I remembered that *I* had brought it up. I wondered why I had.

I forced a laugh—it came out strangled and harsh. "Jesus, Mike, I'm sorry—"

"Don't apologize, man." He sank back into his seat, smiling.

"Must be the kava."

"We'll return to your departed mother later, if you want. Don't you have a job to do in the meantime?"

"Yes, yes." Embarrassed, I put my phone on the table and started recording. Luckily, Devourer didn't leave it to me to shrug off the awkwardness—like a man with a newfound purpose, he picked up the thread from yesterday without prompting.

Devourer: When it came time to make *Mysterium Tremendum,* I was desperately looking for something new, a meaningful path to atone for some of the waste I'd made with my career. You could call it a mid-life crisis. We were just coming out of the big sale period for the previous record, *Dark Matter,* and I just didn't have the sense that I was accomplishing anything anymore.

Me: Was it the sales that bothered you? Critical reception?

Devourer: I think we had moved 11,000 physical copies by the time I had started looking for a new path. That's actual CDs and vinyl. Not bad for a one-man black metal act. The critics were pretty receptive as well. I had appropriated some field recordings—the swinging of a rusted gate, frigid blasts of wind, the sound of an armadillo rooting through leaves and underbrush—to play behind the blistering wall of guitars. Drench the whole thing in reverb, and that was enough to lead some reviewers to believe I had done something unique.

Me: What was it, then?

Devourer: You know, you spend all your life wanting to *be* something. You want it more than anything, and if you're lucky, it's something concrete and obtainable: an artist, a teacher, a doctor, a journalist who makes a living listening to music and musicians, that sort of thing. Only a very small segment of people will eventually fill the role they dream of filling. In some respects, they're unluckier than those who never make it. You always dream that the things you want are tools that will help you carve out your niche in the great edifice of contentment. Then you finally get those things, wait for the unhappiness to dissolve, and it fucking doesn't, man. We're the ones who live to see our aspirations gutted and left to die. The truth is never preferable to a dream.

Me: That actually sounds a lot like burnout.

Devourer: Human desire relies on the absence of its object. Desire is a hunger for what's not there. By definition, it's impossible to desire what you've already obtained. That's why marriages fail unless they're scarred with some form of unhappiness, a trauma that keeps them separate. It's more than burnout—it's the void nested inside the very nature of desire.

Me: So, you felt this...void...after *Dark Matter*. What made the new, experimental elements of *Mysterium Tremendum* seem like a cure?

Devourer: Anyone who wants the answer to that question should read Hunter Hunt-Hendrix's treatise, "Transcendental Black Metal." Hunter's the brain behind Liturgy, a so-called "black metal" band that sees traditional, what she calls "hyperborean" black metal, as embodying something of the void I just mentioned. Hunter calls Darkthrone's *Transilvanian Hunger* the epitome of this—walls of blast beats and tremolo picking, a desolate, affectless nihilism devoid of energy, the inevitable result of turning inside out the puppet that civilization has called God for all this time. Not that black metal's done that, religion has, in its own failure to back up its insistence on God as a literal, physical being. It's all what I call the murder of the mythic. Black metal is just a response to this great, Lovecraftian "correlation of contents," an unblinded look at reality that drives us mad.

Me: So *Transilvanian Hunger* is—

Devourer: What my own music had become: a proxy for suicide. A dream of living death, suspended animation, a garden of quiet, listless agony.

Me: Interesting. So Hunter's solution is?

Devourer: To infuse black metal with energy—"burst beats" instead of "blast beats." It seems ridiculous at first blush, but when you think of it, the static nature of black metal directly correlates with its metaphysics, the all-too-real worldview of its creators and deep listeners. Liturgy doesn't shy away from much of anything anymore: electronics, harps, even rap vocals. It's part of this revitalization of American black metal that Hunter thinks should be closer to Blake than Schopenhauer.

Me: So, what you're saying is black metal should be *happier?* That message doesn't entirely match the aesthetic of *Mysterium Tremendum,* does it?

Devourer: Nor does it match Liturgy's, if you recall. No, "happy" is very much the wrong word. There's liberation in realizing the cosmos is a vast, godless void filled with things we can't hope to conceptualize. There's something profound about seeing through the illusion of faith, then returning to something like a "decayed" faith— a radically changed faith that has nothing to do with God—in the face of truth. It's like madness; it's a phantom that seeks to populate the empty spaces with itself, to induce the imaginary into being, and the only way to do this is through trauma. That's why the music can't be happy. It must remain traumatic. *That's* why I thought black metal was a perfect medium for the numinous. Only I was wrong.

I sank back into my chair, suddenly dizzy. I can't say that I understood him, but I found myself desperate to leave the subject behind. A fevered glimmer in his eyes left me intensely uncomfortable. I could see that he had a secret, a pain somewhere deep inside, gnawing away, driving him to a frenzy as it neared the surface. Back then, it was hard for me to remain in the presence of people who suffer. Perhaps they reminded me of Mom. Maybe that's why I had brought her up.

The Astra had gone dead and dangled uselessly between his lips. As I watched, his eyes drifted up to the ceiling as he floated further into his inner landscape—despite my revulsion, I couldn't find the courage to interrupt. "Sound is a borderland between being and nonbeing—an ethereal thing with no mass, no physical qualities outside of its own movement. It's an emanation of the *nothing*, a conduit between what's here and what isn't, which is why it is a Hermetic creature of thresholds, boundaries, and Orphic descents. Hence its onetime function as a communal language—it strengthened solidarity along ancestral lines that turned national with the emergence of mass civilization. But now, it's been removed of its national context—you can simply log onto any streaming service and listen to sacred hymns alongside East Coast hip-hop and apocalyptic folk or whatever. The musical landscape has always been a mirror of culture. That isn't to say this decontextualizing is bad—the National Socialist assholes are great examples of how communal identity can stagnate—but it does mean that music is an individual experience now. It's no less than the new savior for a civilization of lost souls."

Devourer drifted into silence, gazing through the window to the listless wall of trees. A line of sweat trickled steadily down my back as I shifted in the steel chair. The sudden desire to leave took hold again. The cramped interior of the trailer was unbearable; the undefinable stink of rot and something sweeter wafting in waves from of the kitchen made breathing difficult. I remembered then my long-standing passion for metal, the worship I'd lavished on bands like Mayhem, Mercyful Fate, and Immortal as a kid. That it had all led here seemed unthinkably disappointing.

"Let's get some fresh air," he said, as if he could hear my thoughts. I followed him out into the clearing and watched as he surveyed the black wall of trees. It was almost worse than before. No wind stirred the air, the stillness allowing the heat to congeal horribly in the humidity of the surrounding foliage.

"You hear that?" he said, the haunted smile teasing the corners of his mouth again.

"There's nothing."

"You've never been more right," he said, nodding in satisfaction before motioning for me to follow. We picked our way through the rusted shells of vintage amplifiers, their vacuum tubes exposed to the elements like yellowed fingers. Cables snaked across the ground in complex webs, intertwining with spines of ruined books and the guts of machines decayed long past their recognizable forms.

"You forgot your next question," he said suddenly over his shoulder. It was true. If I ever wanted to leave this place, I'd have to continue the interview. I made sure the phone was recording and continued.

Me: You said you were wrong. That *Mysterium Tremendum* failed to capture the...‟numinous.” How?

Devourer: It's just music, you know. At the end of day, black metal is entertainment. There are a select few who see beyond the guise into the abyss—I've gotten my share of fan mail from people who glimpsed the light that *Mysterium Tremendum* tried to suggest. In the end, though, it wasn't what I wanted. I can't change the world. I can only revitalize my own existence, wake myself up from this sleepwalking spell.

Me: So what comes next? Is this where your next project comes in? Something more...personal?

Devourer: Yes.

Me: Can you give your fans a description of your new direction? Is there a drop date for the album?

Devourer: There won't be an album, man.

Me: What?

Devourer: You said it yourself—this is something more...personal. Call it a performance piece. Not black metal or transcendental black metal or anything like that. If you have to call it anything, call it...black ecstasy.

My head throbbed as we emerged from the junk and followed a path into the overgrown field behind the trailer. I hadn't realized before that the grass was tall enough to easily hide a car. Out of sheer nervousness, I asked him how he had come to live in such isolation. Devourer didn't respond. I watched the back of his head bob with each unfaltering step. I tried again. "Was this plot of land in your family?" Devourer turned around, giving me a sad, empty stare, as if I had grossly missed the point of everything. Embarrassed, I fell silent. He continued to lead me through the grass for longer than seemed possible.

Unexpectedly, the path opened into a mowed space. It was relatively large—fifty feet or so along each outer edge—and in the shape of a triangle. At each corner sat an enormous, high-end speaker linked by cables to something covered by a tarp in the heart of the triangle.

Without a word, Devourer walked over to the tarp and wrestled it back. I came up beside him, ignoring the sense of seclusion that seemed magnified within the comparatively small space. I tried to ignore the terrible, inhuman forms my imagination began to conjure within the wall of grass.

Soon, a table emerged from the folds of plastic, not like the one back in the trailer, but metal, shiny and clean. An expensive laptop was folded on top of it, plugged into a massive generator. Various cables ran from the distant speakers to the generator and what looked like a soundboard attached to the computer. Devourer maneuvered the unwieldy tarp under the table and spread his arms, the subtle smile returning. He hadn't even broken a sweat—I was drenched.

"This is it."

"This is what?"

"The point of connection. A sonic gateway."

Only then did I taste the maddening depths of Devourer's obsession. If there was any money left from the albums, it all led here, to the inexplicable audio equipment tucked inside a neatly mowed triangle in a field of grass. Worse, it was clear that Devourer's insistence on the importance of his next project went far beyond an enthusiasm for musical evolution. There was something tangible now, something I could sense had been the black, throbbing core of everything he said, the silent heart in the middle of an emptied-out forest.

He bent down to enter a command on the keyboard.

"Listen, man," he said over his shoulder, the last words of his I clearly remember, "Why, when I think of escaping this world, do I imagine a descent into hell? Maybe I have the system beat—my heaven is hell, a place of suffering where the body is filled with the purest intensity: the meaningless wail of agony. But beyond the wall of pain is a white band of light, a void only the blind can see after they've torn their eyes away. Only then are we free."

I did not understand what he meant. I distinctly remember blaming the kava tea. Perhaps it was spiked with something stronger, a dose of LSD or DMT. It would explain the things that began happening then. It would explain the way suddenly nothing made sense, why I heard muttering and turned toward Devourer only to see his empty, baleful eyes staring off into the trees, lips unmoving. It would make sense of the way the waning sun took on a new, menacing hue without changing color, a jaundiced, furious glare that I vaguely remembered from my deepest bouts of depression. The way the grass rippled away from the triangle. The way a white cloud of birds rose above the tree line and vanished into impossible heights. And what happened later...the photograph in my hands right now—

But no. I must face this reality with bravery. How long have I spent running from it? How long out of work, afraid to go outside, half-starved on meager disability benefits and drinking can after can of Keystone, mirroring the arc of the sun I never see by a steady descent into oblivion? There's something in the audio recordings too. After Devourer's last words, I cannot deny that the audio suddenly cackles with distortion—I hear a vast, relentless wind that I don't remember feeling carrying inarticulate sounds from impossible distances. I would call the noise the warbling of strange animals if they didn't vaguely possess the cadence of language.

My memories of the end of the interview are confused—untangling reality from hallucination has proven impossible. Later, when the doctors began talking about a "psychotic break," perhaps they were half right. Nevertheless, I did everything in my power to defend the other half. I brought to my appointments peer reviewed articles on infrasound, frequencies well below the limit of human audibility characterized by their ability to trigger altered states of consciousness. I located a book I had stolen from Devourer's trailer titled *AUDINT—UNSOUND:UNDEAD*. From it, I copied passages I found relevant and arranged them in a notebook. Once, after I spent half of a session explaining the West Kennet Long Barrow, an ancient burial site near Wiltshire full of chambers constructed for the purpose of distorting drum rhythms into infrasound, the doctor rudely informed me that I'd have to find another therapist if I persisted in bringing him every instance of pseudoscience I stumbled across. I have long given up any attempt to share or explain my terror.

That is, until now.

I know we didn't stay in the field past nightfall, but I remember darkness, an eclipse of the green-yellow sunlight that pressed against the earth like a slow death. Shapes flitted behind the grass, dark beings scuttling back and forth but never entering the boundaries of the triangle. They made no noise above the inaudible bass that throbbed inside me. I felt it in every bone, like the voice of God.

I groped for Devourer. Was I screaming? Did tears stream down my face? He had moved to a mat near a corner of the triangle closest to the woods. The point of the triangle was aligned neatly with a dip in the tree line, a slight part in the impenetrable wall near the peaks of the pines. He sat there in what I recognized as Padmasana, or lotus position, facing the trees. I staggered toward him, brought back to consciousness briefly by the new point of definite focus.

I swear he said something to me. "The world is filled with less-concentrated swaths of infrasound like this. Whales communicate with it. Animals use it to gauge the occurrence of an earthquake long before the quake itself. It lives in the world like a ghost, a shadow of something invisible living alongside us."

As I play the audio back now, I am assured once more that these words were never exchanged. Yet I remember them clearly, as if they happened yesterday.

Something in Devourer's calm steadied me. I stopped and watched him from behind. He bowed his head, his stillness contrasting with the grass bent by a wind that somehow didn't touch me. I'm not sure why, but I remembered the photo then. The interview came back to me, the magazine, Lucy's suggestion that I catch Devourer off-guard. I unlocked my phone and turned it toward him just as something emerged from the gap in the treetops. I realized, with horror, that the caesura in the wall of pines was left there by frequent passing of the impossibly large thing forcing its way clumsily through the forest.

In blind panic I snapped the picture. I called to Devourer, my voice drowning in the miasma of black ecstasy. He didn't raise his head.

I ran then.

I've been running ever since.

Not that I didn't go back. I'm not sure how many days or weeks I spent in the Motel Six, paralyzed between the urge to rescue Devourer and panicked flight. I vaguely remember a phone call from Lucy.

"What's wrong with you?" she asked. "You sound like you're in trouble."

"It's nothing," I said.

"Did you get a photo?"

"Not yet."

I emailed her the audio recordings with little explanation. "What the fuck is this shit? Are you getting fucked up out there?" she shouted into my voicemail a day later. I didn't call her back. They still used my name on the final interview, attributing the abrupt ending to failed recording equipment. When Lucy threatened to fire me if I didn't respond, I emerged from the dark hotel room to purchase a pistol and a bottle of whiskey.

The ensuing twelve hours is what I still think of when I hear the phrase "dark night of the soul." The soundless sound quivered through the walls, screamed into my brain, while a horde of dark figures raced through the night just outside the curtained windows. The gun passed into my hands more than once—left more than one red ring in the flesh of my temple. I learned then the tremendous strength it takes to pull the trigger.

The next morning, I stumbled to the car, revolver jammed into the back of my jeans. I expected the forest to grow dead the closer I got. Instead, birds flitted through the sunlit gaps in the canopy while squirrels recklessly dashed across the road before me.

Soon I was there. Three deer standing in Devourer's lawn froze for a moment before bounding into the trees. I searched the trailer first and found nothing. I finished the bottle of whiskey before walking into the grass.

I don't know how long I walked. Two hours, four. I traced the expanse of the clearing until I was sure I had covered every inch. It wasn't there. I don't know how else to put it. Devourer's sonic gateway had vanished, leaving behind nothing but a ragged, unkempt clearing in the woods.

Compelled by some unreasoning urge, I swiped *AUDINT* from the cabin. By the time the world had noticed Devourer's disappearance, the interview had long fallen out of the infantile, momentary consciousness of the industry. I was never connected to the vanishing, never questioned. Or perhaps just never found.

I can't express what comes over me when I hold this photograph between my trembling fingers. A mixture of awe and terror. If someone's innocent questions regarding the fate of black metal legend Mike "Devourer" Lowry leads them here, it is with pity that I affix the following image to this file. If it is something more, I envy their luck. If you look hard enough, you can glimpse the eye-studded amalgam of flesh and jagged bone, a blend of biology locked in agony. And the antlers, great, majestic emblems rising above the trees like the torn and wrathful hands of an incarnate god. Yes, look at the proof of my account, the source of my newfound resolve. I've found my tremendous strength at last.

the rubber man

SUCH A SMALL thing, the bug guts on the window, smears of yellow and green that make Kaire feel dirty when the sun gleams through them. It would take nothing to clean them off, a matter of seconds at the gas station while she stands there waiting for the tank to fill. But events have a way of accumulating inertia; tasks resist completion more fiercely with time, as if every minute leaves a leaden residue.

There's plenty left to do, and Kaire feels it defines her in some vaguely unflattering way, a testimony to the neuroses that have rooted into her foundations, weakening all she's worked to build. The sale of her house, for instance, isn't finalized, a failure represented by a stack of paper on her desk back in Michigan. It waits, as the buyers do, and the realtor, a talkative woman named Sam who reminds Kaire uncomfortably of her mother. Kaire hasn't the heart or the courage to tell them she doesn't plan to return. Let them think it's a working absence for as long as they will. The truth will dawn on them eventually—or, rather than the truth, a set of assumptions that doesn't resemble the truth at all, speculations over an event they couldn't possibly understand.

As Kaire pulls into the harbor, the sun mercifully shifts to the passenger side window, divesting the smashed bugs of the terrible light that turns them into brittle leaves of fire. The stink of the ocean thickens the air, and far in the distance, a strip of menacing blue clouds blend with the indefinite expanse of gray water.

The failure to be on time doesn't quite weigh on her like it should, or perhaps it does, but the weight fits too easily against a static wall of other failures for her to notice. Tyrone's been waiting for her in his old Classmaster for an hour now, if he's still waiting at all. Kaire slows down, absorbs the gentle stillness of the empty boats docked in rows. A cat sleeps on a parked car, curled up luxuriously in the half-light of the day. Gulls pass overhead, dipping into the harbor and emerging with silver fish dangling from their beaks.

One could almost imagine something like "peace" here, she thinks to herself, and Kaire imagines the thought should inspire more regret than it does. Instead, she feels hollow and weightless, like an empty box—it's what she's come to expect from herself, the resounding tedium of nothingness.

Mercifully, she locates Tyrone where expected. He's busy with his car, an old blue Honda with a trash bag pulled over the passenger side window. He's bent over the trunk, shifting the weight of something around. Frustration strains his weather-toughened features until he sees her pull in.

"You sure about this?" he asks when she hands him her duffle bag.

"Of course." There is no hesitance in her voice.

‡‡

There is unease, the smallest tug of it, as Kaire watches Tyrone's Classmaster vanish over a swell. When she sees it again, it's but a splash of red, a speck, and then nothing. Worry is to be expected. The island's terribly isolated—nothing for miles in every direction, even the harbor a mere suggestion of a glow against the gloaming. Tyrone was upset to be returning so late—rightfully so, considering the weather—but his scowl softened when Kaire added two extra hundreds to the small stack of bills in his waiting hand.

A single light illuminates the concrete shelter at the center of the small island. Kaire turns toward it as the wind hits her back, bursting from the line of storms now flashing blue and white high overhead. The small structure is all that's left of a defunct lighthouse, demolished years ago for safety concerns. The thunder reverberates within the sidewalk beneath her feet, and something large scuttles across the toe of her shoe, a roach or a silverfish, populations of both thriving between the shadows of stones. She surveys the sky one last time, jagged with clouds, and hoists the strap of the army cot onto her shoulder. It will be a long, dark night, but aren't they all?

‡‡

Kaire sets up the cot in a corner. The shelter reeks overwhelmingly of fish, but she knows she'll adjust quickly. Green swaths of moss extend up the walls, almost to the ceiling. Finger-thin rivulets of water trickling through spaces in the concrete gleam in the dull light, and the generator fills the structure with a gentle hum. Thunder rolls through its foundations, churning Kaire's gut, and the storm continues with renewed fury. The interior is warm, uncomfortably damp, but already the island has begun to do its job. Kaire is forgetting Michigan, the house, her position as project manager, even Roman. Her attention is on the task at hand, the instructions printed on the plastic MRE, the process of mixing, squeezing, and pouring. To her surprise, she finds the simple meal enjoyable.

She tucks the spoon into the plastic wrapper and rolls it up, ready for the single trash bag she hopes will last her the next two weeks. The rain strengthens audibly against the concrete walls, and the lightning momentarily fills the space with a pitiless blue light.

Kaire unzips the duffel bag and locates an uncrumpled manila folder tucked between immaculate rolls of clothes. She opens it, removes the few sheets of paper inside. Each features an aerial photograph of the island, an irregular rocky shape with the shelter square in its center. She wonders what it looks like now—the surf uncalm, white foam swallowing rocks growing locks of moss, the insufficient dock on the west side swaying where the support beams have weakened with rot. She reflects, for what could already be the hundredth time, on the sheer strangeness of being here; an island, by all odds, impossible to locate. No matter how long she searched the coast on Google Maps, she should have never found it. Over two thousand miles of coast from Maine to Florida to explore and she recognized it within minutes, hitting print and jotting down the coordinates with a hand that trembled. That it was called Icarus Island seemed all the more fitting. A miracle since, according to reason, she should've never dared to hope it was real.

"Here I am," she says to the empty room. A peal of thunder rattles the bars at the windows, but nothing else. She repeats it, hoping for something to mark her homecoming. *That's what this is, isn't it? That's what you want this to feel like.*

Somehow, she is no longer so certain.

‡‡

In the morning, the incomplete tasks return, a chorus that demands attention with the narcissistic insistence of a child. Things like the note she never left Roman and the certainty that he's noticed her absence by now. It's possible that he's already beginning to panic, or what passes for panic if such an emotion could be said to exist beneath his wry disregard for everything that isn't work. There's an email waiting to be written to Kaire's supervisor, an explanation of her sudden absence coupled with an admission that she doesn't plan on returning to her position as project manager. She thinks about it as the sunlight pools into the room, first in a corner that gathered rain from the night before, then spreading as the day advances. She decides that there's nothing to say, and that this is the root of her inability to address what must be addressed. How could she begin to explain what resists translation into clear, pragmatic concerns?

"What's the problem, Kaire?" She imagines this in Roman's sleepy baritone. And she'd say what? *A sudden resurgence of adolescent insecurities? An inclination to overthinking bordering on paranoia?* And what would *he* say? He'd never tell her she's overreacting, having learned from his ex, as he never tires of pointing out, to avoid the "o" word like his life depends on it. He'd sooner recommend—calmly, ever so calmly, and without the slightest hint of pain—seeing someone, a therapist. Not bad advice, she admits, except for the implicit assumption that Kaire's concerns are *wrong*. Therapy is always normative—it necessarily posits a *right* and *wrong* way of navigating the world—and her increasing feeling of hollowness, the oppressive suspicion that life is a role played for the benefit of everyone but herself, isn't something she's ready to write off as depression and anxiety. *Don't fool yourself,* she chides. *You've given up* everything *to entertain this.* "Writing it off" *was never a real alternative. Not for you.*

Kaire extracts her phone from last night's jeans. Much to her disappointment, it hasn't lost reception and is already accumulating missed calls, several from Roman. She walks outside and looks at the ocean, flat and pristine, a sharp contrast from the foam of yesterday's storm. High up in the sky, something catches the sun. She squints to see it, shields her eyes as her heart begins to pound with a mixture of terror and excitement that begins to fade the moment she identifies it as an airplane. She looks around her island, at the mossy rocks drying in the sun, the gulls and occasional crane dipping into the water. A fish leaps in the distance and vanishes back into the depths.

A right way and a wrong way. It's crazy, what she wants to do. She doesn't *feel* crazy though. It doesn't take too many hours on the ID channel to realize that cell phones—even dead ones—can be located, if one wants to locate them badly enough. Her impulse, she realizes with some surprise, is perfectly *rational. How can one be both rational and crazy?*

She flings the cellphone into the sky. It spins sideways, catching the sun like a metallic black bird, and vanishes with barely a ripple into the ocean.

‡‡

Nothing happens. The day is stifling hot—the humidity is terrible, and there is nothing to do, so Kaire sits on her cot in the shelter and reads and rereads the deed to the island, which was handed to her just days before in an old motel near the harbor. She walks around outside, watching the giant roaches flit between the shadows of the rocks. She watches the sky and sea for a while before returning to her cot. Around midday, the wind picks up and the sound the waves make against the rocky shore lulls Kaire into half sleep. She dreams of the storm from the night before, sees the lightning again as it throws a blue gleam that lingers too long across the filthy concrete. The light is gone and returns, this time casting a silhouette across the floor. Kaire shifts to check the barred window above the cot. An owl's there, eyes like large black mirrors. She jolts awake, a scream already lost somewhere in her throat.

‡‡

Tyrone had mentioned summer storms in his polite attempt to dissuade her from what must seem to him like a deeply inadvisable course of action, but the fresh line of clouds at nightfall, blacker even than yesterday's, catches Kaire by surprise. Already the wind moans against the shelter, which Kaire can't bring herself to think of as a house. Not yet.

She beats an early retreat, hiding from the relentless spray of surf that invades everything, drying her lips with salt that stings the cracks in them. She's sunburned, her flesh resonating with a warmth that will soon become a pain. She lies on the cot with one of the novels she brought and rereads the same paragraph for half an hour before setting it aside.

Still nothing happens, but what did she expect from this place? Nothing was promised, everything was risked. She wonders for the last time if Roman truly did anything to deserve her leaving. Nothing outright, certainly—if the only thing wrong with a man is his perfect adjustment to the demands of his job, is it fair to blame him? Roman was—*in the past tense already?*—opportunistic and bitter, galvanized by a deep sense of entitlement, qualities his partners at the firm collectively renamed "ambition" and "drive." She thought of the listless surface of his calm voice as a mask, a layer of plastic concealing a ruthless cunning that served him well as an attorney, less as a partner.

But leaving Roman is not something Kaire can bring herself to regret. *Deserving* has nothing to do with it. If she subtracts the desires of others and follows the unnamable impulse that feels much closer to an identity than her assigned roles as project manager and partner, she'd find herself right where she is now, on Icarus Island. For once—storm and sun and the overwhelming smell of fish notwithstanding—she feels more human than puppet.

A flash like ice floods the room, followed in an instant by a cannon shot of thunder that Kaire feels throughout her body. She glances at the window but nothing's there, just long weeds battered by sheets of rain. She closes her eyes, wondering if she'll ever fall asleep easily in this space that isn't a space, this home that is very far from a home. But her intensifying sunburn won't allow her to lie comfortably in one position, and something rustles somewhere in the dark, something living, perhaps awakened by the storm.

She listens for a while, waiting for the caesura between thunder cracks to hear the scuttling of movement against concrete.

Is this what I'm waiting for? she asks, and suddenly she remembers something from her childhood. She calls it the Rubber Man.

Where did that *come from? A horror movie? One of Dad's TV shows? A book?* She can't remember, but she clearly sees his eyes in her mind, circular pools of black that glisten with a light that isn't quite visible, like the silver beam of a star reflected from a labyrinth of mirrors deep underground.

And when the generator dies, terror renews her for a second sleepless night. She watches the window, but nothing comes. Just the insistent rustling, on and on until the sunlight collects once again in the pool of rain in the corner.

‡‡

She moves the heap of seaweed using shirts as makeshift gloves. It's bunched against the corner farthest from the door, the apparent remains of a particularly rough storm that once left the island entirely submerged. She pushes it away, ignoring the rank smell of sea slime and decay. Returning to the corner, she finds the hole.

It's protected by an iron grille, long gone to rust. Broken rungs of a wooden ladder descend into perfect darkness. For a brief moment, vertigo seizes her—the hole could be limitless, the entrance to an underworld system beyond comprehension. Kaire shines a flashlight down into the depths, finding the floor closer than she imagined. Relief, followed by disgust when she notices the black piles of rat feces.

"Explains the noise at least," she says to no one.

‡‡

She's almost asleep when she hears the sputter of the Classmaster. Kaire grabs a muck-smeared shirt and pulls it painfully over her burned shoulders.

"What are you doing here?" She doesn't bother to hide her irritation as she storms into earshot. Tyrone looks up as he struggles to lash the boat to the warped, moss-covered dock. This time, his smile doesn't come quite as easy.

"I'm sorry, ma'am, but it was necessary for me to check on you. Your phone doesn't seem to be working."

"Bullshit," she says. "I told you I wanted to be left alone."

"I know, but look," big hands splayed out before him, a gesture of helplessness. "It didn't occur to me at first, but I got worried. After the storms—"

"Who's looking for me, Tyrone?"

The big man sighs and stares at his feet. Kaire tries to remember where she slipped. Did she forget and use a credit card? Did Roman find a copy of the deed? Surely a missing person's case in Michigan wouldn't entail a thorough search clear to the other side of the country.

"It's...your car. They ID'd it back at the harbor, started asking questions about someone who might be a danger to herself."

Kaire just stares at him, angry and frightened...far more frightened of the people looking for her than the island or the rats or her childhood Rubber Man. What did they do to people who tried to drop from the grid? Did they force them into behavioral health units? Kaire's mother had ended up in one after attempting suicide with sleeping pills. Was this any different? Wasn't Mom trying to drop off the grid in her own way? More importantly, would it *seem* any different to *them?* Even if she avoided internment, Roman would be there to coax her back into her old life, and he wouldn't be easy to evade a second time. The thought made her cold, even in the heat of the sun.

"I'm sorry, Kaire," Tyrone says, softening. "I just thought I'd find you...you know."

"Look," she says, "I'm not a danger to myself or anyone else. I own this island. This is *my* property, purchased fair and square. If I want to spend the rest of my life out here, that's my right."

"I'm not saying it isn't. Not at all. I just...wish you had told someone where you were going so they wouldn't have sent the police around."

"Nothing to worry about, Tyrone. Look." She pulls the rest of the cash out and hands it to him. "Let me see the month out, okay? Keep them away until the end of the month, then you can come and get me and I'll assure them I'm fine in person. Are we clear?"

A sadness fills him at the sight of the money. He takes it, lifts it to his face. He shakes his head, but his voice is steady and resigned. "So long as you leave me out of this, miss."

"Not a word, Tyrone."

"Is there anything you need?"

She shakes her head. Tyrone shrugs and unties the boat, spending the last moments on Icarus Island carefully scanning the terrain.

"Hey, Tyrone?" Kaire asks suddenly. "What's *under* the shelter?"

"As far as I know," he says over his shoulder as he climbs back into the Classmaster, "nothing at all."

✜✜

And Kaire, having handed the last of her money to Tyrone, won't be heading to Michigan to finalize the sale of the house anytime soon. That would be *insane,* because she's already inflicted irreparable damage to that other life she's left behind: the loss of a job, loss of a relationship, a house—and it wouldn't be a return to normalcy so much as a walk of shame, no prodigal daughter's welcome home. It's *all or nothing,* she realizes, and puts all her faith—perhaps foolishly, *insanely*—in those images she printed from Google Maps, images that led her *here,* to Icarus Island, images from a memory she still can't place but that has persisted throughout her life: the aerial view of the island, so distinct and clear and resurfacing at work one day out of the blue. A coworker had just returned from a coastal vacation and was showing off her snapshots. In the background of one was a tiny bait shop, painted pink but weathered and quaintly decorated with fishing net, large colorful shells, and seaweed. And it was the smell, somehow—the slimy reek of the ocean—that Kaire only had to imagine in order to summon the buried memory like a rogue wave God knows where. The island seen from above. From an impossible vantage point. Kaire's never ridden in an airplane or helicopter, and the island of her memory is awash with a pale green glow that she had always assumed emanated from above.

It's possible, she realizes with a deep disquiet, she was mistaken about that. Perhaps the light came from below.

‡‡

I can no longer tell this story like a story. On the evening of the second day, I scribbled what's written so far into a composition notebook, hoping to achieve a reflective distance that would determine my next steps. Instead, I've become frustrated with my inability to render it accurately—"it" being the tedium of the eventless days and the nagging, heat-crazed thoughts that fill them. I've been thinking about my grandfather's vacation house, for instance, a modest cabin burrowed in the side of a mountain in Colorado. I've been thinking of the smell of pines, the gentle snap of a wood fire, and the dreams that would torment me late into the night every time I stayed there, dreams that felt too real, of hands grabbing my feet; dreams of waking up to find my bedroom surrounded with strange, almost human faces. Dreams that weren't dreams at all, like the owl outside my window, backlit by dusk on the eve of the worst nights, and the quiet terror that would fill me as I gazed into the mercurial pools of shimmering darkness that were its eyes. The owl lies at the center of everything I've said before, a black hole ringed with a gleaming galaxy of consciousness. Articulating this from a third person perspective was somehow impossible.

One more note before I begin my journey:

The storms returned again last night, renewed once more with a ferocity I wouldn't have thought possible. I tried to read but couldn't. On into the night I could hear the surf breaking against the rocks. Soon the ocean began to reach the shelter, and I became afraid that the island would be submerged. Although the corner I've found for my cot remained dry for the two preceding nights, water found it at last, dripping down from a hidden breach in the ceiling. I pulled the blankets over my head, wishing the tempest away. I almost regretted my decision to stay.

Then a flash of lightning filled the room, and everything plunged into uncanny silence. Through the fabric of my blankets, the light seemed more green than blue, that same pale glow I recalled from my memory of the island. The light didn't subside. I could still hear water trickling along the walls, but the roar of the surf had vanished entirely, and the wind outside had calmed to a low restless breeze. I pulled the blankets away—the unearthly light filled the interior of the shelter, illuminating the moss and puddles of water still forming beneath cracks in the ceiling. Only after some moments passed did I notice the darkness beyond the windows. The light, somehow, was coming from inside.

I thought then that I was dreaming, even though the realization didn't give me the usual power to consciously influence the dream's course of action. The rustling returned, louder than before, intensified in the sudden stillness following the storm. I stood and crossed the room to the hole. The green light filled the space below, which I could see now wasn t a cellar at all, but a long hallway. Despite my fear, I lifted the iron grille. The ladder was useless after the third rung, and I dropped the rest of the way. I remember feeling oddly heavy, as if I were in a trance.

Rats scampered away when I hit the ground, lots of them, knocking over something large as they vanished into the shadows. The segment of hallway directly beneath the shelter was green with moss and ruin. The floors were tiled, and the walls were painted dark in a style that reminded me of the 70s. Empty sockets for fluorescent lighting lined the ceiling, next to sprinkler heads protruding from gutted panels like metal spiders.

The hallway branched into several others, some walled and others dug directly into rock and dirt.

The green light didn't come from any single source, an omniscient glow that gave everything the sheen of a dream. Suddenly I remembered the Rubber Man and didn't want to go further. I remembered the strange, burning darkness of his eyes and his skin, gray and glossy like rubber. I remembered his long probing fingers and the metal wand he held to my forehead, and I suddenly felt like screaming. A muttering began, something like a voice but lacking the contours of language, drifting from one of the side tunnels that appeared to descend sharply. I think I said something out loud, something stupid and panicked, and that's when the air rippled with gravity.

It's hard to describe. Impossible. Somehow, the moment was weighted with importance. Anticipation filled the air, as if I were expected to make a decision before an audience. As soon as I recognized this, I heard footsteps approaching from somewhere within the labyrinth.

That's when I started jumping for the ladder. The footsteps fell closer and closer, approaching from one side. I didn't dare to face it. I was sure I'd see it, those terrible empty eyes and its thin lipless mouth. I jumped higher. I screamed. I felt it approach, sensed it just beyond my shoulder, an electric terror that was almost like touching the dead. Finally, I caught one of the rungs closest to the ceiling and pulled myself up.

And as if it had never stopped, the storm resumed. I stood, perplexed, startled to hear the waves crashing suddenly against the walls of the shelter. The door blew open with a fierce gust, and I saw something lift into the air from the shore—a large bird, a light, I couldn't say which. It was gone in an instant. I closed the door and returned to my cot, already resigned to another night without sleep.

‡‡

The hallway is real. In the sunlight, it's still there, branching paths and all. Perhaps this shouldn't surprise me as much as it does, but I still half expected my experience of the night before to be more dream than reality. The green light is gone and there is no hint of movement aside from the occasional scurrying of rats and roaches.

I have decided to explore this subterranean maze. For once, I've made a plan: I must find the Rubber Man and put a close to all this. I need to know *why*. No more half-remembered hints, no opaque lights in the dark. I'm not getting any younger. It's time for the plain, cold *truth*.

I've packed a bag with the rest of the MREs, flashlights, first aid kits, blankets, and this notebook. I vaguely regret the loss of my phone, if only for the camera, but it doesn't matter. I'm standing now in the segment of hallway beneath the shelter. Wetness and decay persist as each pathway burrows deeper—the smells down here are difficult to describe and impossible to experience without nausea.

On the evening of the third day, I hereby begin my descent. I choose the tunnel that carried the voices, the one that drops sharply. This is not going to be easy.

‡‡

Nothing has happened yet. The climb is much worse than I thought. Every surface is slick with moss, and several times I've begun to slip, only to slide into the face of rocks protruding in the dark. I try not to imagine the moment there's nothing to break my slide. How could any being climb this surface? I'm afraid that returning the same way will be out of the question. I can only hope that the Rubber Man will restore me to the surface the moment I've learned what I've come here to learn. Meanwhile, I continue further into the darkness. There's been no sign of the green light.

‡‡

More slime, more stone. Something large scampered over my hand, not a rat, but insectile. A roach? Far too large, it seems, although I've found that roaches *do* achieve intimidating proportions here.

For many minutes I heard what I thought was a tapping far below me. I imagined the Rubber Man and his metal wand, which he used in the dreams of my childhood to fill my mind with unbidden images. After a long and exhausting struggle, I found that the rhythmic sound was simply water dripping onto a large stone.

A fear grips me occasionally now, one that ambitiously oversteps the horror of last night's dream. It's this darkness, so terrifyingly complete and all-devouring. I imagine a great nothingness before me, an expanse of empty rock reaching depths I can do nothing to predict. It makes my head spin. I must stop for a moment. I must try not to think.

‡‡

Things are not going well. I've rolled my ankle and am struggling more than ever over these increasingly large stones. Worse, an occasional draft from below carries the smell of standing water. I'm afraid the path will fall away at any moment, plunging me into a vast subterranean lake. In addition, one of my flashlights suddenly stopped working. I have one left. I am considering turning back.

‡‡

Surely it's been miles since I've turned back, and something's been following me since. At first, I listened for regular footfalls, the deliberate step of the Rubber Man. Instead, there's scurrying: frantic, unintelligent, and persistent.

For hours I've fled from the sound, but it only comes closer. Somewhere along the way, I lost my grip on a moss-slicked rock and slipped, further injuring my foot. I hobble at a ridiculous pace now, and the scurrying continues to gain on me.

I hope it's rats. I truly do; a mass of writhing furry creatures fleeing an incoming tide that regularly floods the lower portions of this cave. Not, for the love of God, seeking me out in *hunger,* an alternative I can neither bear to consider nor shake from my thoughts. There's nothing to do but continue. I've already wasted too much time.

‡‡

There is darkness beyond darkness, silence beyond silence, solitude beyond the thresholds of isolation. It's a darkness of the soul, a darkness that makes existing easy to forget. I turn and the endless night is populated by faces— different than those who used to fill my room in my grandfather's vacation cabin, but similar somehow, formed from the same fabric of nonbeing. I cry out and they vanish, leaving my echo to reverberate against the spaces overhead far too vast to make sense. I am certain it's been too long, that I should've surfaced by now. When I return, perhaps I'll discover mere hours have passed. Perhaps days. In this darkness beyond darkness, such boundaries dissolve. I am here, an abject being alight with pain, and here, a lumbering vortex of scampering, squealing, and scurrying, a multiplicity rising to the surface like the hungry mouth of a thousand rats.

‡‡

Somewhere along the way, I have taken a wrong turn. The path slopes down again, and the restless noise of living things is before me as well as behind.

At one point, my bad foot slipped, and I flailed in free fall before my fingertips found a rocky ledge. For one harrowing moment, I dangled over an invisible depth. Somehow I was able to gain a grip with both hands and haul myself back onto the rock. Even with the beam of the flashlight trained at my feet, it's impossible to see the sheer drop until I'm nearly upon it.

I see that my moment of opportunity has already passed. Even calling it "my moment of opportunity" is a misunderstanding. It was merely a moment, nothing more. There are only moments upon moments, each discrete, impenetrable, and mysterious. The Rubber Man was never a thing of answers. Only a mystery blooming into further mysteries, or mysteries altogether forgotten the moment their magic ended. It's a fundamental misunderstanding to ask for more. I can see that now. I can at least see that, if nothing else.

There is no destiny. Beauty, perhaps, but not destiny.

The closest thing to destiny is the sound of mandibles, a white maelstrom of teeth. I can only hope that I have time to starve. I've tossed my pack into the abyss to hurry things along. Maybe it would be a good idea to follow it. I can only hope beyond hope that they're further away than they sound.

If anyone finds this, tell Roman I regret nothing.

endemic

IT WAS A long time after Mom left before I could bear to visit the old Tule Creek place. By then, curiosity had gotten the best of me, and I quit believing that she would return. I had my own miracles, Chrissy and Veronica, to believe in. Still, I supported my brother's decision to keep paying taxes and utilities on the place. Letting it go after it had sat so long collecting dust, a memorial of debris to a woman I felt less and less sure had ever existed, seemed a sin.

I picked an afternoon when Chrissy was feeling extra morose and Veronica wanted to finish reading a novel. The trip was routine by now—every couple of months or so, even if Veronica kept telling me it was morbid. "It's not like that," I'd say, even though it was. "I'm trying to organize all the junk she has in there so we can sell it." We weren't hurting too badly for cash, but my reputation as a penny pincher helped the lies go down a little easier.

What I left out was the fact that I was still searching. I didn't feel guilty for the lie of omission—what's the point in bringing up what you can't begin to explain? Maybe if the police had bothered to look more thoroughly, the gnaw of this lingering lack of closure wouldn't exist. Maybe I still felt that she wasn't the kind of woman to leave without a goodbye. My brother didn't think she was, although his assumptions took a much more sinister course than mine.

The chain had been cut and the meager piles of junk near the front door had shifted again. I wasn't surprised, though I did search the place with my heavy Maglite on the ready. Break-ins had become common since around '99, when word finally got out that Professor Kandice Sawyer wouldn't be coming back. The house was empty except for Mom's junk. None of the burglars could seem to manage more than a few items at once. All I noted this time was the absence of the Shop Vac I had brought with me a few months back. I can hardly blame them. Mom was a pack rat, and I'd be the first to admit that the mess is intimidating.

The sheer quantity of items was enough to keep me from getting too sentimental. If Mom had scribbled down a note and left it on top of a pile, it could take years to find. The home I had known as a kid was immured in the remainder of an unfamiliar side of a woman I once thought I knew like my own flesh. I couldn't make heads or tails of the pieces; there were simply too many to form a coherent picture, like the fragments of a thousand unrelated puzzles packed into a single case.

Chrissy had asked me to look for a record player. I took interest in anything at all as a good sign in my daughter. I assured her that I had spotted a nice Victrola next to a pile of dishes. As I ambled into the kitchen, I knocked a stack of books from the bar onto the floor—books with titles like *Grizmek's Encyclopedia of Ecology, The Origin of Species,* and *Principles of Population Genetics* that the thieves never bothered. As I stooped to gather them up, I noticed the rim of a small plastic container tucked between the back of the couch and the bar. Curious, I picked it up and lifted it to the sun burning yellow through the old window shades.

It had a label: "Endemic Species #8, Crickshaw Cavern, June 1998." Inside were two thin red worms. They appeared to be dead, but something electric rose inside me.

I knew enough about Mom's work to recognize the importance of the words "endemic species." "Crickshaw Cavern" meant nothing, but the date was one I'd never forget.

‡‡

That night, after arriving home later than usual and slumping onto the couch to avoid disturbing Veronica, I had the dream again. It had been a long time, but it came back easily, as if it had never disappeared. It's been three weeks since anyone's seen her and Dad keeps telling us it's nothing, she's always only cared about herself. I'm at the Tule Creek house. Something in me can't accept that she'd vanish without a trace. I bang on the door, angry that she doesn't just open it. "Why are you doing this?" I yell through the wood. "You're worrying everyone sick." Nothing happens and I keep bashing the door with the palm of my hand, threatening to kick it in. Eventually I do just that. Inside, the house is as dark and cluttered as ever, and I rush along the paths worn between the heaps of junk toward her bedroom. She's not there, but I keep screaming her name and sending papers, books, and clothes sliding to the floor in the wake of my search. At some point, I'm ready to give up. I turn to leave, tears burning my eyes, when the TV switches on. I follow the static back into the shadows of the living room. I could've sworn it was empty before, but a hand now clings to an arm of the sofa. I approach it from behind. "Mom?" I whisper, and when I see her, the skin pulled pale and gray across her skeleton is alive with movement. I'm not relieved, since it's the wrong kind of movement, as if she's an empty vessel filled with something else. Her eyes are flat and dead, and somewhere far away but coming closer I hear the sound of a vast, roaring wind.

✛✛

I took my time unpacking the junk from the Tule Creek house, saving the best for last. When I brought the Victrola up to Chrissy's room, I basked in the rare smile it earned.

"Do you have any records?" I asked, even though I had noticed the steady stream of packages she'd spent her allowance ordering online. She made an honest effort not to roll her eyes as she indicated the stack of vinyl on her desk.

"You know they make CDs now," I said. This time, she couldn't help herself.

"Dad, we're in the streaming age. Keep up."

Downstairs, Veronica eyed the half dozen lamps on the dining table and the stack of books with open disgust.

"What?" I said. "I thought you'd at least like to dig through the books before I sell 'em."

She humored me with a patient smile before lifting the first title from the stack. "*NATO ASI Series, Ecological Sciences, volume 35?* Thanks honey. That'll follow *Fall of Giants* beautifully."

"Hey," I teased, "figured you may want to broaden your horizons."

"You might consider broadening your own. How many more times are you going to go to that old house full of junk anyhow?"

"It was burglarized again," I said instead of answering her question.

"Excellent! Did they take anything this time?"

"Just my vacuum. Hate to disappoint you, but there's still plenty left."

Despite herself, Veronica was sifting absently through the books. I savored the unguarded display of her innate curiosity I once found so attractive. "Here," she said finally, lifting a worn paperback. "King's *Four Past Midnight.* I'm pretty sure this one has 'The Langoliers.' All is well."

I smiled and turned to the coffeemaker. I didn't have time to pour a cup before Veronica asked, "Hon, what's this?"

The levity was suddenly gone from her voice. In her hands was the specimen container with the dead worms. Apparently, I had left it on the table with the books, an oversight I wasn't prepared to pay for.

"Oh, just one of Mom's specimens, I guess. You know how important endemic species were to her—according to the label, that's one in the flesh. What's left of the flesh, anyway."

She frowned, and for a moment I worried that I'd have to defend my decision to bring the thing home.

"So, this has been in the Tule Creek house *the whole time?*" she asked.

"Well, yes. What's wrong?"

"Then how are these things *alive?*"

She brought the specimen closer to me. Sure enough, the twin red worms writhed together in a tangled double helix, as if they were collected fresh from the earth just an hour before.

‡‡

Could they survive nearly 20 years without food or water? If so, what revived them from yesterday's dry and brittle state of undeath? "Vampire worms," Veronica suggested. "They smell our blood." We laughed, but the lingering idea soured the morning for both of us.

I waited for my wife to settle with a book and for the steady drone of something harsh that didn't seem to be music to drift from Chrissy's room before retreating to the office. Luckily, summer and my long vacation were both approaching their terminus. I had reams of reports to read before returning to work. My absence would hardly raise notice.

It wasn't long before I found a Wikipedia entry on diapause, a state of dormancy initiated in some worms and insects to survive unfavorable environmental conditions. There were instances, I discovered, of it lasting quite a while. The yucca moth—a pale, winged creature, glittering with a fine layer of silver dust—had been observed emerging from diapause after 19 years.I picked up the specimen container and held it under the desk lamp. The red worms weren't large, but they were a far cry from the brittle strands of long-dead tissue I had found at the house. What had stimulated them? Sunlight?

Could it be that Mom had stumbled across something undiscovered? I remembered her telling me about Movile Cave, a pocket of water and gasses discovered beneath a featureless desert in Romania. Movile stank of Hydrogen sulfide, the odor of swamps, indicating the microbial deterioration of organic matter in oxygen-poor environments. "The smell of life," Mom called it, and the life inside Movile was unlike anywhere else on the planet. Every leech, louse, and water scorpion that covered the walls of Movile was uniquely adapted to the cave's isolated atmosphere, an atmosphere quite different than Earth's. It was filled with creatures unique to its ecosystem, little samples of alien life.

Mom wouldn't hesitate to point out that most examples of endemic species aren't quite as dramatic—Darwin's Galapagos marine iguana and the Nilgiri blue robin are endemic, severed from the world's evolutionary history of life by geographies of extreme isolation. But since its discovery in the 80s, Movile always held her captive. Up until her disappearance, she traveled the world exploring obscure cave systems, slave to an obsession that Dad never got around to forgiving, if only because it was a convenient distraction from his own shortcomings.

A tapping on the faintest edge of audibility drew my attention to the container. The red worms thrashed madly against the plastic, inspired to a new level of activity by something I couldn't sense. I simply watched them for a while, bewildered by the possibility that these small creatures were all that would remain of my mother's fascination. What greater discovery had she been nearing in the summer of 1998? Could it have been so incredible that it swept her up along with it? Or had something more sinister cut her short? It had been a long, long time since I'd ever hoped to find the truth.

I turned to my computer once more. To my surprise, "Crickshaw Cave, June 1998" yielded results. I followed a link titled "Mystery Surrounds Fatal 1998 Crickshaw Ranch Drilling Accident" to a notification stating that the page was no longer available. Stifling my disappointment, I searched for Crickshaw Ranch. A listing for a private ranch outside Chasm, a small town not four hours away from the Tule Creek house, appeared. At the bottom of the page was a phone number.

I wheeled quietly over to the door as I dialed the number on my cell, listening for the subtle sounds of Veronica listening back. What passed to Chrissy for music still wafted down the hallway, but the quiet breathing I didn't truly expect beyond the door but feared nonetheless was mercifully absent.

As the call rang, I realized I wasn't at all sure what to ask. I didn't have long to worry about it. Soon enough, a robotic voice alerted me that I had reached a phone number whose voicemail had not been set up. The call ended and all was silent. All except for the quiet clicking of the worms.

‡‡

I'm kicking the door again, demanding to be let in. Fire blisters the horizon, and the sounds of human screams waft across the empty plains. Something impossibly large in the distance lumbers through the clouds, and I realize that this couldn't have been what happened. In a flash I know that I am dreaming, but it does nothing to stop the panic. "For Christ's sake, let me in!" I scream—I don't want to be here when the impossibly enormous thing finds us. The door is much harder to kick in this time, but eventually the hinges give way and I'm inside. Through the windows, the grass bends violently in a wind I cannot hear. A light cast from behind a pile of books flickers against the living room ceiling. It draws me into the black interior. As I round the stack, I see mother, crouched in front of a fire made from books and stray papers on the carpet. A backpack is splayed open before her, its contents disgorged onto the floor. Specimen jars, a video camera, climbing gear, and flares, she runs her fingers nervously over each object in some inscrutable inventory process. When she hears me behind her, she turns. Her movements are jagged and animal. The burst capillaries in her eyes savagely reflect the flame. "The stone," she whispers. "Can't you hear it singing?"

⸸

If we hadn't reached the plateau of indifference most long-standing marriages tend to find, I would've been ashamed to wake up on the couch again. It happened often enough that Veronica wouldn't be particularly suspicious, even if I couldn't recall how I ended up there. I let the smell of coffee lure me into the kitchen, where my wife had already taken her place at the table.

"Rise and shine, sleepyhead," she said without enthusiasm.

"Hey... Guess I nodded off at some point."

"I, on the other hand, turned in super early. Getting old, I suppose."

She turned to the window and said nothing more. Outside, the sky was burdened with clouds. The tall grass shimmered in the distance with a wind that hadn't yet reached us, and the aura of expectant stillness inspired an insidious discomfort in me. I was so absorbed in the feeling that I nearly didn't notice Chrissy walk into the dining room.

"Look who's here, hon."

"Hey, I gotta eat sometimes too," Chrissy said, a rare glimmer of lightheartedness in her voice.

"Well, what sounds good?"

Chrissy shrugged and headed to the pantry to browse the cereal. Veronica continued to stare out the window, ignoring the coffee in her hands, still accenting the air with flourishes of steam. She remained motionless when I walked up behind her. Her shoulders recoiled against my light squeeze.

"Jesus, honey, what's wrong?"

When she turned, her smile didn't quite hide her worry. "Oh," she began, "it's probably nothing, but early this morning there was a van parked at the end of the drive. It stayed there for about an hour, then drove off."

I looked at the driveway, empty and filled with sunlight intensified by the contrast of dark clouds beyond.

"Probably nothing. It's just..." she turned away as her voice trailed off, rubbing her eyes with her palms.

"What is it?" Chrissy asked behind us.

"Nothing," I said a little too loudly. I smiled, trying to soften my misstep. "It's probably the Wi-Fi company. You know how the Internet's been lately. They're probably just testing the connection."

From their van? For an hour? It seemed unlikely, but I found myself inexplicably eager to put the whole thing out of mind. I poured a coffee and retreated to the living room. It wasn't until I had sunk into the couch that the night before began to loom in my thoughts: the red worms that came back from the dead, the ranch with a name matching the one on a container from the Tule Creek house. A part of me wished that I had stayed away, allowed the past to be nothing but the past, particularly since I was powerless to make it anything else.

Too late, I thought as I stared stupidly at the number on my phone's missed call alert. Before I retreated again to the office to return the call from Crickshaw Ranch, I already knew I'd be leaving. The hard part would be deciding which lie to hide behind.

‡‡

As happy as I should've been that Chrissy wanted to come along, even if only to sift through her long-vanished grandmother's junk for vinyl, I was relieved that she didn't want to talk. There were too many uncomfortable questions that would demand answers soon enough, the most dreaded of them being "Why aren't we going to the Tule Creek house?" For now, I was happy to let her take over the Camry's Bluetooth while I pretended to be absorbed in thought. It was less painful, for once, to be what we now were: two individuals with personal concerns utterly irrelevant to the other.

In silence, I mulled over the brief exchange with the woman who identified herself as Cheryl Crickshaw. After a moment of uncertainty, I had decided to approach the question directly. I asked the quiet voice on the line if she was familiar with a college professor named Kandice Sawyer. The voice disappeared long enough for the silence to become uncomfortable. When it returned, it had a new, harder edge.

"Who are you?"

"I'm her son."

"This isn't the place to talk."

"Well...Where is?"

But she had already hung up.

She had clearly recognized Mom's name. I had little doubt that the Crickshaws knew what had happened to her. The need for secrecy, along with the fact that whatever had happened remained entirely outside what little existed to constitute an "official narrative," didn't bother me as much as it should have. Thanks to my brother's penchant for conspiracy theories, the idea of a government cover-up was easy to entertain, even if I didn't fully believe it. I focused on the only detail that gave me hope: that Cheryl hadn't explicitly declined to speak in person.

Nine Inch Nail's "Head Like a Hole" began playing from Chrissy's playlist, filling the car with darkly brooding synthesizers. Although I was closer than ever to discovering what happened to Mom, I felt more uneasy than relieved. I quietly hummed along. The distraction was welcome.

When Chrissy noticed, a bewildered smile crossed her face. "Dad! I didn't know you knew Nine Inch Nails."

I couldn't stifle a laugh. "Just how old do you think I am, young lady? This is closer to my era than yours."

Suddenly, the garish wail of police sirens erupted from behind us. "Shit," I said as I flipped my turn signal. I checked my speedometer. We were well under the limit. "What the hell is he doing?" I made an effort to swallow my anger as I braked gently for the shoulder. Chrissy turned off the music.

The police car was coming in fast—too fast. I edged over further, leaving plenty of room for it to pass. Instead, it rushed boldly up behind us. The dawning realization of a possible impact surfaced only at the last minute. I reached over and grabbed Chrissy's shoulder.

Just when disaster seemed inevitable, the cop swung around us and onto the street, clearing our back bumper by what couldn't have been more than a foot. It blasted its horn as it sped off, leaving behind a sour haze of seared rubber.

The sudden silence was a second shock. It was a while before either of us could speak.

"What the *fuck?*" Chrissy shouted.

"I know, I know."

"Can you fucking *believe* that?"

"Chrissy, language," I groaned.

"Scared the...hell out of me. Jesus."

"It wasn't a trooper. We'll stop at the next town and report this. I didn't have the presence of mind to grab a license plate, did you?"

"I...I tried," she said, wiping tears from her eyes. "It...didn't have one."

‡‡

We had largely recovered our calm by the time we made it to the small, half-abandoned town deep in the Texas Panhandle. We pulled into a local burger stop before searching for the police station. When the carhop, a frail woman with a toothless smile, brought our food in two greasy sacks, Chrissy unplugged her ear buds and tossed them aside.

"So I guess we're not going to the Tule Creek house?" she asked over the noise of crinkling paper.

I didn't miss the accusatory undertone, but I can't say it wasn't expected or deserved.

"Sorry, kiddo, not yet. I have something to take care of first. I promise we'll make it there on the way back."

She looked out the window at the empty rows of parking spaces. Beyond the asphalt, the rusted remains of an old car peeked out from the wall of grass that had been allowed to swallow it.

"So you're having an affair."

"What? No, Chrissy. Is that what your mom thinks?"

She shrugged. "It's hard to tell what she thinks. All I know is she's lonely."

"Yeah, well, we're all lonely, Chris. It's called growing up."

She turned to me then, a hurt look in her eyes. I realized once again that I might've handled this whole thing better.

"Look," I said, twisting to face her as best I could. "Remember Grandma? My mother? I know you probably don't—you were so young when she disappeared, and no one's talked about her in so long. She was nuts about you, Chrissy. You should've seen her face when she first saw you. The tiredness in her eyes just...melted away, something that rarely ever happened."

"Brown hair, hazel eyes," she muttered. "And that may have been from a photograph somewhere...but that's it."

"Well, you know how Uncle Dan says she never would've run away? I think I'm close to finding out what *really* happened."

"But the police said—"

"Nothing. The police said nothing." Chrissy jumped as I smacked the steering wheel with the palm of my hand. "That's where they'd have me leave it. That's where your mom wants it to stay: in the past. But it's my *mom*, goddamn it. What if she needs my help? What if there really is another story, one with a motive and some sort of rationale? What if there's more to existence than this horrifying emptiness that swallows people without a trace? Who wants to live in an insatiable, blood-hungry universe like *that*?"

I shook my head, forcing the tears back that threatened to flood my eyes.

"If it were Veronica, would you ever give up? If a decade passed, or two, or even more, would you stop looking? Despite her shortcomings, and even if she were guilty of a thousand more, would you really want to forget?"

I shoved the burger back into the bag. Feelings that had simmered quietly for too long rose readily to the surface. I understood now why it was better to lie to Veronica. Like a wound, the truth exposed the parts that hurt to the jagged contours of the world outside. Vulnerable and empty, I sagged against the steering wheel and fought back the horror of solitude that appeared to envelop the world from a fanged horizon.

I didn't expect Chrissy's hand to find my back. With all the awkwardness of a teenager, she let it linger pointlessly before pulling it away again.

"I understand, Dad," she said. "I wouldn't give up on Mom. But I also wouldn't want to give up on you or the people who need me while they're alive. Look at me." She shook my arm and I sat up, miserable but slowly recovering. "I'm with you, okay? Let's find out what we can, but we go home when it's done."

‡‡

We drove around the town for half an hour before giving up on locating a police station. Run-down shops and long-abandoned gas stations filled the odd spaces between empty lots and ragged houses. Antique cars that couldn't have been touched in years littered driveways cracked with rogue patches of grass. In front of a grocery store, we found an old man emptying plastic sacks from his car into the trash cans in the parking lot. When I asked him about the police station, he stared at me uncomprehendingly until I drove away.

"There's nothing to do about it, I guess," I said, noting how much lower the sun hung in the sky than I had hoped. "We best move on." Chrissy, bored but sympathetic now, nodded. She didn't seem to mind when I mentioned that we'd likely have to skip the return detour to the Tule Creek house.

I set the GPS to Crickshaw Ranch, some thirty miles into the middle of nowhere. As we drove out of city limits and into the surrounding sprawl of small, knotted mesquites, Chrissy dialed her mom. The call rang uselessly before going to voicemail.

The nervous sweat of my palms unpleasantly wetted the worn plastic of the steering wheel. In the panhandle of Texas, one gets used to the feeling of isolation—some call it "freedom"—but the closer we drew to Crickshaw Ranch, the more the great, empty expanse seemed like a hungry maw, ready to suck unwary wanderers into the erasure beyond. If one could walk off the edge of the world, this would be the place to do it.

We drove on as the road tightened, losing a lane on either side. Great slabs of sandstone jutted from the fists of malformed brush. The wind picked up, stirring a haze of dirt that glowed red with the first suggestions of twilight. After a while, Chrissy turned off the music and stared into the passing landscape. Everything fell weightlessly into the deep silence.

When the narrow strip of asphalt suddenly vanished beneath us, giving way to gravel that soon turned to dirt, I checked the GPS. The signal had given up long ago.

"Dammit," I hissed. There was no way to turn around without backing the car into a sand-filled ditch on either side. "We keep going," I said. "I know we're headed in the right direction."

The sun sank lower and lower as we jolted over the uneven road. My hopes of making it back before dark vanished with the gloaming and I resigned to the necessity of finding a motel back in town. As much as I knew it was my own fault, much worse was the prospect of admitting my deception to Veronica.

I told Chrissy about the change of plans. "Hey," she said, "at least we'll have time to see the Tule Creek house tomorrow morning." I did not doubt that I owed her at least that.

I had all but given up hope when a light suddenly reached us through the dark. It vanished and reappeared as we dipped in and out of depressions in the road, remaining fixed as we advanced. "It's a house," Chrissy said, and in a moment the vague outlines of a tall structure emerged against the lavender sky.

"Maybe this is it," I said, "although it's too late to go knocking on doors."

"Wouldn't hurt to try," my daughter countered cheerfully, as if the strange evening had finally awakened her curiosity.

Soon, we parked in front of the house. It was large but old and weatherworn. The merciless panhandle wind had eaten away at the paint, and even in the waning light I could see that the yard was littered with large, angular bits of scrap metal. If I wasn't so uncertain about my ability to find my way back to town in the dark, I wouldn't have gone to the door.

"Stay here," I told Chrissy. "Try to call your mom again."

"Yeah, right," she said, and got out.

‡‡

Much to my surprise, a smiling old man in work-worn overalls opened the door within seconds of the first knock.

"Lemme guess: y'all must be lost."

"I'm afraid so," I said.

"Well, come on in." He stepped aside, revealing a dimly lit hallway flickering with the light of a distant television. "The name's Thomas—you can call me Tom. May as well have a drink while we figure out where it is you need to be. I'll tell you straight away, you're a ways away from just about everything out here."

"I don't doubt you there."

He laughed politely and extended his hand. I took it as Chrissy cast a questioning look my way. I introduced her as the man heartily guided us inside.

We followed Tom down the hall and into a kitchen that branched from the main corridor. The house wasn't immaculate, but the man appeared to maintain some semblance of order. Everything had its place, even if, like the model car I caught sharing a shelf with various cookbooks culled from discount bins, its place was unorthodox.

"Have a seat," he said, pulling out two stools from the bar.

"Thank you, but we really don't want to put you out."

"Nonsense," he said, fetching two Bud Lights and a Coke from the fridge. "As far off track as you folks are, directions can take some time."

I thanked him and savored the cold, carbonated jolt I had almost forgotten. It was my first beer in years. Chrissy sulked warily over her Coke as Tom settled his considerable bulk into a stool on the opposite side. He took a long drink, wiping his mouth with his sleeve.

"We're looking for Crickshaw Ranch," I began. "GPS led us in this general direction, but I'm afraid I didn't realize we had lost the signal until we were well off the beaten path."

I was unprepared for the look of surprise that quickly overtook Tom's jovial features. He shook his head slowly and paused for another long drink. "Well," he said, choosing his words carefully now as he stared at the bottle in his hand, "you may just be less lost than I originally suspected. You're about as close to Crickshaw Ranch as you can possibly get. It's only about another half-mile before you reach the fence line. Except," he lifted his eyes to mine as he leaned over the bar, "ain't nobody can get inside."

Tom got up again and ambled to the fridge, dropping the already empty bottle into the wastebasket on the way. I met Chrissy's curious gaze and shrugged as he cracked another beer.

"You ain't the federal type," he said, oblivious to the irony that I was, in fact, a federal employee, though of a quite different breed than he meant. "They don't generally bring their family along for the ride." As he settled in his seat once more, his infectious grin had returned. "Reporter?"

"More of a private investigator," I said.

He accompanied a nod with a low chuckle. "Crickshaw Ranch attracts a very, what you might call 'niche,' demographic. Not many people know about it anymore. Even folks in town have largely forgotten the whole thing. It ain't no Skinwalker Ranch, I tell you that. You can hardly even find anything online, as I'm sure you're aware. No," his face shifted, darkening with angular lines of frustration, "they've locked this one up and thrown away the key, I tell you."

Chrissy's eyes widened with surprise, and I'm certain my own expression mirrored hers. In just a few sentences I had already learned more about Mom's disappearance than years of official efforts had revealed. The empty space that had loomed over my adult years finally began to take on color—vague and sinister, but a welcome change from the incomprehensible darkness it was beginning to replace. I found myself wishing Dan were with me, confirming at last his worst fears which everyone else had dismissed as delusions.

Our surprise wasn't lost on Tom, who nodded in approval. "Yes," he said, "you aren't the only ones who've looked into old Crickshaw. That's why I moved here, you see, to keep an eye on the place. I'd wager I even know a bit more than you folks, though not as much as Cheryl, of course."

"I spoke to Cheryl Crickshaw on the phone, if that's who you mean," I said. "Although she wouldn't say much."

"Arthur died about ten years ago," Tom went on, absorbing my implied question without pause, "and Cheryl hasn't gotten out much since. It's a miracle to get her to say anything at all, even though half of what she does say is plain madness. It's really taken a toll on her, this whole business."

"I wanted to ask her about someone who went missing in '98."

"You won't get much useful information, I'm sorry to say, even if you could get inside, which is impossible now. Someone padlocked the gates several years ago, either Cheryl or the plainclothes characters you still see milling about every once in a great while. There were more of them back when it happened, '98, like you said, but they've mostly gone their own way by now."

"What happened, exactly, in 1998, Tom?"

The old man looked at me, then turned to Chrissy. With subdued laughter, he finished another bottle.

I looked down at my own, noting with surprise that it was already empty.

"Y'all really are brand new to this whole ordeal, ain't you?"

I nodded, and he responded with a deep sigh.

"We're gonna need something a little stronger to get through this," he said, reaching for the glasses and bottle of Wild Turkey at the end of the bar.

Tom's story still spun in ghoulish colors as Chrissy helped me onto the fold-out bed in the guest room early the next morning. What had genuinely interested me at first now took on horrifying dimensions in my drunkenness—it was a surreal pastiche of contradictory accounts, and I am still far from confident in my ability to distinguish truth from the wild distortions refracted from Tom's words by my intoxicated imagination.

1998 loomed large in my troubled consciousness as I listened to Chrissy's even breathing turn into soft snores. In a maddening loop, I replayed Tom's account of the drilling accident on the Crickshaw farm, during which two immigrant workers died. In the local papers, a lack of proper equipment was cited as the culprit, along with an unexpected gas explosion—regrets were offered for the loss of life, but family never turned up looking for bodies. Oh well. Life goes on.

Except some people reported gunfire on the ranch—a lot of gunfire, and from automatic weapons. Almost everyone noticed the uncharacteristic presence of military aircraft in the area over the ensuing weeks. When the concerned and generally idle citizens of the small, dilapidated town came to the ranch to inquire further, they were turned back by groups of nonuniform strangers who lined the property in knots less than a mile apart. When the subject came up around town, it was clear that no one believed they were Arthur Crickshaw's men.

Queries filed at the small, local police office that were initially greeted with enthusiasm by the town officers soon turned cold—the sheriff eventually went so far as to deny that he had ever heard of any strange occurrences at Arthur's. As time passed, the quiet Texas town slowly drifted back to normal.

In the small hours, the reeling of my mind kept me from sleep. When the throbbing pain blossomed red and fierce in the center of my skull, the more incomprehensible elements of what may have been Tom's story took precedence: the way Arthur stumbled into town in the following years, drunk and raving about the cave in the middle of his property filled with strange insects—large, white scorpions and spiders without eyes. Muttering to anyone who would listen about an ancient stone, perfectly round and matte black, older than the earth and housing creatures from far, far away.

Arthur eventually quit coming to town, but he still tried to tell his story—or did he? Was this part of Tom's narrative, or were my own nightmare mixed in by the indistinct borderlands of sleep? Either way, in my head is the image of old man Crickshaw broadcasting the story in Morse code on a shortwave radio, broken phrases and tantalizing fragments for the few who had fallen into obsession over the mysteries of Crickshaw Ranch.

The soft light from under the door vanishes. I no longer hear Chrissy breathing. I reach out into the darkness. My hand touches a cold, damp surface, and a smell like rotten eggs suddenly fills my lungs. Something slithers across my fingers. I fall back, my mouth open but unable to make a sound. When I turn, Mom stands beside a man I don't recognize. Their flashlights are trained on a large, spherical mass that doesn't reflect the beams. After a moment, the man says, "Note that the water hasn't eroded it at all. This cave...it has to be millions of years old. There's no way this...rock...should still be here."

Mom looks at him for a moment before saying "Well, congratulations, Doctor, on your *own* future publication. Seems like this has been a profitable little journey for everyone involved."

"No...you don't get it, Kandice. This thing *shouldn't be here.*"

As they stare silently at the massive stone, a constant sound rises into audibility. A low, buzzing drone.

Mom says, "God, that fucking noise. Do you hear it, Brian?"

"If this cave is millions of years old, it's an infant compared to this rock," the man says, ignoring her.

"Are you okay, Brian?"

He draws closer to the stone. "It's like a window to another age—can't you feel its timelessness? Can't you sense the sublimity of the infinite? Nothing like this exists on the planet. This...thing is older than the Earth itself. I'm certain of it."

"Jesus, Doctor Shaw, you're freaking me the fuck out."

"You don't need me to tell you. Feel for yourself."

The man Mom called Brian reaches toward the rock and places his hand against it. He closes his eyes, seemingly in pleasure. After a moment he shudders with what looks like the shock of pain. He opens his eyes and quickly withdraws his hand. It's crawling with masses of red worms.

‡‡

Someone shook me. It took longer than it should've to recognize Chrissy. She was unnaturally pale and distraught. "You were screaming in your sleep," she said.

I sat up on the fold-out bed, fighting the sickness that swelled inside like the surf of a poisonous ocean. The pain blotted out the dream from the night before, but the fear it inspired still surged through the impossible ache.

"Let's go," I said.

Chrissy draped an arm across my shoulder, steadying me as I rose to my feet. We lumbered awkwardly through the big empty house. The TV that had been left on all night was off, but there was no sign of Tom. In the kitchen, I made a note thanking him for his hospitality on the back of a torn envelope. The front door was left wide open, and nothing moved in the dense forest of rusted scrap metal beyond. We scanned the horizon, empty and barren except for the dark patches of mesquite. The man was nowhere to be seen.

"Can you drive?" I asked Chrissy, choking down a fresh wave of nausea.

"I have my permit, Dad. Relax."

"I'm not sure we're any less lost."

"We'll just go back the way we came. It's no big deal."

"I'm sorry Chrissy. Let's go..." I didn't get to "home" before sleep overtook me again.

‡‡

Mercifully, my sleep was dreamless and uninterrupted until the car stopped. "Wallet," Chrissy said, shaking my arm. Achingly, I fished it out of my back pocket and handed it to her. As she opened the door, I tried to regain my bearings.

It was hot and the sun was nearing its zenith. A group of laughing college-aged boys stood outside my window smoking cigarettes. Two of them leaned on a "No Smoking" sign attached to a cage full of propane tanks. As my eyes adjusted to the brilliant white of day, I found that we were parked outside a gas station.

Chrissy soon returned with a sack of water bottles, a packet of two Advil, a small carton of orange juice, and a bag of beef jerky. "Thanks," I said as she handed the items to me. The hunger and thirst came all at once, and I tore into everything as she pulled the car around to a gas pump.

As the sour mist that enveloped my body slowly subsided, I began to recognize my surroundings. I had eaten at the rundown Tex-Mex place across the busy street a dozen times. The highest buildings of the small but highly praised university a few blocks away peeked tentatively above the uneven wall of elms. "We're not going home, are we?" I said when Chrissy got back into the car.

"Hey," she said, "you owe me. The whole reason I came is to check out the Tule Creek house."

"Can't argue with that. How'd you find it?"

"GPS, genius."

I was recovering, but still too exhausted and full of guilt to comment on her attitude. After last night's overindulgence, I deserved much worse.

"I'm good to drive," I said.

"Don't worry about it. I need the practice anyway." We pulled out of the parking lot and onto the main street. "No wonder you don't drink," she said, glancing at me with half a smile.

"Yeah. It's bad."

We drove in silence as buildings became scarce on either side of the road. The elms vanished, replaced by wide expanses of grass. An orange tint to the distant horizon promised an oncoming wind filled with dust.

I found my thoughts wandering away from the Tule Creek house ahead. Instead, I imagined the cave, far behind us now and hidden somewhere in the rock and mesquite, a black hole into which my mother descended. Who knew what she saw down there. I wondered if there were other places like that, terrible secrets tucked in the wilderness that only a handful of people knew to look for, places watched by people like Tom, straining to glimpse weird lights in the night.

"There's another reason we aren't going home," Chrissy said.

"What's that?"

"That car."

I craned my neck to the rearview mirror. Far behind us and partially obscured by the heat simmering from the asphalt, a gray car appeared over a distant hill.

"I wasn't sure before, but now I'm certain. It was following us well before the gas station."

The fear in Chrissy's voice worried me, but I refused to let it show. Time, for once, to be the adult. "Did you call your mom?" I asked.

"No answer, but I left a message."

The dust storm in the distance took on a darker shade the further we drove. The wind picked up, rippling the grass in wide, sweeping arches. Soon, fierce gusts rocked the car. Still the vehicle remained behind us.

"There's only one thing to do," I concluded. "Pull over."

I wasn't sure who to expect: the police, the government, or worse? The confrontation promised to be unpleasant. Calmly, I opened the glove box and fished for the handgun I kept loaded inside. I pulled the holster out, knocking the drivers' manual and a few pens to the floor. Chrissy stared at me, eyes wide with fear. "Just in case," I said, and tucked the weapon between the center console and my seat.

As she pulled onto a tractor path that terminated a few yards off the road by a fence, I leaned down to pick up the spilled items. When my hands touched a cylindrical, plastic canister, I froze.

It was the red worms. Had I taken them with us? I couldn't remember. Inside, they writhed more furiously than ever, knocking against the container with a tiny but palpable force. I quickly slipped the thing in my pocket.

It took a long time before the car finally reached us. Each second passed with agonizing slowness. If it weren't for the distracting noise of the wind and preternatural gloom outside, the wait would've been unbearable.

To our surprise, it zoomed right past us. Before I could glimpse a license plate, the gray car had already vanished in the swirling mist of red dust.

"There," I said, "just our imaginations."

We must've known our relief was unreasonable, but we embraced it all the same. I kidded Chrissy about her determination to see the drab old Tule Creek house, and Chrissy muttered, "You should at least learn to hold your tongue better than you do your liquor." Our laughter took on something of a mad aspect out there in the hideous sandstorm. It was heartfelt, but neither light nor jovial. It was the desperate laughter of fear.

By the time we pulled into what should've been the shadow of the great, empty house, the sky was blood red. We rushed through the deafening wind to the porch, the collars of our shirts pulled up over our noses, still giddy with the sense of impending calamity. The padlock was in place, and Chrissy shouted something that I couldn't make out. I took the keys from her, and with a satisfying rattle of falling chains, the door gave way and we spilled into the entryway.

"Christ," I said, pushing the door closed with effort. "This is the worst sandstorm I've ever seen."

"This place really is a dump, isn't it?" Chrissy was already captivated by the heaps of debris looming near the darkened corners of the ceiling.

"It's a regular treasure trove. I think there were some old records in the kitchen." I pointed the way, and she vanished in the deep sepia light straining through the windows.

Outside, the roar continued. Idly, I picked through the books I had begun to stack by the door last time. I quickly found that previously innocuous titles like *The Caves of Carta Valley* and Nevada Barr's *Blind Descent* now possessed sinister resonances. I had to put them down. We needed to get *home*. The amateur detective work could wait for another day.

Suddenly, I caught a murmur of something else in the din of howling wind. An engine, faint but certain. I raised the blinds of the nearest window.

Nothing but the furious swirl of dirt whipping through the grass beyond. Yet I heard it again, the muffled sputter of a vehicle.

"Chrissy!"

When she didn't answer, I quickly made my way through the gloom to the kitchen. Along the way, I toppled a box with my knee, sending its contents rushing to the floor. In the dim light, it looked like a mass of small worms clumped into an impossible knot. A second glance revealed a generous heap of loose change instead.

"You okay?" Chrissy asked from the dark, startling me all over again.

"Christ, yes, Chrissy."

"What is this?" She lifted a black, rectangular box.

"Looks like a VCR, kiddo. Have you never seen one before?"

"I thought it may have been an eight-track player," she said, turning it over in her hands. "What does it do?"

"It plays tapes. Video tapes."

"It has something inside." Shrugging, she handed it to me.

"Look," I said, "I thought I heard something outside, Chris. Why don't you try to call your mom one more time and let's wrap things up here."

"What did you hear?"

"Sounded like a car."

Chrissy nodded and began walking back toward the kitchen. "Stay close," I warned as she disappeared around the corner.

Shifting the bulk of the VCR between my hands, I noticed a slight weight sliding back and forth inside. I rotated the machine until I found the face and pressed aside the flap concealing the inserted VHS. On the label, I could barely make out the word "Crickshaw" half submerged in the dusty mechanics within.

I stood there staring stupidly at the black box in my hands. How often had I walked past this thing? How many times had I assumed this piece of junk would take me no closer to uncovering the incomprehensible rift Mom's vanishing had left in my life? It didn't matter and yet it did. Was there something out there, I wondered, some controlling force that withholds all secrets until our desperation is ripe?

I traced the power cable connected to the VCR to confirm that the metal prongs were not bent. The house was full of TVs, but I was certain the main set in the living room still had the input cables the VHS player would require.

Slowly, I made my way into the gloom, groping the walls for a light switch. I found one next to Mom's buried sofa, but when I switched it on it burned out in a flash, plunging the room into a darkness somehow deeper than before.

Something crashed against the walls outside and I found myself wishing that I had locked the front door behind us. The intensity of the storm suddenly increased, and the walls groaned against the force of the wind. Overhead, another crash and the clink of crumbling glass sounded from the upper floor.

"The wind," I muttered to myself. "Nothing but wind."

The insufficient light filling the living room churned restlessly. I knelt before the TV and sorted blindly through the mess of cables beneath. It wasn't long before everything was plugged in. I hit the power button and the old set sputtered to life in a rush of static. Still holding the VCR in my hands, I pressed play.

A ghostly green light spilled into the room as the interior of a cave filled the screen. There was a chamber, a vaulted expanse split down the middle by a small stream. Despite the profusion of green glow sticks strewn across the floor, all that remained visible of the ceiling were the tips of large stalactites.

An uncanny familiarity swept over me as the camera continued to turn, finally resting on a large, perfectly spherical stone half submerged in the heart of the chamber.

I barely heard the third crash as Mom walked toward the stone, zooming in slowly until the blackness filled the screen.

"Look," she said, her voice distorted and distant, but more real than the voice in my nightmares that had served as her proxy for all these years.

She leaned over the rock, dangerously close now, and suddenly the matte surface gave way to an incomprehensible depth. As the camera tilted further still, a dazzling array of unfamiliar stars swam into focus.

All was still. Over the wind of the storm outside, I heard another, more desolate wail.

"The call of the void," Mom said in a quiet voice, "the song of a larger world outside."

Her pale hand dipped into the field of vision and came to rest against the stars. It didn't flinch as the thin, red worms appeared, burrowing through her flesh and into her veins.

"Dad?"

I hit the eject button and tossed the tape aside. I tried to ignore the terrified throb of my heart against my temples as I turned to Chrissy.

She held her cell phone out to me. I took it. "Veronica?"

"What have you done?" my wife asked in a voice I'd never heard before. "There are men here looking for you. They're all parked outside right now. You need to—" a loud crash cut her short. My breath stopped as I heard the muffled sound of rapid movement. "They're coming in," she whispered. "They're—" and the line went dead.

I stood there, absorbing the impossibility of what I had heard. It took everything I had to calmly hand the phone to Chrissy. "We need to go now. Call her back while I start the car."

"Wait, what's going on?"

I turned to the door. I thought of nothing but the gun in the console. The tape was already no more substantial than another bad dream, a mere symptom of the real and inevitable forces set to punish my curiosity.

The front door had blown wide open. In the tall grass just beyond the gravel driveway, casually dressed men unloaded machine guns and gasoline cans from twin unmarked vans.

In an instant, the world I hoped for had shattered.

I didn't move until the bullets ripped the air around me. Splinters from the doorframe stung the exposed skin on my arms. As I stumbled back into the house, I fell into Chrissy, landing together in a confused heap on the floor.

I kicked the door closed and scrambled to my feet. I wedged a chair beneath the doorknob just as the second wave of bullets screamed through the walls, tearing through the piles of junk, which retaliated with clouds of dust.

"We have to hide," I said, feeling for my daughter in the dark. When I found her, my hands came away wet.

In the red light, I saw the hole freshly bloomed in the middle of her forehead.

The bullets didn't stop. They never would, I knew, not until the last traces of the thing that had crawled from the bowels of the earth so long ago were finally erased.

They should've burned this place sooner, I thought, despite the hopeless sobs that choked me. They should've fixed this long ago. I twisted the cap to the specimen container.

I coughed on the dust as I dipped my fingers inside. The pain of the red worms entering my flesh was intense, but I didn't move away.

I let them in.

And the long process of transformation began.

ABDN-1

I AWAKEN LIKE a scream.

It's hell for both of us, like shaking off a deep sleep on a cold morning, a simile arising from the experiences of my human host. The transition is a shock that doesn't deaden the senses, an invisible fire dancing across nerves that refuse to die. The insidious panic of an illness that lends every passing moment the metallic edge of pain.

Brian, the human counterpart, isn't having an easy time. A vital alert flashes across the screen projected inside his helmet. He tries to control his breathing, but he feels me inside him. I try to make myself small and quiet. He's no good to us if he loses it now. His eyes roll restlessly across the stars as he retreats to his "safe space"—there's sunlight there, and a dock stretching out into an expanse of pristine water. He goes there with the readiness of training. It only helps a little. I do my best not to interrupt.

For Brian, just like the rest of them, it's an uncanny sense of violation, a hidden gaze burning from within. They scan the horizon even though they couldn't say what they're looking for. This horizon—Brian's horizon—is empty except for the spattered pinpoints of starlight. Like the rest of them, he searches. Like the rest of them, he doesn't realize it's already too late.

Despite all the times I've done this, awakening never gets easier.

"Walker one," a woman's voice says, "medical has detected a sudden elevation in blood pressure. Is everything alright?"

Brian lets his gaze rest on the empty circle in the distance, the small nothingness devoid of stars.

"Yeah, I'm good. Just got a little spooked is all. Call it vertigo."

"Yeah, well, we all have reason to be a little spooked lately. Still, I think command is going to want to follow procedure on this one."

"Christ, Sarah. We need these mining plates in place already. I'm fine, really."

"Don't even tell me you couldn't use the rest, Brian. The backup team is already suiting up and medical is waiting for you at the airlock. Just cut the tough guy act and get your ass home."

Relief washes over him, yes, but there's something else, something that isn't me. *What if this isn't about my blood pressure?* he wonders. *What if it's not medical waiting, but a different team altogether?*

Quiet now, don't be absurd, I answer, and it works its way through the sinews of his anxiety like a *pharmakon* (the ancient word comes back to me unbidden). I'm not accustomed to dispensing cold comforts, but we need him in the best of shape. After all, we have such a long distance to cover in so short a time.

‡‡

He doesn't activate the sleep medications uploaded to his health regulator, even though the medic instructed him to. Once he's in the room, he logs into the system and begins deleting files. It's a ridiculous measure, but I try to appreciate his urgency—all symbiotic relationships require sympathy, and I ought to be accustomed to such concessions by now. There's the corpse, after all, moldering deep in storage in a pool of blood. The gash across its throat still smiles up at the ceiling of the chamber from between two steel crates. We both imagine for a moment the surprise of the storage attendant who may eventually stumble across it. The search for the missing crew member began nearly 48 hours ago—I can feel Brian's panic rising like a swollen growth.

His fingers dash madly across the holographic projections of files as they vanish from existence. It's unclear how he thinks the texts will connect him to the corpse in the hold, but it's difficult to expect rationality from him. I can see that he's been cracking at the seams for so long, undergoing a process of deterioration that the calculating persona of a skilled mechanic hides well. Perhaps he still feels me inside and he imagines he's made a mistake. He's right, according to his own limited perspective, but pretending to have never read the grimoires, religious texts, odd treatises, and novels of extreme violence won't make the slightest difference. They, after all, are just fictions, mere fantasies that suggest the gap he sought and nothing more.

Brian pauses as a flurry of voices erupts over the intercom. His backup crew is ready to disembark. He shudders, but it's truly not in shame. For a moment he imagines he's with them, peering out the airlock into the starless circle. He's been told that distress is common—none of his trainers hesitated to remind him that the mission's object still lies well beyond the full understanding of science. A black hole is a closed system that cannot be measured from the outside. Its very existence is only detected by the effect it has on surrounding celestial objects. A great rip in the fabric of space and time looming ever nearer—who can say that nothing stares back?

"Try not to think about it," a woman whose name he has trouble remembering said long ago. "Just do your job and come home quickly." With that, she downed the rest of her Merlot and drew him close.

The unexpected memory pains him and it pains me in turn. Oh, what I wouldn't have given, eons ago, when I first awoke in the hellish torture of time, to unburden these humans of their worthless sentiments. I have learned since that they can be valuable, so I take the woman and make her my own. I study her eyes, happy little emeralds dazzling above the caress of a smile, and the curves of her body that quicken Brian's pulse. In his mind, their bodies entwine, and somewhere I can sense the humid expanse of the ocean. What frail little details are these, already fraying with disuse. I won't erase her—a mistake I've long unlearned. Our greatest resources are often their most minute details.

Brian's fingers hover over the one document it would be wise to delete. I don't urge him on. He reads it slowly, despite his fear that the communications sector could be reading along with him: "I'm so lonely, even with Joshua," it says. "We trade our despair, remembering those we left behind at the colonies and wonder who else they've learned to love in our absence. We discuss the texts we've found and the worlds beyond they suggest—yes, we talk and talk as the hours continue to sag with inertia: about the inevitable abyss between us, between all beings, and the solitude held together by the dead weight of routine. None of it does any good. I must be losing my mind—"

Brian closes the journal without deleting it. I remind him of the sleep medications. Reluctantly, he activates the device attached to his shoulder. I suggest the bottle of spirits under the cot as well, and slowly he forgets the things I want him to forget. I fill him once again with the woman, this time adding my own ancient memories of the Mediterranean. The air sours with salt, softened by the incense burning on the fireplace mantle in his mind. I infuse the gray with color, and his pain quietens. As he drifts away, I turn to the body hidden deep in the ship to initiate the miracle.

‡‡

"Do you hear it?" Cade asks the room. No one looks at him.

"It's a distant scraping, like something's trying to climb to the surface. It's just beneath the static. Listen!"

A shiver sparks somewhere within my human vessel, but he wisely maintains his silence. The monitoring team exchange unreadable glances as the projected screens refuse to deviate from the standard glowing ring of Hawking radiation.

Janice finally risks pointing out that the black hole cannot emit sound.

"I get it—even photons can't get out. But if we consider quantum alternatives, who's to say that a black hole can't emit some form of nonlocal exchange of information?" His brow is knotted in confusion as he stares at the ring on the monitor.

I urge Brian forward and he places a hand on Cade's back. Something passes between them, and I can only imagine that it's some manner of understanding. The outer boundaries are cracking, and they have both felt it in their own limited way. The others will see soon enough. For now, they interpret Brian's intercession benevolently.

"Please," Cade says, turning to him. "Tell them that you hear it too."

"Quiet," Brian says. "You need rest. It's been a rough week for everyone. We'll need you in shape when we set up the Hawking mines."

In his mind, Brian silently poses a question to the room: *Can you finally see there's nothing wrong with me?* This pleases me greatly. It's uncommon to find a subject so complicit in my deceptions. I fill the man with gratitude and color it with the voice of his colleagues—*Yes, we are proud of you, Brian. You have done so well.* To my satisfaction, his hard knot of desperation weakens ever so slightly.

What I don't show him is how the body in the hold has begun to change. Joshua's contours are shifting, indistinct. Miles inside the depths of the ship, he flickers in the crimson light like a faulty projection. Later, the monitoring team, temporarily distracted by Cade, will determine the surges of radiation an anomaly from a distant pulsar.

When medical staff enters the room, the crowd shifts, exposing Cade.

"You're telling me you can't hear it?" he asks, a new pitch in his voice.

No one looks at him as the medics escort him out of the monitoring room. Brian, in a moment of admirable calculation, shakes his head regretfully.

"Well," says Gemma, breaking the silence, "there's one, if we're still not counting Joshua."

"I don't know," Janice says, settling back into her workstation. "Joshua didn't really seem the type. I could see Cade cracking a mile away."

"Why the past tense?" Brian asks, somehow managing to minimize the tremor in his voice.

"Given the length of his absence, it's more than likely that Joshua was a—"

Gemma silences her with a glare.

Looking into their memories, I see that it was no secret to the crew that Brian and Joshua were close. Their long hours spent together poring over texts hadn't gone unnoticed, even if the intensity of their communion had.

"One out of ten," Janice says. "That's statistically how many of us will break."

"Really, do we have to dwell on this now? Let's get back to work," Gemma pleads.

"Do you," Brian says, leaning toward Janice, and I'm not quick enough to stop him, "think I'm the 'type' to...you know..."

"Honestly, I could see it happening."

A young technician named Steve laughs and shrugs at Brian. "You know how Janice is, man. No fucking filter."

Much to my pleasure, Brian responds with laughter of his own. I must force him to be more careful.

‡‡

Time is a hole. The human awakens, proceeds to his workstation, and spends the hours affixed to a screen made of light. Only an occasional murmur interrupts the silence. Rarely, the outdated melody of a song briefly fills the room before fading again. The lights never dim outside of the proscribed hours of darkness. I fill Brian with the woman, adding details from my past to his own broken version of things. He sighs, lifting his face to the alien scent of incense that hangs in the air, so different from the prosthetic chemicals used in the crew's hygiene products. "Do you smell that?" he asks a woman who passes him in the corridor, and she gives him a strange look. I project these things into the approaching black hole, marking the trail with black rose buds that only he can see. As the ship creeps closer, the collective disquiet deepens like a shadow.

‡‡

When the pain finally subsides, I see the message before it's distributed. The old powers inside me fill the space recently obscured by suffering while Brian debriefs a repair team on possible faults in the mining panels. "We absolutely have to run diagnostics on the intake monitors," he says, even though his mind is filled with visions of moons eclipsing their suns across the universe. "The slightest miscalculation will destroy the data, and we can't leave it up to the internal stabilizers to correct everything...." He doesn't notice as I frantically drink the ancient warmth, gulping it down in great, famished gasps. The message becomes clearer with my increasing strength until finally I can reach out to the busy woman on the command deck who dictates it. I read along as she conjures words on the projection in front of her:

Greetings Minecorp employees:

As we simultaneously enter the twelfth year of our voyage and the final stages of installation near ABDN-1, we may find it easy to forget important protocols amidst the general spirit of celebration. Your hard work and dedication to the company has earned our gratitude, but vigilance is more important now than ever. Over the next six time-cycles, we're due to embark on a task integral to the perpetual maintenance of cosmic habitation. Every Minecorp employee must maintain awareness of our mission's importance.

Remember that you are contractually bound to *report any suspicious psychological states to medical staff immediately.* The human brain is our company's most valuable and fragile asset. Like any computer, it requires frequent testing and calibration. That is why we are issuing a two-part initiative, mandatory for all Minecorp employees aboard *Gabriel 22.* Over the next 24 hours, we will issue a mild sedative to every staff member. It will be administered automatically by your health regulator packs. This is intended to reduce emotional strain related to your upcoming tasks, and shall be followed by the completion of a psychological questionnaire—

I leave the woman to her work and search on, through long and dimly lit corridors left mostly vacant by each crewmember's workstation confinement. It isn't long before I find the pharmacy behind the physician's lounge. Inside, a young technician calibrates dosages for the upcoming sedative administration.

I have learned much over the past few thousand years. Of all the procedures of priests, tribal elders, and physicians my human counterparts and I have suffered, the application of chemicals has proven the most powerful.

I take the young girl's mind. Her pain is brief, but the confusion will last. She struggles alone, unheard by the bored doctors discussing experimental film on the other side of the wall. I force myself in until pink foam drips from her lips. I do not relent. As her mind finally darkens, I fill it with my own and turn to the screen.

Sedatives will not do, and I command her to cancel the dosage. Before she does, something lingering in Brian's consciousness catches my attention. A glimpse of a conversation with Joshua: "If we had anything like *that* on this hunk of shit," Brian's mutters in a darkened room, "we'd cross the gap in no time." A laugh from Joshua, then, "I'm sure they have something like that, and lots of it. We just can't get any." The synchronicity of the connection amuses me greatly.

All those long hours of deep space ennui and intellectual restlessness have brought him closer to me than any host before. In truth, there have always been those who are sympathetic—they are the easiest to find, gleaming as they do like red stars in the night—but the way the darkness of space seems to mute the agonizing pulse of time...it's strange how like us humans have finally become.

I find the letters DMT and enter the administrative override sequence.

I feel Brian interrupting his lecture to wonder silently if Joshua would've had to die if they had obtained access to chemical alternatives. It cannot be helped; I can no longer fully conceal my actions from him, but I hide myself the best I can so he can continue speaking.

It doesn't matter what could've happened, I tell him. *The results are always the same.*

And this time, the atonement shall be final.

I can't see the end. I can only follow my impulses. It's a matter of faith, and I surrender blindly to it as I schedule the dosage and leave the technician to reel in her inarticulate madness.

‡‡

A sound like a scream echoes from storage. A thousand screams. The disharmony of a multitude congealing painfully into one. For now, no one is close enough to hear it. It echoes against the placid steel of the ship's interior, traveling empty corridors lit by dim red lights that no one has walked in hours. The scream is inhuman, but nevertheless filled with joy and unimaginable pain. The vast empty caverns of the storage sector almost swallow it.

‡‡

Although Brian is miles away in a sector plunged in scheduled blackout, he is the first to hear the creature. I find it fitting that he immediately turns to the countdown monitor at the foot of the bed: "ABDN-1: 43 Hours." The whites of his eyes roll in fear as the distant wail erupts once more.

I allow the warmth of the woman's flesh to fill his mind, but his thoughts turn stubbornly to Joshua and the grinning gash he tore into his own throat with the broken glass of a bottle. The nameless woman's flesh melts, exposing glistening sinews that reflect the empty expanse of stars surrounding us. Her emerald eyes empty, and mirror images of ABDN-1's blank ring replace them. I must do something. I take a risk.

"Quiet, Brian," I tell him in a voice that he can hear. "You are safe. The screams will not hurt you."

Deep in the darkness of the ship, something large moves.

"Who are you?" he asks the empty room.

"I am your intercessor. I am the comfort called forth by your friend's sacrifice."

"No," he says, sitting up to bury his face in his hands.

"I am your advocate. I am the Redeemer."

"No," he says again, although he knows it's true. The thing in the darkness screams again as it tests the strength of its insectile appendages. It lifts itself upright, chattering madly from a permanent grin that Brian would surely recognize.

"Yes. Rejoice, for your salvation is at hand!" And slowly, I peel back the veil.

‡‡

I have more than earned this moment of triumph. The ancient philosophers wrote that art is a visitation from the gods, a kiss from divine winds imperceptible to the mute stupidity of the grosser senses. In their ruminations our work first took shape. Oh, how we have slaved to bring them to knowledge, to feel that their small and furtive movements echoed a grander restlessness beyond the stars! How long we whispered in their dreams of things beyond their reach. How we have labored to show them the fractal resemblances spontaneously infecting existence like a cancer. Relentlessly we filled them with pride and possibility, an invitation to dare press beyond the circumscribed borders of imagination limited by nature. Promethean task, indeed, and now the recording of it is all that's left. We submit this account to the annals of human achievement, the penultimate statement of their striving.

We showed them the secrets of the universe in glimpses they called madness until they better understood. We gave them their freedom from physics and called them from the depths. Behold, the era of the superhuman.

‡‡

Janice falls suddenly silent while her colleagues laugh over their lunches. Steve notices first. "You okay?" he asks. She can't pull her gaze from the projection screen. No one else notices the anomaly in the data. They try to wake her, snapping fingers in front of her empty gaze until they notice the urine pooling at her feet. She watches as the Herald emerges from ABDN-1. I can only imagine its beauty, the yawning rift that dreams desire into being.

Miles away, Joshua crawls from the hold, finally equipped to guide His charges home. His song liberates the minds of the crewmembers who respond to the breach alarms. They stand silently as He spears them with the sharp ends of his appendages and lifts them to his maw. They wait like dolls as He sucks them dry. One by one, wasted husks of flesh and bone clatter to the floor.

‡‡

When Brian finally staggers from his chamber, he's like a child. Colors he's never seen before dazzle his senses as he lurches precariously into the hallway. The coordination of wills is difficult, although this clumsiness will also pass. Already our boundaries are blurring, like two cells devouring each other. We are an autophagic event that will result in something greater than both of us.

I direct him to the flight deck. He barely notices the wailing sirens and the panicked retreat of his crew members. Some of them carry weapons, and they knock him out of the way when he stumbles into their path. "Get the fuck back in your cell," a captain screams at him, and he can't help but laugh at the terror in the man's voice.

I protect him from what I can—the memories of the long, black interim outside of time, the horizons clipped from the past like photos of an alien history, scenes of blood and death and torture at the hands of stupid but well-meaning men. Still, some leaks through, and he groans at the expanses opening like cosmic wounds before him. Limits, he realizes, were always comforts.

He hardly sees that he has opened the door until he's standing next to the pilot.

"The time is now," I tell him. "Do you want to see Joshua?"

Something distant stirs inside him, a vague sense of loss and yearning as deep as the hole that devours space right outside the flight deck window.

"It's terrible...and yet wonderful at the same time, isn't it?" he says in his new innocence to the young man.

The pilot pales when he sees Brian's face, drained of color and twitching ecstatically. "What are you talking about? You aren't supposed to be here."

"Vast, deep, and powerful. Like the ocean," Brian shrieks. The pilot recoils as Brian sinks the broken neck of a bottle into his throat. Blood spurts from the man's carotid as he crumbles to the floor. Brian gently nudges him away and approaches the control panel. From the data I've collected, he enters the command code. A low roar surges through the steel as the engines fire. Within moments, ABDN-1 swallows the stars as the ship accelerates.

"More," I hear Brian say as I say it too. We speak in tandem now. We. I. The two that became one that became nothing that became all.

When the regulator packs begin to hiss with the sudden dosage, everything changes. The walls of the ship dissolve and something resembling a lavender sunrise spreads across the gaping hole in time and space looming over us. The Brian part of me turns to the tempered blend of light and darkness and suddenly I remember her name.

The name carried on the perfumed breeze that erupts from the light at the end of existence, the name that is situated in a history that grows blurred at the edges and fades with the ship—the faint whispers of a trajectory that points at the sun blossoming beneath the swirls of light thick with scars. The name hangs in the sky like the traces of an explosion and the traces become lines that meet in a pyramid against what was once the event horizon.

The ship recedes into invisibility. Now it is part of a forgotten time, a time that was plagued by inadequacy and pain since the beginning. The remaining crew members gape in wonder as they take their first steps across the dizzying black, steps lent to them by a savior who is no longer a beast of unimaginable terror, but a man, Joshua, who points to the brightening sun.

I turn to Him, my beloved Joshua. He smiles—a real smile that isn't a jagged absence of flesh—and I watch as the light overtakes us and beyond, stretching back to the name echoing across impossible distances. I know that I'll see her too—she'll have a special place in the interim, a seat in the trinity as we wait for time to return and gnaw away at the light once more.

At last, we have succeeded—I, Brian, the matrix of the human and the divine, hereby affix this endnote to the beginning of the new cycle of being.

m.Other

I'M TALKING TOO much. I'm always disturbed by how easily I slip back into this stream of chatter, rushing forward with the urgency of a discreetly sublimated anxiety. It's unprofessional, an open display of my own lack, a naked request for love. It wouldn't be so bad if I could terminate the transgression once I notice it. But somehow, I can't.

"Your father," I tell the blonde woman, facing away from me on the couch, "idolized your mother because he developed a conscious sexual attraction to his *own* mother at a young age, which triggered a vigorous repression at the implementation of the castration complex and corresponding incest taboo."

I'm horrified at the words—horrified at the pleasure I take in their articulation. Their lack of therapeutic necessity sickens me. "Soon after, to be sure, he learned where babies come from. His mother fell from grace in his eyes—from a chaste saint one moment to a whore the next. He probably exhibited infantile signs of aggression, including pronounced regressions in which he attempted to revive the state of lost innocence."

I know this is an open abuse of my position, this showboating. But, of course, the woman enjoys it. They always do. This is what they imagine they have come here for. They expect omniscience from me. They need me to unveil the invisible secrets of human behavior in a stunning display of intellectual acumen. How are they to know that these cheap "revelations" are exactly what must be withheld?

"Thus, he formulated two distinct but consistent versions of his own mother: the virgin and the whore. Neither alternative is empirically realistic. Nevertheless, his conception of women is vitally colored by this division. Your mother was a saint to him. He worshipped her, certainly, but her suffering arose from his inability to truly *desire* her."

The stunningly attractive analysand nods, running her delicate hands excitedly along the cushioned contours of the couch. She turns to face me, and I smile, in no way discouraging the encounter. *The situation is too damaged to repair*, I tell myself. This session will cause more therapeutic harm than good. I should terminate it immediately. I should—

"That's *very* impressive, Doctor," she says in a lazy, southern drawl manicured to suggest horses and a large, spacious estate. "For the life of me, I've found my father impossible to understand. He often accused me of being too friendly with boys in my youth. He was *very* hard on me. I suppose I've assimilated some of his criticism, being always so devoted to my husband as I am, despite all his...shortcomings."

Scratch a virgin... "Well," I reply, in a concerted attempt to hide the drunken ease of self-satisfaction from my voice, "I'm glad we have been able to address that issue. It is undoubtedly a central edifice in your, as you call it, 'castle of anxiety.'"

"Yes," she says, smiling. She considers something carefully. A blush warms my face. Surely it's *me* she is considering, for I am not an ugly man, and I know all too well the romantic power of the analyst over the analysand—*especially when he opts to abuse it,* an accusatory voice adds.

"In fact," the woman continues, turning to face me, "you've been more help to me than anyone I've seen before. And I've seen many, many psychoanalysts. Some quite renowned."

But we've only had three sessions. We haven't even begun! I know I should tell her this, but I can't bring myself to break the spell, no matter how cheaply purchased.

"Well, I am honored to hear you say so," I reply.

She nods and looks away. Something new crosses her face. Something dark—so dark it unsettles me. I place the notepad on my desk. Her brow furrows and a long-borne burden is visible in the pouches under her eyes. It is the look of someone in mourning. *Now is not the time to be gallant,* I tell myself, but it is too late. I've already stood and walked around the couch, smoothing my Armani jacket before sitting next to her. "Mrs. Tillman?" I ask.

She looks at me sharply, flashes an embarrassed smile and quickly wipes the corners of her eyes.

"Oh," she begins, "I was just on the brink of asking you a silly question...but you have enough on your hands, consoling weepy women like me day in and day out."

"Not at all," I say sternly. "It is my *job*, Mrs. Tillman, to help you in any way that I can. I implore you to ask me your question." *Absurd! Reprehensible!*

Mrs. Tillman smiles again, without surprise, as if she has expected my cooperation from the beginning. I fear, suddenly, that I haven't sufficiently concealed my attraction. *That's what you get for playing this game, old man.*

"It's my daughter," she says between sobs. "She's... bedridden. She's locked herself in her room and nothing persuades her to come down. And so beautiful. It's a real tragedy. Glenn and I have paid for a whole *community* of professionals throughout the last few years: neurosurgeons, psychiatrists, psychoanalysts, even, I admit, a priest or two—none of them have been able help her. It has gotten so bad that she will only communicate by email. Her exposure to a host of prodding minds has only made her more withdrawn, I'm afraid. She will admit only one housekeeper, a woman who has been with the family since Julie was a child. I have been on the brink, Doctor, of losing hope. But *you—you* are someone special. It's true. I can sense it."

Alas, look what you've walked into. My high spirits ebb as the description continues. For a moment, I imagine that *I'm* the one who's been duped. Then again, her distress seems so urgent, so genuine. I balance a hand on her shoulder.

"What are her symptoms exactly, Mrs. Tillman?" I ask.

"Doctor," she says, with broken-hearted desperation, "it's *me!* She *loathes* me, her own *mother!*"

⁜

I awaken more drunk than usual. Somewhere in the middle of my effort to get up, a depleted bottle of Disaronno clatters off the nightstand and into the stack of Heineken empties. The edge of an approaching hangover magnifies the gashes of sunlight screaming into the bedroom through the venetian blinds. After a glass of tap water from the kitchen sink, I immediately call my secretary and cancel my appointments for the day. How unthinkable this would have been only a few years ago! But now, Kaci makes no comment, accepting unexpected cancellations as a matter of course. I weave into the study, spilling water here and there along the filthy carpet. With one sweep I send an avalanche of Heinekens from my desk to the floor, clearing a space in front of my laptop. I unlock the screen and close a paused porn video. I used to be so organized, so dedicated, so *together—*

I open my email and scroll through the wasteland of spam messages, trying to forget the contours of my gradual decline: how I gradually became calloused to the practice, how the collection of Lacan's seminars and the newest translations of Freud, once proudly shelved above my desk at the office, have gathered a thickening layer of dust. The theory, so enthralling in my postgrad days, long ago degenerated into a bland, halfhearted dogma I find all too easy to exploit. I'm constantly faced with my inadequate command of the analyst's only true gift: empathy. *You should've quit years ago.* But how can I? What distinguishing mark would I then bear to differentiate me from the mass of other pointless people?

I discover an email from Mrs. Tillman sent yesterday evening and our conversation gradually resurfaces: the horrible session, the psychotic daughter.

Dr. Keller, below is Julie's email address. It has been communicated to her that you will be in touch soon. I want to again thank you for agreeing to a consultation under such unusual circumstances. As discussed, I will forward your tripled session fee at the end of each week. To express my gratitude, why don't we discuss your initial thoughts over a glass of wine at Tonio's after you chat with her? My treat.

I get up and amble to the fridge for a morning Heineken. *Excellent! Perhaps yesterday wasn't a waste.* I look at the empty beer bottles and piles of dirty suits waiting for the cleaners. There's a lot of work to be done...*after you chat with her.* Of course. I hurry back to the computer and type an introductory email to Julie Tillman. I quickly outline my qualifications and express my desire to mutually construct the foundations of a virtual safe place. I decide to begin by asking her what kind of music she likes. All the while, I try to ignore the nagging moral aspect of composing the email just to get the girl's mom into bed.

Before long, I'm struck by how much *easier* it is to write a session than to personally administer one. I'm aware that online therapy sessions are becoming increasingly popular, but now, seeing potential materialize on the screen before me—Maybe this is the answer! I'd never have to leave the apartment again! Perhaps this is close enough to an early retirement without the shame of total surrender. And with Mrs. Tillman coming over for an occasional toss in the sheets—what more could I need? By the time I hit send, I've finished the Heineken and entirely dissolved the headache. I even whistle a fragment of Queen's "Bohemian Rhapsody" on the way to the kitchen for another beer.

Mommaaaa

‡‡

To my surprise, Julie responds to my email within minutes. *The girl must sit there all day, simply waiting.* I take a swig of the beer, spilling a little on my undershirt before opening the message.

Hi doctor Keller. I don't listen to music sorry.

No music? How is that possible for a kid her age? If she is truly psychotic, it's possible that music triggers a painful hallucinogenic response. Or perhaps music functions malevolently in the organization of her paranoid worldview. I generally don't work with psychotics, so I'm not entirely confident in these speculations. In any case, I need to get her typing. Mrs. Tillman, after all, is going to want to discuss more than her daughter's dislike of music over ribeye and wine.

Hi Julie. We don't have to talk about music. What do you enjoy?

I stare at the screen, expecting another rapid reply. Sure enough, a new message appears within moments.

Doctor Keller, if you really want to know, you have to watch the film.

Below Julie's text is the link to a video. I immediately notice her use of the word "film" in lieu of the more age appropriate "video" or ' movie." The word does not seem like an accident, since Julia is far too young to have grown up with "film" mixed liberally into the vernacular soup. It seems less likely to refer to strips of cellulose triacetate than to evoke a specific genre often preceded by terms like "experimental" or "avant-garde." Then again, I am a psychoanalyst, not a film expert. Perhaps I'm reading too much into this.

Most peculiar is her omission of the prepositional phrase "about me" proceeding logically from "to know." Without orienting the sentence around knowledge of *her,* the object of knowledge is left indefinite and, perhaps, universal. Could this be intentional? Didn't I ask about *her?* Did she purposefully eschew my specificity and imply the possibility of knowing something *greater* than her through the video? A matter of *gnosis* over knowledge? If so, it has a certain paranoid logic. Paranoiacs often imbue mundane aspects of the world with supercharged significance, often intermingled with deeply malevolent undertones. It is also common for schizophrenics to suppress explicit references to the self, although she didn't refrain from the first-person pronoun in her initial email message.

I try to mentally sift through psychoanalytic approaches to psychosis. The gulf of time between the present and the postgrad years of intensive theory shows in the slowness of my recall. Laboriously, an idea solidifies, a rough paraphrase of some book I once read: *An analyst must attempt to absorb the psychotic's delusions. He must convey to the analysand a willingness to take them seriously. Only when the analyst appears engaged with the psychotic's worldview is there any hope of therapeutic progress.* I type

If I watch the film, will you answer more questions?

and hit send. Her response is immediate.

Yes.

I sigh. The link opens a download option, which I approve. I look at the running time of the video on the scrollbar. It's nearly three hours long. *Christ.* I get up and walk back into the kitchen. I certainly don't feel like watching a video. Thai takeout boxes cover the entire surface of my Weston Home dining table. Dried noodles trail from their unfolded lids and adhere to the table surface like dead tentacles. "I really should be cleaning this shit up," I mutter to myself. But if I don't formulate *something* to say to Mrs. Tillman about Julie, there won't be any point in cleaning at all. *Besides, what else are you going to do today? Drink?* I grab three Heinekens and return unwillingly to the study.

‡‡

A mob. A writhing mass of mundanity. A street sign names one of the streets at the intersection "Hell." The other remains unnamed since the scene is shot at an angle perpendicular to its sign. Under the "Hell" sign, people cross back and forth in thick, heavy streams. The crowd mingles in a multicolored wash of jackets, raincoats, and shopping bags. This is Julie's film. This is what I've been watching for fifteen solid minutes now. There certainly is no accounting for taste.

I'm on my fifth Heineken and starting to feel a little drunk. I've been formulating an interpretation, and all I can come up with is Jean-Paul Sartre's "Hell is other people," but this seems trite. Nor does the fluid motion of the overall composition hint at such a misanthropic line of thought. Of course, what matters most is *Julie's* interpretation, not mine. The question is *Who or what am I supposed to be "knowing" right now?*

There are no cars, parked or otherwise in this seemingly busy intersection caged between indistinct gray buildings. The sky is a dusky orange and sunless.

As I get up to grab another beer, I find that the slow, continuous flow of the crowd has left its stain on my vision. Luminescent globules swim from my peripherals like oily floodwaters invading a riverbed. I sit back down in front of the laptop and crack open the Heineken. The pulsating mass still flows hypnotically toward the center of the screen.

I decide to write Julie later this evening and tell her I watched the whole thing. It's not as if the film will be difficult to summarize if she presses for a reaction.

I lean forward to close the laptop. Immediately, I'm driven back into my chair by an irresistible fatigue. "What the fuck?" I mutter to the empty room. My vision swims. I feel like I'm well into a second six-pack and a pint of Disaronno. A static rush blooms inside my head, as if I'd taken a hit or two of good hydro, a feeling I haven't had since college. The overall sensation, while disorienting, is far from unpleasant. I relax and open myself to the blurry euphoria. My eyelids are leaden and before I allow them to close, I look at the computer screen. The crowd ambles wordlessly on like ghosts. Except now, they are staring at me.

‡‡

I'm standing in shallow water. I can tell only because my feet are wet and cold up to the ankle. Everything is submerged in utter blackness. I can't see my body.

I begin to walk aimlessly and the ripples at my feet catch a glimmer of faint, red light as they expand into half-moons. There is no sound, not even the baseline pulse of my own heart. I try to shout, straining to articulate a cry that penetrates the darkness, but nothing happens. I imagine, for a moment, that I've suddenly fallen deaf.

I walk on, groping for something, anything, for what seems like a long time. Suddenly, I stop. A nearly imperceptible change has occurred in my surroundings. The faintest of drafts kisses the stubble of my beard. It's coming from below. I risk a few more cautious steps. The crimson ripples retreat from my footfalls but vanish before expanding to maturity. Something is directly ahead. The ripples terminate at the distance of a yard in front of me.

Now two feet.

One.

The upward draft is now a low, frozen breeze. I extend my right foot forward above the water, expecting to find a wall...

Panic surges through my abdomen. My knees buckle involuntarily, and I stagger back.

It's a hole, perfectly hidden in the blackness.

I make a failing attempt to repress the nauseating surge of vertigo. I tumble backward, barely breaking the fall with my hands. The splashing water lashes my exposed skin with daggers of ice. I begin to hyperventilate. The short, futile gasps of air distort my thoughts into a fevered pastiche.

In the throes of my fear, I unexpectedly recall an image of my mother. She's leaning against the edge of the sink, hovering over a pile of unwashed dishes which have begun to emanate a sour miasma. Mother usually kept the chrome sink not only dish free, but sparkling, careful to avoid even the common water stains that I've never been able to eradicate from my own kitchen. The stink means something is wrong, and from the look of things, something has been wrong for a long, long time.

I regain control of my breath. I turn my head and scan the impossible darkness.

I move my hands in the water at my sides. The slight crimson crests of ripples skitter nervously into the black. I lift myself to a crouch and stretch my hands in front of me, grazing the shallow water for the lip of the void.

Mom is crying. With one hand she covers her eyes. With the other, she grips a dishrag in a trembling fist. I approach her cautiously, reaching out to her, wanting her to turn, sparing me the agonizing tension of discovery. What is she hiding under her hands, under her eyelids?

The freezing water suddenly falls soundlessly away from my fingertips. The panic tries to reassemble but I sink my teeth into the tense muscle of my tongue. I lower my open palms onto the perfect edge where the water turns suddenly vertical and crouch, looking down into the invisible deep.

I touch the hem of her dress with my thick, sticky fingers. She turns. Deep crevices mar her facial features. Her pupils are black and swollen, fattened with the consumption of her once-green irises. Pools of tears collect in the hollow between her nose and cheek.

In the void, the dim, crimson light reflects against a hundred uneven surfaces. At first, I think they are bubbles, walls and mountains of quivering bubbles, gurgling up from the churn of perpetually falling water. But they are too solid, too uniform in size. I can barely make out small black circles in the center of them. They are eyes. Thousands and thousands of eyes.

‡‡

I wake up in the office chair, covered in a cold, sick-smelling sweat. At first it seems I have not slept long. It's still early in the day—the sun illuminates the closed blinds hiding the east window of the study. Only after I walk into the kitchen to grab a beer do I notice the date on the digital display of my stove. I realize that I slept through the afternoon, the night, and into the next morning. "Shit," I mutter as I hurry back into the study to check my cell phone. As expected, there is a missed message from Kaci.

"Doctor Keller, this is Kaci. Johanne is here in the waiting room for her eight-o'clock appointment that she rescheduled after you canceled on her yesterday. It's eight forty-five now, so—"

I delete the message. It's ten fifty. I'm sure the little bitch has figured out by now that her vacation has been extended. I don't bother to call back. I down a significant portion of the cold Heineken to quell the thought.

I look at the computer, and suddenly yesterday comes back to me: Julie, the film, the bizarre dream, Mrs. Tillman...

Mrs. Tillman's invitation to Tonio's. Mrs. Tillman nodding in admiration as she bathes in the silver rhythm of my Freudian yammering. Mrs. Tillman's bare ass, bent over the side of the king-sized, four thousand-dollar Stearns & Foster mattress in the bedroom (where I never sleep). I almost forget the dream somewhere in the expanding panorama of erotic fantasies.

I reawaken the dormant laptop screen. The film is there to greet me, paused on a mass of incomplete strides. I shudder and move the cursor to close the tab when something catches my attention. I lean closer to the screen. "What the fuck," I mutter, not believing.

In the middle of the crowd, between two anonymous shoulders, a strand of gold-tinged, brown hair rises slightly in an invisible wind. It curls around a familiar face, streaming casually down the front of an equally familiar corduroy jacket. She gazes ahead, frozen in the middle of a trajectory of unknown purpose. But it is wrong. I *know* this is all wrong. I take a quick inventory of the landmarks onscreen, the Hell sign, the buildings, the street devoid of vehicles—*no, this place is unfamiliar. I had never seen this scene in my life before yesterday. Yet there it is. There she is. It's impossible.*

She's not weeping like she was in my dream. She seems normal, as if she were walking home from an afternoon of grocery shopping. She always walked everywhere, with that same thoughtful look, at once engaged and distant, always the queen of some opaque universe within. *But how the fuck did she end up on my computer screen?*

This isn't a scene from her life—I know it isn't. This isn't a snapshot from our rural hometown, and she never once mentioned acting in a film. She always hated the television, in fact. She believed it was the devil's choice tool of influence.

I rewind the video a single frame and Mother disappears back into the mob. I play it at normal speed and she fails to reappear. I rewind, fast forward, and hit play a dozen times. I slow the video down to half speed. Quarter speed. She never reappears between the two shoulders. I press the heels of my hands irritably into my eyes. Perhaps I'm beginning to drink too much.

⁑

I'm sitting at Tonio's, dressed in my best Armani suit and staring blandly at the champagne bubbles rising unsteadily from the bottom of my glass. I'm fifteen minutes early to my meeting with Mrs. Tillman, and nowhere near as happy about it as I imagined I would've been. *But that's life, isn't it? Anxiety is the realization of desire—the closer you get to what you want, the more you fall apart inside. That's what makes this dead, empty world go 'round. Don't you know that?* There is something else, though. Something... deeper.

Physically, I don't feel well. I had spent the rest of the morning watching Julie's film, scanning the mob for that golden-brown streak of hair again. I know I didn't imagine it. I am *certain* my dead mother was in the video. The whole thing lacked the unsteady liminal character of a hallucination—it *must* have been real. Nevertheless, I couldn't find her. In despair, I had finally closed the video and switched to my email. At the head of a column of spam, I was surprised to find an invitation from Mrs. Tillman to a "preliminary" meeting regarding Julie.

A stunning young waitress appears at the table to ask if I want another champagne. Normally, I would've enjoyed leaning toward her, inhaling her cheap perfume as I crack a self-depreciating joke about alcoholism. Tonight, I just shake my head and she moves on to the next table. I can't imagine why Mom would've been in the film. Nor can I imagine why Julie was so insistent that I watch it—unless she knew, unless she *intended* for me to see—

I jump as Mrs. Tillman pulls her own chair out and sits across from me. I stand, embarrassed. "Forgive me, Mrs. Tillman. I should've—"

"Nonsense," she says with a dismissive wave, "You seemed to be rather deep in thought. I didn't want to disturb you."

I mutter an additional apology as I ease back into my seat. Mrs. Tillman looks *stunning*. She is wearing a low-cut black dinner dress that leaves little to the imagination. Aside from slight crow's feet around her eyes (which, I decide, add character to her charms rather than subtract from them), her skin is remarkably well-preserved for her relatively advanced years. I find myself openly grinning when I notice the pearl necklace. *You are a fucking dog,* the inner voice suddenly chides, a voice I have always associated, in an inversion of the paternal cliché, with my mother: *Fucking animal. How long did you spend reading Simone de Beauvoir in grad school? How many times have you railed against the inherent misogyny concealed cunningly within the structures of capitalism? How many papers did you write with the feminine pronoun in lieu of the traditional masculine? After all your academic posturing, here you are, drooling like a regular fucking Charles Bukowski over one of your fucking patients—*

"What's the matter, Dr. Freud? Are you suddenly at a loss for words?" Mrs. Tillman teases, a smile accompanying an exquisite blush.

"I'm sorry, Mrs. Tillman."

"Please. Call me Janet."

"Janet...I was just thinking about...how lovely you look this evening."

"Well, let's hope that's *all* you were thinking about, Doctor. You must remember, I am one of your *patients.*"

The glimmering lilt of excitement in her voice indicates she is open to becoming more.

"Of course, Janet. I meant no disresp—"

"Of course not. Now," she interrupted, catching the eye of a waitress and signaling her with a half-raised finger, "tell me about Julie. What have you discerned so far?"

"Well," I notice I'm shifting in my seat uncomfortably, compulsively flattening my tie against my stomach with a nervous right hand, "I really haven't had much time to communicate with her yet—psychoanalysis, at least successful psychoanalysis, can be a long and arduous process, as I'm sure you have—"

"Yes, of course, Doctor. I am aware that you haven't found any *answers,* per se, at such an early stage, but certainly you have developed a few hypotheses—" Janet smiles at the approaching waitress and orders champagne and a salad. I follow suit, even though I'm far from hungry.

"Indeed," I continue, "I have entertained a few theories of my own. One appears to outshine the others, however. Your daughter—and remember, this is only, as you put it, a 'hypothesis'—exhibits patterns that correlate to a paranoid personality type. A paranoid personality can manifest symptoms to varying degrees of severity. I think that your daughter's paranoia is very severe, characterized by extended episodes of psychosis—"

"Paranoia? Psychosis? Doctor, are you sure?"

"I'm not sure at all. Let me emphasize again that this is strictly speculation. I wouldn't dream of hazarding a diagnosis at this stage. But her schizoid withdrawal and her extreme preference for highly ritualized exchanges over spontaneous intrapersonal interactions point to paranoia, if not full-blown schizophrenia. Tell me, Janet—you mentioned before that she mistrusts you specifically. Does she exhibit this same mistrust toward others?"

"Well...perhaps, but not to the same extent. She goes into hysterics when anyone enters the room besides Cathy, the housekeeper, as I mentioned before. Her behavior indicates that she mistrusts others, don't you think? Although she has taken a rather intense liking to you, Doctor."

"To...me?" The waitress returns with twin glasses of champagne. I stare at mine, noticing the fresh bubbles rising from the bottom of the glass. There are hundreds of them, miniscule globes glittering like wet eyes.

"Yes, Doctor."

"Devin, please. Call me Devin."

"Devin. Such a nice name. She told Cathy all about you—showed her your introductory email and said that you were going to help her, Devin."

"Well, I intend to, but we haven't really discussed much. She sent me a video, or a 'film' as she called it, appended with explicit condition that I watch it before we continue the therapy."

"Oh, yes," Janet says, nodding and tilting the champagne glass to her full lips. "Oh, yes—the film. Did you watch it?"

"I did."

"What did you see?"

My mother. A darkness deep and unfathomable. A thousand eyes, beckoning me to an endless fall—an endless fall into a blackness so complete my ontological boundaries blur as I rush into the expansive silence. A descent into insanity.

I shrug, ignoring the clammy sweat of anxiety dampening the back of my silk undershirt. "A bunch of people walking across an intersection."

Janet smiles. She stares at me for a moment, studying my face. She no longer seems attractive to me as I resist the urge to wipe my forehead with my dinner napkin. A hot, irritable blush burns my cheeks.

"Yes," she finally says, "it's rather silly, isn't it?"

‡‡

I type the name Mathias Osbourne into the Wikipedia search bar. Nothing. I know the spelling is correct, since I wrote the name on the back of one of my business cards. I switch to Google. Personal profiles on various social media sites immediately fill the screen. On the third page of search results, I find him. It *must* be him. I click the link bearing his name and find myself looking at a short bio on a website entitled Silent Motorist Productions. The website hasn't been updated in years, and a quick glance at the "About" page indicates that Silent Motorist Productions is (or *was*, by the look of things) an upstart art collective, unified by both their extreme obscurity in subject matter and general residence near New York City. I follow a link to an online fundraising campaign that expired nearly the same time as the last page update.

By the end of dinner at Tonio's—a smoldering fajita dinner that Janet enjoyed heartily while I pretended to, chewing slowly on the tender strips of steak so as not to exacerbate my nausea—it was clear to me that Janet would not accompany me home. She was sociable enough, but kept the conversation almost fanatically relegated to the topic of her ailing daughter. I did my duty, rambling on to varying degrees of accuracy in the classical psychoanalytic discourse. A certain coquettishness on her part kept me from entirely losing hope. When she politely declined my offer to escort her to her car, my heart sank. She must've noticed my disappointment, and promptly assured me that this would not be our last encounter.

As I shook her hand, she paused, gave me a sidelong glance, and said, "You know, that movie—or whatever you call something like that—is quite important to her. I can't understand why, but something about it resonates very deeply with her psyche. She talks about it to Cathy. Cathy told me once that Julie claims it was directed by a man named Mathias Osbourne. I haven't been able to discover anything about him myself."

She turned to me then, dropping, in a sudden moment of vulnerability, the cultured visage she had donned so cautiously all evening, and gripped my extended hand in both of hers. "Please, Devin. Find out what you can. Watch the film again, carefully. I am convinced that it is some sort of key, some hint to the structure of her strange, tortured reality. It may inspire just the stroke of insight that gets us out of this mess." I promised to give the matter my attention. She smiled and left the restaurant without another word.

Mathias Osbourne is one of a dozen transgressive poets, painters, and filmmakers scraped up from the bottom of the mass of resentful, disillusioned, and impoverished liberal arts majors in New York City who make up the Silent Motorist collective. Not much activity seems to have ever been attributed to them outside a few local exhibits.

Despite my promise, I'm not doing this for Janet's sake. Certainly not for Julie's either. Although understanding the psychotic's worldview could serve as a basis for establishing an open dialogue, I'm not naïve enough to believe, like some psychoanalysts still pretend to, that unveiling some core, unconscious aspect of a psychotic's delusion will magically, in a mythical moment of Freudian integration, eradicate the barriers between this world and theirs.

Mathias' biography is frustratingly unilluminating. He studied musical composition at Julliard before dropping out in the middle of his second year. After that, he turned to experimental film.

The golden-brown strands of hair, the indifferent gaze, hidden, somehow, in the throes of the crowd, as if she walked Hell Street every day of her life to pick up milk and eggs at the corner market.

A description of Osbourne's "theoretical concerns" follows his bio. One passage seizes my attention:

Osbourne's goal is to utilize film to capture the erosive effect of a malevolent Other. Rather than positing alterity in the classical opposition across ethnic boundaries, Osbourne suggests that capitalism internalizes the dynamism of alterity, transforming peers into objects of scorn or pity. Rather than emulating our fellow workers, according to Osbourne, we imagine that we are superior to them. We remain aloof from the system, wise to its trickery, undeceived, unlike our less intelligent, more gullible counterparts. In Osbourne's analysis, however, we despise the mass only because we fear it.

The womb of the tomb, the darkness populated with disembodied eyes, glistening in the red light of an invisible fire. She is down there, isn't she? Somewhere deep in the maw of the beast, she is down there, I know it. I can hear her whispers on the frozen breeze.

Our illusions of superiority to the blank, dead mass of our workday peers masks an unconscious terror of the subjugation of our individuality to the dissolving forces of collectivity. In capitalist society, we live tyrannized by the mirror image of insignificant anonymity we see reflected to us from across the cubicle. Osbourne utilizes crowds in his films, often accented by subtle (and sometimes subliminal) suggestions of violence, to represent this fear of the mass Other (or, to use his own notation, the "m.Other").

I close the Silent Motorist webpage and stare at the screen. I lift a Heineken to my mouth and drink until it is empty. I grab another and do it again. I open Julie's email and, after a moment of hesitation, follow the link to the film. *No, I wasn't born yesterday. I was born long ago—and everyone who was there, besides me, is now dead. No one alive can remember my beginning. Yes, Mrs. Tillman, I'll watch it again, closely. But it's not for you. Not for you or your crazy daughter. This is for Mother.*

‡‡

When I wake up the film is still playing. Empty beer bottles line the desk. *How is it still playing? It's only three hours long, isn't it?*

It is night. The screen is brighter than it should be. Images of the walking crowd project onto the bare walls of the study in a full panorama.

Like the lamp Mom put on the nightstand when we were kids. It would slowly rotate, dragging the phantom shadow of Little Red Riding Hood across the wallpaper—the head of the wolf, half-buried in the grey branches of the forest, followed closely, never falling behind, never losing ground—

I hear a hundred footsteps, as if I am in the middle of the intersection myself.

There was never any audio before. It was always silent—

The crowd generates a soft, inarticulate murmur formed from sounds only shaped like words. I stand, dizzy and swerving. as a man in a grey overcoat brushes against my shoulder. A woman passes my other side from behind. She is wearing a pink tank top and jeans, carrying a large shopping bag in her right hand. The baseline drone of muttering voices increases. An older man in a tweed jacket nudges me gently with a leather briefcase as he passes. I am near the middle of the intersection. A woman pushing a baby carriage glares at me. I try to apologize for my unsteadiness but, like in the dream, I can't seem to make a sound. I wave my hands ineffectually as a young couple unlock their hands to circle around me. The word-like sounds become clearer, although they still convey no meaning. They well up in a harsh, glottal cacophony of phonemes. Their collective faces are furious, twisted, scarred by deep harrows in angular daggers of flesh.

And suddenly, the crowd thins. The drone of demon voices quietens.

And there she is.

Mother lies on the asphalt. She's on her back, propped awkwardly by her elbows. Her face is twisted in pain. I run up to her. Her legs are spread apart and a dark swath of blood stains the front of her denim skirt. I'm screaming for help. Screaming without voice into the deep, cosmic silence of the empty intersection. A breeze emanates from her body. A cold breeze. A frozen breeze from the place where her shirt casts a shadow, sheer blackness between her legs.

I stop. Tears burn my eyes. She looks up at me. Her furrowed brows shift from an arc of pain to a hard edge of malice.

Her eyes are red, recalling the dream. But they are not tired. They are full of an unnamable energy, a dark, swollen capacity, hungry for destruction. She grins, her jagged teeth covered in blood, and pulls the hem of her skirt with her fingers. Between her legs, the round, veiny surface of a head protrudes and rests on the street. Blood pools black and thick beneath her. The sinews in her legs twitch and convulse as she forces the thing out. It tears her viciously, but she doesn't scream. Thick globs of matted gore follow the tiny legs and feet. It doesn't breathe. It wears my face.

I fall to my knees.

As the ragged hole in my mother expands, swallowing my field of vision with an impenetrable darkness spangled with constellations of glistening eyes, the voiceless murmur returns, rhythmic and biological, the groans of sex or laughter.

‡‡

I'm falling.

I can't stop falling.

The well is endless.

I will fall forever.

An angel appears to me, bathed in deep, crimson light. I watch her step into my study, high heels shuffling bottles of Heineken from her path a few feet from my face.

Darkness again.

Darkness and the eyes.

It's Julie.

Somehow, I know.

She doesn't look sick.

She's wearing an expensive black dinner dress.

She glows blood red, a beacon in the blackness.

She's gorgeous.

"Jesus Christ, this place is a mess," she says.

I try to explain.

"Don't bother, Devin. You won't ever speak again, not intelligibly, at any rate. And your pathetic gurgling is frankly unbecoming. I know you can hear me though. I hate to barge in like this, but I have a serious character defect—I simply must have the last word, every time."

I ask for help.

"Quiet. You deserve this. Do you think insanity is a game? You think it's nothing but a quick lay? My mother and I have plenty of experience with 'professionals' like you. Everyone has a switch, you know—everyone is just a small push away from the abyss. Mathias, my brother, discovered a way to expediate the process. It shouldn't be surprising to a shrink like you."

I try to apologize.

"Jesus, quit that, will you? It sounds horrible. It stinks in here too. You've shit yourself, haven't you? Get used to that. It'll start to burn something awful after a while."

She comes closer. I'm falling, flailing madly for something solid to hold on to. Julie doesn't fall though. She hovers in the circle of her crimson glow, immune to the awful forces at work in this place. She's inches away. A half smile forms as she leans forward to whisper something that erases my last vestiges of hope. When she's done, she turns and dissolves into the darkness.

she

THE FIRE BURNED everything, right down to the half-dozen tenants unfortunate enough to be at home that night. Still, even as the firefighters sifted through the rubble the following morning, the rising mood of celebration robbed my solemnity of its sincerity.

"They fucking found him, Clem," Chief Brenner muttered to me over the phone as I watched flakes of ash from the Evesdale apartments dance in the pink dawn. "We don't have a positive ID, but the man had a steel case full of surgical knives exactly like those used in the killings." Never had I heard the soft-spoken, sixty-year-old cop struggle so hard to contain his excitement.

I was more than willing to leave that morning. Things at home hadn't been good since Darla had taken to heavy drinking, often combining her beloved Barefoot rosé with a few Xanax. On most evenings, I'd leave the office to find her unconscious on the couch with the Trinity Broadcasting Channel still screaming at full volume. I mulled over the idea of contacting Darla's shrink regarding the blatant abuse of the meds, but what could come of it? My wife clearly hated her life. If sharing twenty-eight years of a normal marriage with me has left her cold, I felt little confidence that severing her steady supply of drugs would foster newfound affections. The smell of smoke still stained the air as I drove to the office.

Hewitt was already hovered over his computer when I walked in. He spun his soggy frame to face me, a fever in his eyes.

"I thought it best to pull some security footage," he said, a bit breathlessly.

"Is the metal suitcase at the lab?" I asked.

"Do I do my job?"

"FBI?"

"Let's look at the footage first," Hewitt hissed, rubbing his temples. "This is our town, goddammit."

I slumped happily into the seat next to him, entirely unaware that the boundaries structuring my existence would soon dissolve like cinereous fingers of smoke.

‡‡

In the footage recovered from an exterior camera of the pharmacy a few blocks away from the Evesdale apartments, the wraith of a profile enters the frame at 10:43:33 PM, CST. He simply hovers there for a while—a full four minutes—unmoving. I wondered then, as I often still do, what he was thinking. His journals, an aphoristic log of musings written in a tight scrawl on the pages of a cheap Moleskine notebook discovered later in a compartment of his metal suitcase, leave no doubt regarding his penchant for patient observation, a characteristic that undoubtedly served him well on his hunts.

The sketch of a man finally shifts at 10:47:45 and edges nearly out of the camera's lower limits toward the illuminated circle of a streetlamp. He walks slowly. In all things, he acts as if time stretches on into an inconceivable horizon.

As he reaches the glow, he pauses again, and I can't help but recall this short passage of his:

I admire the way the lights from the streetlamps press gently against the darkness. No soft halo quite reaches the next. The boundary of the night seems to brook no transgression. Yet they skirmish on, the pale and the black, in this empty corridor of the town. Ah, love. Love is like these lights: a soft resistance that cannot help but fail. Night is the symbol of inevitability, since all it requires is a momentary lapse of light and it effaces everything like a deluge. The night forever waits, like me, for the sun to flicker out in a wisp of smoke.

It is certainly to some variation on this theme that he stands unflinching, half-submerged in the night he hopes will reign supreme.

I remember how Hewitt impatiently rapped his thick knuckles on the desk, worried that the murderer would turn back without entering the light. When he did finally enter and, astonishingly, turn to face the camera with the metal case plainly in hand, we both erupted in cries of victory. The man's hollowed cheeks, weak chin, and high forehead were distinct, and we were certain that, with a little sharpening of the image, we—or, more likely, the FBI—would go as far as to discover the color of his eyes. If our confidence that the lab would uncover DNA evidence on the knives proved warranted, we were on the cusp of knowing who had shaken Hawthorne so brutally over the years. Beat officers had begun to mill about the station, and several approached to see what the excitement was about. I took a moment to call Darla, but the call rang on uselessly until finally I hung up.

The image the FBI later released to the media was from this point in the footage. It was the clearest glimpse we would get of the man, but not the last. At the time, Hewitt had turned his back to the screen and was busy explaining the significance of the metal case to the officers, while I was vaguely distraught by Darla's failure to answer the phone. We both missed the second figure's entrance, which the FBI eventually classified and excised from the public footage.

‡‡

She enters the frame at 10:55:21. I call her a "she" because he does, and there's no way to determine otherwise from the video.

The man faces the camera momentarily as he scans the circumference of the streetlamp's illuminated pool. All the while, unseen even by him, another figure hangs within the obscure borderlands of light and dark. It's difficult to notice the blank, ovoid shape until it moves. When it does, the man recoils in fright. It's possible that she simply caught him by surprise, although I now find myself inclined to believe that he never fully acclimatized to her presence.

We discovered her while reviewing the footage a few hours after our initial breakthrough. At first, we bent toward the screen, trying to identify any lines of recognizable facial features in the dim and distorted light glowing from the computer. The man appeared to address her directly. He even ran his hand along her bare head. "An accomplice?" Hewitt asked in an uncomfortably loud voice. The man's features were clear even though he had drifted to the far corner of the light to greet his companion. When we realized that hers remained blank despite their presumably equal distance from the camera, our appetite for conversation died.

Minutes passed while the man leaned over the empty face of his unmoving companion. Hewitt grew restless. "Gotta be a burn victim or some shit, but wouldn't we have noticed if someone like that lived in town?" Irritably, Hewitt shifted his considerable bulk, earning a wail of protest from his chair. At 11:07:07, the man shrank away, and the thing clambered momentarily into the light.

Hewitt involuntarily shoved himself away from the desk, emitting a low, panicked groan. My insides froze, and a gnawing cold sawed into my spine.

The creature's movements were irregular, ungainly...animalistic. Her thin limbs jerked unnaturally as she lumbered into visibility. She was much taller than the man and bent sharply at the waist. She wore no clothes, and her body was the same colorless canvas as her face. These characteristics, combined with the odd spaces between her joints, gave her the horrid aspect of a large, pale spider.

Quickly, she scrambled back into the dark, but that glimpse was enough to change something in Hewitt. He paused the video and stared at me before retreating wordlessly to the break room. In the ensuing weeks, he wanted nothing further to do with the case. He reviewed evidence and answered the FBI's questions only with visible reluctance. I, on the other hand, couldn't tear myself away. I called Darla only twice more over the next few days, secretly relieved when she still didn't answer. "Perhaps she's gone to her parents," I told myself.

At 11:10:10 PM, both the man and the woman vanish into the night.

‡‡

Patience is the key. The human organism is besieged by constant pain. Before I fall asleep, I focus on the tiny pricks and pinches that dance across the surface of my body. If I cannot locate these miniature agonies, I imagine fleas filling the spaces between the sheets, and like magic my flesh erupts with the gnawing of a thousand phantom mandibles. I pace the hunt by the measure of this ambient pain. If I forget for a moment the throng of ghostly stings, I know I am falling into the dread numb of haste.

When the feds arrived, they commandeered the metal case along with its nightmarish contents and began scouring the debris of the Evesdale apartments. They were already familiar with the murders and didn't ask for many details. Mrs. Thatcher's corpse had just been discovered the week before, disemboweled and draped across the branches of a withered pine like the rest. A serial killer had been postulated long ago, and they'd monitored every new report with extraordinary care. The fact that the killer's charred corpse, still gripping the metal suitcase, was already extracted from the fire and waiting in the forensic pathology lab for proper identification seemed to eliminate the need for any meticulous methodology the FBI had demonstrated when the killer was still at large.

The fire department had already determined the deadly blaze's origins. It began in the west wing they said, in precisely the room the murderer's remains were discovered. The apartment belonged to Ms. Dell, a striking, green-eyed blonde woman of about seventy. The FBI, reasonably enough, wanted to prove that the killer had started the fatal fire and to locate his mysterious accomplice.

The latter goal was possible only after we discovered another security tape, this time from an ATM on Eve Street, one block away from the apartment.

‡‡

It is not a scent, of course. It's more primordial than that, a chain of events connecting the edifice of fate to our inconsequential shuffle through the late-night streets. Each of their eyes are faintly reddened by capillaries carrying our presence; they were conceived, every one of them, with two latent shadows lurking in the thick of a distant and final night. We are not usurpers of the natural order, as you would have us believe. We are the final destination. We are the hands of the dark, hands that feed the hollow maw waiting beneath the light.

At 11:18:32 PM, the outline of the man materializes in the sinister red glow of a blinking stop light. He walks slowly. It is clear, given what I've read of his journal, that he always waits for random events to reveal his victims. 11:19:46 introduces a car. The man has nearly reached the crosswalk. The vehicle, a new Jetta, speeds by, bursting through a puddle left from the previous night's rain. It is likely that the driver didn't see the man, who seems to possess a talent for blending inconspicuously with the shadows.

The man watches the car swerve into the parking lot—clearly visible from the stoplight—of the Evesdale apartments. If you allow your imagination to color your interpretation of this moment, you can almost see the man smile as a second figure rises from the dark. Her long, uncertain limbs are unmistakably those of the first video, although it seems impossible that she followed the man, since she never appeared in the lengthy stretch reddened by the pulse of the stoplight. I tried to suppress the chill that crept along my limbs as I realized the implications of this.

Although the man doesn't move his mouth, the uncanny pair appear to confer for a moment. What passes between them in these moments of weighty silence? The journals never say. If they are anything similar to the frightful silences I know, they are brimming with possibilities drenched in blood, gleaming with landscapes clipped from creation beyond creation. But the man doesn't tell us. If he was subject to dreams beyond the primacy of the night, he doesn't attempt to put them into words. Who can blame him?

⚎⚎

I've always been married to the night, but the union was arranged. Our relationship is one of convenience, since the limpid dark is my guide's permanent abode. She's there now, I see, stepping into the hesitant circle of the streetlight, the canvas of her plastic feet scraping against the concrete as her empty face spasms inquiringly in my direction. Yes, my dear (I do not say love), I'm coming.

What the ATM security footage captures at 11:23:30 sent the FBI rushing to the stoplight where the man and his "guide" made their final exchange. They returned with a body bag sagging unnaturally in the middle. I demanded to see inside, and the agent cast an inquisitive glance at his supervisor before firmly denying my request. Toward lunchtime on the same day, I was approached by a suited agent I hadn't met and told politely that my assistance with the case was no longer required. "We've ID'd the killer from dental records, and I've just received a call confirming that the

DNA samples obtained from his surgical instruments match those of several victims," the man said with a wan smile. "We are prepared to publicly release this information within days, and we want you there by our side to deliver the good tidings. Of course, the strict secrecy of what you have seen is imperative until we tell you otherwise." I was boiling in my own fury, but I forced myself to nod. When he clasped my shoulder, I wanted to pummel him to pulp. "The best thing you can do," he concluded, "is go home and get some rest."

"And why not?" I asked myself as I drove my old Mustang out of the parking lot. I did rather look forward to a night alone—I was certain at this point that Darla had left—and the urgent need for a night of deep, uninterrupted sleep wasn't vanishing, despite my steady intake of coffee and cigarettes. Still, the final moments of security footage kept surfacing in the unstill waters of my mind like a bloated corpse, displacing the more natural concerns of self-preservation. So many questions still lacked answers. What is she? When he started toward the Evesdale apartments with sudden purpose, why did she block his path and refuse to move? Why did he become angry, and why, when he opened his case and pulled out the hatchet, did she not flee? Above all, I wanted to know what was inside the body bag. Surely all the answers were there.

And certainly, I realized with fresh anger, I would never know. Whatever remains of the humanoid creature the FBI had found would surely be whisked away by invisible authorities before morning. I tried to resign myself to the fact that I would never see inside the bag.

Of course, I was wrong.

The house was empty. That Darla didn't even leave a note vaguely surprised me, but I was too tired for alarm. The call to her parents could wait for the morning. For now, sleep drew me to the empty bed, and the night was pure and dreamless.

‡‡

I had a chance at happiness—only one, to be sure, but its loss still burdens my dreams with urgent clarity. Oh, how I've sought you in the eyes gleaming with pain, only to watch it fade as I dig deeper and deeper into the secrets of being. I first met you as a child; an aunt had given you to me, a mistake intended for a niece close to my own age. I loved you immeasurably. Mother, in her characteristic blind fury born from the immutable totality of her worldview, wanted you gone, so I hid you among the other toys. Your brightness tarnished the others, and soon your limits became the circumference of my own immense joy. The secret of you burned like an undying light, a field of purest white. That you were made for little girls made no difference to me. I could've died happy. But for Mother. If only she could understand! From my hands she sent you to the fire, reducing poetry to ashes like a tiny mirror held to life. I reached for you, burning my own fingers in desperation before she dragged me screaming into my room. As the lock snicked behind her and the days became indistinguishable and dull, I first tasted hate. I've long unlearned that hate, my lost little phoenix. Only the quiet inevitability of duty remains, and though there is no hope, I dream of you always.

The call from Darla's father the next morning was unexpected.

"Clem." The old man's voice was heavy with worry. "Darla's gone. She said you've been having trouble, and she's been staying with us for a while. What's going on between the two of you is none of my business, but this morning the guest room was empty and there was no note." I told him I hadn't seen her, and we both agreed that this wasn't like Darla. I decided not to mention the pills and drinking.

Darla's was the first of many surprises on the day following my return home. The rest would accumulate on my answering machine. According to Chief Brenner, the serial killer, Hank Malthus—a Hawthorne native—had burned first. His proximity to the fireplace in Mrs. Dell's apartment suggested that he had caught himself on fire, or that Dell had shoved him in as an act of self-defense, although given the woman's age, this seemed unlikely. No trauma, other than suffocation from smoke, had befallen Mrs. Dell at the hands of Malthus. A call from the man I had spoken to yesterday revealed that the Jetta in the ATM's security footage was Dell's.

They eventually called it a murder-suicide. The details of the killer's last moments were convoluted and inconclusive. No one really knew what to make of them. But Malthus was dead, and that seemed good enough for the FBI and the grieving citizens of Hawthorne. They never mentioned his "accomplice."

In truth, the fire would remain a mystery without one piece of evidence. At the end, when everything fell together through the growing cracks in my mind, I would see it clearer than the beasts that burned through my childhood nightmares into my daydreams: Mrs. Dell looked like Malthus' mother. They shared the same green eyes, the blonde hair stricken with bolts of silver, and the general beauty of a woman who refined rather than succumbed to the harsh trials of age.

What truly happened? Suicide? Madness? So many things in this life are simply unbearable. A glimpse from the pivotal fire that reduced Malthus' doll to ash could've been one lash too many.

As I hung up on Darla's father with the promise to call him the moment she arrived, I didn't yet know these things, just as I hadn't yet heard the sounds in the garage. When I did hear them—the crackle of plastic and the thump of something heavy—I thought my wife had returned from a shopping spree. Oh, the innocence we can afford when we are unaware of the limitless dark surrounding our tiny spark like the swell of a soundless storm.

"You need to call your father," I said as I flicked on the lights. The large, black bag in the middle of the concrete surprised me. Why did it look familiar? What was it doing here? I rubbed my eyes. Had my mind leaked, allowing the worlds of work and home to bleed together?

Against my will, I stepped forward. Next to the bag was the infamous steel case, splayed open to reveal the little black book resting across the silver sheen of blades.

"This is what you wanted, isn't it?" a soft voice asked.

No, I cried, not making a sound.

The bag was open. Standing over it, I could see the blood pooling onto the concrete along creases in the plastic. Mounds of gelatinous tissue trembled as I reached inside. I could no more stop my hands than I could the vomit that rose into my throat and dribbled onto my clothes.

Behind me, footfalls. "Know that this is real," she said.

I turned my head now, calmly, even though my mind was white with screams.

I saw my wife, horribly thin and bent sickeningly at the waist. Her once-recognizable facial features were now expressionless holes in a lifeless canvas stretched over the plastic frame that had recently filled the bag.

"I have heard your calling," she said, "and have brought you the hunt."

I couldn't scream. I couldn't run. As I stumbled unwillingly toward her, the desire to do either slowly faded.

An involuntary sigh crosses my lips. Such a feeble thing, this light, and yet so bold. There is no viciousness, only a sad longing in my urge to put it out. My faceless guide, sensing my silent intent like an instinct, scampers from the light and into the dark. When I do not follow, she scuttles back, lifting her mud-soiled face devoid of features as if to peer into my own. I sigh again and stroke the mannequin gently along the lower curvature of her face far too rounded to suggest a proper chin. She has yet to learn to savor the hunt. She has yet to drown in the languid patience of nocturnal predators, borne from the assurance that one day they will inherit the earth. She's a child, innocent and divine, like all things ennobled by flame.

the enucleator

DESCRIPTION OF THE "home" page:

There is a body in a hallway.

The shot is from above and angled as if recorded by a security camera. Black walls and white tile floor. In the peripherals of the shot, the hallway stretches on and on, illuminated by small lights in the ceiling. The head and shoulders of the body lie just outside the beam of the closest light. A pool of dark liquid has formed beneath the corpse's distended abdomen.

The body has been there a long time.

Description of the "home" page following Trigger Event 1 [five minutes of no activity at home page]:

The lights flicker off. Darkness.

Trigger Event 2 [thirty seconds of no activity]:

Another segment of hallway, identical in design except for a small protrusion in the wall. The lights flicker briefly but do not go off. The narration begins, a deep, warm voice thickened with fatigue. At the time of transcription, audio analysis has confirmed a positive match with the voice of celebrated architect E.C. Gomez.

GOMEZ: This is where I'll sleep. It's a modest space, exactly like the other "beds" I've dispersed throughout the structure. I don't wish to sleep too comfortably. I'll be compelled onward, you see, even though I'm certain to regret this feature soon. How ironic, this lapsing of the future into the present. It's a fitting touch, given the nature of my project. Already, the delirium is setting in, this reaching back of a path not yet traveled, only to be traveled again, like walking backwards in time. You see? I hardly need to inhabit the space itself. Mere contemplation is sufficient, the mental thumbing of the ragged edge that lifts the mask away from the sickening tangle beneath.

Trigger Event 3 [thirty seconds of no activity following the end of narration]:

A still image of Gomez's face fills the screen. This is the only photo of Gomez known to the public following his enucleation. Here, his injuries are shown with no covering. Ragged scars ring his hollow eye sockets, some running deep into his cheekbones and jawline.

GOMEZ: You remember this, don't you? Gaze upon your work, your masterpiece. I only wish I could see it myself. The pain still awakens me. I feel it always, as if the blade is inside me again, scooping away an aspect of my form that once seemed an undifferentiated expression of being itself. How I failed to recognize the fragmentation of the body, how little it suggests a state of completion. It's a malleable surface, a network set to project the changes it undergoes into the mind. There's nothing so human it can't be bent or subtracted into something else. You see, in taking what you thought were the best parts of me, you took nothing at all. If I were interested in consoling myself, perhaps I'd end these ruminations here.

Trigger Event 4 [thirty seconds of no activity following the end of narration]:

The hallway fills the screen again. After a few moments, another segment of identical hallway replaces the first, beginning a long montage of hallway shots presumably from within the same structure. With each viewing, the shots change order. Lights flicker at altering intervals, indicating a continuous livestream. Dead ends are revealed, paths that double back on themselves recur with alarming frequency, and with time the terrible vastness and complexity of the structure begins to dawn on the viewer.

Without Trigger Event 5, the alternating hallways shots continue interminably.

Trigger Event 5 [type command "I'm a great admirer of yours." Press Enter key]

The (partial?) playthrough of an unidentified first-person maze game begins. A crude 3D outline of a long and winding hallway appears, which the "player" immediately begins to navigate. Some of the textures are incomplete and filled with static. No discernible correlation exists between the "game" layout and the "real" passageways shown in the livestream. The playthrough continues over the course of the proceeding narration.

GOMEZ: You remembered the first words you said to me. Congratulations! Let me encourage you to pause for a moment to admire my certainty that you'd make it this far. This labyrinth of mine wasn't cheap to build, especially given the multitude of contractors employed and the utmost secrecy to which I've bound them. Retroactively concealing it within the substructure of one of my less famous pieces wasn't easy either. That should warm you a little, that you're worth all this bother.

Nevertheless, flattery isn't my way, nor is it what you need. I'm aware that you've run up against the inevitable fact that my eyes haven't given you what you sought. They are organs, after all, inert sacks of fluid, despite the symbolic resonance your psychosis has imbued them with. When you packed them in your little cooler (I distinctly remember the sound and sweet smell of ice), I couldn't persuade you of what you've since learned from experience: they are bits of flesh, nothing more. You stole my *physical* eyes when you meant all along to steal my *vision*. An easy enough mistake to make, when you're within the spectrum of schizophrenia.

I sense your disappointment. I sense your longing and want nothing more than to restore to you the gift that slipped through your fingers.

When you took part of me with you, we became inseparable, you and I. Although, in my terror that you'd return to me, I initially resisted this identification with you, time has only strengthened it. I'm linked to you, like it or not. Your scalpel is eternally sheathed in my flesh.

I have taken you on as a model, of sorts. I have fashioned my work against the fabric of your blank, unconsummated longing. I have been reoriented by tireless creation against the nothingness between us, the impossibility we face of ever truly being alone.

The game vanishes, replaced by a table beneath a dim light. For a moment, nothing happens. The table is empty and limned by a thick wall of shadow the light utterly fails to penetrate. Then, something stirs. Zoomed in, it's possible to see dark liquid dripping onto the table.

A bare arm emerges from the dark. It rests on the table, palm up, while the other hand descends on it holding a knife. Gomez's face appears, the shadows cast by the light above deepening its eyeless hollows and stark, angular scars.

He is covered in blood.

He works meticulously with the knife, carving something into his arm. With all the blood, it's impossible at this point to determine what it is. The narration resumes.

GOMEZ: You know what this is, don't you? It's a bridge made of flesh. An outstretched hand. As you are aware, my father and mother were both actors. Their legendary infatuation had already cooled by the time I was young, and I had a recurring dream where I was running after my mother, calling her name inside a vast featureless room, all gleaming white and infinite. Something was carrying her away from me. She was draped over the shoulder of a creature I could never quite see. I heard her calling back to me from up ahead, around bends I couldn't make out. I couldn't reach her, couldn't glimpse more than a wisp of hair or the tips of reaching fingers. This is what I remembered when I entered the contest that brought me to the attention of the academe. With that dream in mind, I built that miniature city with its endlessly transmuting topography, its hidden panels and shifting dimensions. Even when I began to drift, when my later designs emphasized function over mystification, the dream was always there, that beautiful, innocent toy, hovering in the liminal darkness of a deleted space.

You are haunted by nightmares, like me. There are two kinds of haunted people: those who transmute their ghosts into work, and those who rage impotently against them. I was the former, you the latter. Now we are a symbiosis, a dual being of both work and rage. You have accomplished that. I am *your* masterpiece. You are mine.

Do you know where to look now, my friend? Can you guess where you'll find this broken face of mine, this violence that has changed your rage into work and my work into rage?

Trigger Event 6 [thirty seconds of no activity following the end of narration]:

The screen becomes dark for a moment before the montage of shots within the empty labyrinth resumes. This montage appears to serve as a waiting room between trigger events and deserves a brief commentary, since this is where the viewer spends most of their time. There are more than a few of us who have shared hundreds of hours with these silent hallways. Some have followed an inner calling to sit, pen in hand, and record angles, intersections, dead ends, and redundancies, an impossible effort carried out in hopes of composing a map of Gomez's masterpiece. Landmarks are sparse—occasional piles of human feces, roughly identical—and the stark, uniform aesthetic increases the viewer's disorientation. Only in rare cases can it be confirmed that a previous camera angle has been repeated (a small step that gets us nowhere in itself).

We have found it instructive to imagine Gomez—old, blind, and nearly crippled with exhaustion and pain—wandering these halls with no hope of escape. The lights are not for his benefit. They are for ours (or, if we strictly follow Gomez's intent, the Enucleator's).

Some of us have seen something in the hallways. Just a glimpse, nothing more, but something. We have one who swears to have seen a hand, differentiated by a monstrous light. All sightings of the creature—fleeting and unsubstantiated as they remain—have been described in terms indicating an emotional response of intense unease.

Trigger Event 7 [type command "Mirror," Press Enter key]:

The table reappears. Its surface is entirely covered with blood. This time, Gomez can be seen circling around from behind the camera and moving toward the thickest shadows in the back of the room. He stands still for a moment. His wounds have only partially healed. His flesh is swollen, and scabs cover most of his nude body.

When he turns to the table, he holds two jagged pieces of glass. He sits heavily into the chair to take a series of preparatory breaths before attempting to wedge the shards of glass into his empty eye sockets. The narration begins before he's fully fitted the first piece into place. The process becomes increasingly difficult as the glass becomes slick with blood.

GOMEZ: "A mirror into reality," a "reflection of our deepest fears." Ha. Remember what the critics wrote about the Crystal Library? I'm sure you do, given your admiration of that one. I seem to recall you telling me it was your favorite. Strange, how I can still hear your voice, crystalline and soft, tinged with an anxiety I found remarkable at the time, given the context.

I believed them then—that mirrors reflected the viewer's inner as well as outer facades. I was naive enough to frame this as a confrontation, as though some psychological work was being done in my castle of mirrors. "A library of selves," is what I'd said on multiple occasions. How cute.

I should've paid more attention. I should've noted the anxiety that would overcome the guests as they arrived for the viewing, as they turned to take in their multitudes echoed throughout the dimensions of the house's interior. I don't even have the excuse of calling my inattention juvenile. I was out of school by then. A professional, already on the way to fortune.

In truth, the mirror doesn't reflect anything of the human at all. It multiplies the human past humanity. It flays and kneads the human to proportions that are *truly monstrous*, dimensions residing well outside of representation. It's this glimpse of heights that become depths in their extremity that give mirrors their destabilizing power. *That's* what made the Crystal Library uncanny. It wasn't their own neuroses people saw in their reflections. It was their own inhumanity, their abject endlessness.

Only, that "inhumanity" *is* your humanity, don't you see? That's why the Crystal Library resonated with you. You, out of all others, *do* see your true form in the endlessness of mirrors. Your monstrousness has already consumed your humanity; your rage—even against me, the object of your love—is a towering multiplicity, a reverberating structure of flame primed to blacken every surface. You are *seen* in the Crystal Library, by me, by the structure itself, and the monster it subsumes.

Do you understand my gift to you now? Mirrors are no longer necessary. I've changed my exterior to match yours—*I know you've seen it too.* Now we turn to the interior, the prison, the dungeon, the grave, the mind. It won't be long before I enter the labyrinth. We have exhausted our roles in this myth. The last one we must play together.

Trigger Event 8 [thirty seconds of no activity following the end of narration]:

The more we watch the montage of hallways, the more we glimpse the figure within. It has become quite an object of fascination among the staff.

There was a time during our contemplation of Gomez's website when we found it necessary to summon the Enucleator from his duties. He entered our quarters, hiding his hunger the best he could, though we could see it within him, burning like a petal of cold flame. He clenched his scarred, roughened hands at his sides and forced his eyes to meet ours, battling his terror with admirable determination.

When we told him we found the labyrinth, he said something quite remarkable: "This is where you've always intended me to go." We considered this, and decided such words necessitated a hollowing. As he was escorted to the hollowing, his screams echoed through the hallways, recalling in the minds of his fellow harvesters the unbearable joy and terror of the Great Work.

Trigger Event 9 [type command "Icarus," Press Enter key]:

The table appears once more. The blood on its surface appears to have coagulated and a halfhearted attempt has been made to wipe it away, ultimately smearing the mess into clumps. The darkness surrounding the table is alive with movement, which we assume to be Gomez until he appears in the light, carefully holding an open glass container filled with clear liquid. He places it on the table before him.

His flesh still isn't healed, although enough of the swelling has gone down to hint at the dazzling intricacy of the pattern that covers him. The mirrors in his eye sockets occasionally catch the light, forcing the camera to readjust its exposure settings. He seems to mutter to himself, his mouth forming repeated shapes that might be "ash, ash, ash."

Right before the narration begins, Gomez produces a lighter and touches the flame to the liquid. It erupts into a brilliant pale gleam, a restless combustion that recalls white phosphorus. He grabs the glass and quickly lifts it to his face, pouring the flame into his mouth. Already, the container glows red and has melted to his hand, adhering to the skin even while Gomez thrashes in agony.

His face vanishes behind a shower of sparks. Smoke fills the room. The viewer can tell where his mouth is only by the blinding concentration of light burning inside it. Gomez collapses as the following narration begins.

GOMEZ: This will be my last monologue. I'm sure you understand why, given the future recording of my transformation you're currently witnessing.

My only regret is that I know next to nothing about you. Who *are* you? Do you have a mate? What about children of your own? Do you work at some menial, unassuming job that in no way reflects your inner dimensions? I was never what you'd call lonely, my friend, my brother, my *enucleator*. In my younger years, after I obtained all the comforts society dispenses, I surrounded myself with lovers and adorers. A few of my relationships were even what you'd call passionate, "serious."

I remember your hands—dirty, pitted things familiar with work (though what kind, I'll never know). Your face, during the short opening of the door, when I thought you were housekeeping, was already locked inside that fascinating diametric of shyness and ferocity. Your eyes were blank, significations of a terrifying emptiness as far from human as the infinite play of mirrors. You are *nothing*. I imagine that, if they find you here with me, they will be frustrated in their attempts to historicize you. You've wound your way to me without touching another soul, I'm certain of it. A being with no past, no ring of influence, an absence shimmering with menace.

I've only recently understood that I am nothing too. What have you built with my eyes? Nothing. What have I made here for you, for *us?* Nothing.

What am I saying? I am an artist, a world-famous architect. My exit was *bound* to be dramatic. I could've hung myself in my penthouse, but what would that leave behind for you? For the world?

I am ready to go now. After enough time has passed for me to fully transform, this website will activate. Eventually, you'll find it. Only *you* will make it this far. And when you find *me,* well...the cameras are programmed to track *your* transformation in turn. You'll be the first thing the rest of them see. You'll be the entranceway, the ornate edifice at the beginning of the underworld.

Trigger Event 10 [thirty seconds of no activity following the end of narration]:

There are no discernible exits in Gomez's labyrinth. We do not find this entirely surprising, since entrances and exits are an integral aspect of navigating the daily world, the very realm of existence Gomez seeks to undermine in his work (this is the work's only flaw, that it does not embrace the social context surrounding it). Entrances and exits facilitate movement from one space to the next, entailing a process of exchange, a flow of ideas, an endless distribution of capital across a market that is projected onto our spatial surroundings. The ease and accessibility of entrances and exits is of utmost importance to pragmatic concerns.

Gomez's disruption of "flow" between entrances and exits indicates a breakdown in logic. It implies a stasis. It is this very element that signals his movement beyond the symbolic world of the everyday and into the borderlands of the nonhuman.

How little he understands, for one coming so close.

His eyes have been put to good use, as have the multitude of organs and limbs our harvesters ferry to the warehouse without interruption. It all goes into the Great Work, which doesn't reside in a nonhuman, imaginative sphere. It is here, connected to the society surrounding it, a vital node of entrances, exits, pathways, tunnels, words, songs, and dreams; a profound being of unending connectivity, a mantra of terrible vitalism.

At last, one of our viewers has seen Gomez's final form—his mouth is a well of ash, his eyes black mirrors, the labyrinth carved across every inch of his flesh, pulled tight and dry over his skeleton, mold spreading like a flower from the area where the moisture of his body has seeped into the wall. Unwittingly, he has become an imperfect saint, modeling with his flesh the Great Work.

Description of the "home" page:

There is a body in a hallway.

The shot is from above and angled as if recorded by a security camera. Black walls and white tile floor. In the peripherals of the shot, the hallway stretches on and on, illuminated by small lights in the ceiling. The shot lingers here for a while before switching.

There is another body, slumped in a shadowed corner where the wall meets the floor. The bottoms of its shoes extend into the light, visibly bearing the logo of the shoe company.

Then there is another. This one is freshly bloated, still full of organic gasses. The viewer can see where it gnawed away part of its own hand.

Then there is another. And another.

What ensues is a montage of hallways filled with corpses. In some places, the stacks have begun to liquefy near the bottom, leaving dark pools that attract swarms of flies. The corpses are of all sexes, all ages, and in varying states of decay.

Even within this sterile, insulated environment, the Great Work has found a foothold.

the golden thread

PLEASED TO MEET you, kid. Go ahead and have a seat right there. Don't mind the mess. I'm putting my affairs in order, I guess you could say. That makes it sound like I'm preparing to die, doesn't it? How strange you must find that. I'm sure you're making note of the colloquialism, filing it mentally as "evidence" in case it turns out to be more than a subtle malapropism. Hell, maybe you aren't. Maybe you wouldn't have even noticed if I didn't point it out. That amuses me. You'll learn to be more observant than that, I'm afraid. You'll learn soon enough.

No donuts?...No, you didn't miss a memo, kid. I guess you could say we had a different way of doing things back in my day. Never in my life have I shown up to my first day of work without a dozen, mixed. It's just plain rational. You want to get off to a good start, don't you? I see you've donned a nice jacket and tie, so I know you do. What better way to make an impression than by bringing breakfast? I used to be a breakfast man: "the most important meal of the day," I'd always say. It matters less and less, you'll see, but still, manners are manners. On my first day, I ordered donuts from the geezer behind the cash register at that shit hole of a gas station. Get a look at him? Creepy fellow, isn't he?

By the way, how did the process go for you? It takes some getting used to, certainly. This is the only job you'll ever have that requires you to scan an ID card in a fucking paper towel dispenser, I can promise you that much. And the descending staircase that opens behind the toilet? It put my hair on end the first few times, I tell you. They could at least light the goddamned thing, cheap bastards. But this particular site's been on the backslide for years. A damned shame, I suppose, but I honestly can't blame them for forgetting about a patch of bare dirt in the empty sprawl of a massive mesquite forest, can I? I strongly recommend working up to jogging that subterranean kilometer of hallway, by the way. It's the only decent space you'll find for ironing out the godforsaken restlessness.

...Just hold your horses, son. We'll get to that. I'm aware that you haven't been briefed. I was in your shoes once too. There's all the time in the world, you'll find. Yes, pretty soon all that bullshit outside will start to fade. Time has its own way of operating around here, and I mean that in more than one sense. Speaking of, I'd bet HR fed you the line about "taking a breather"—doing something "easy" for a change, and you bit right into it, didn't you? I wasn't born yesterday, kid. I know how things work around here. You've run into trouble out there, haven't you? What was it? A divorce? Drowning in child support and death threats from a crazy ex?

...Just plain old burnout? No shit? Get tired of lifting paper and fetching coffee for the corporate office? Shit, don't bother explaining, kid. I don't care, it's none of my business. Well, I'd like to say you've come to the right place. Maybe you have. I'm not sure about much anymore.

I'd hazard a second bet that the first thing you noticed when you parked outside that fecal excuse of a gas station was the sky...No? Maybe you're in the right place after all. Got a sensible hunk of goo between your ears, haven't you? Not too prone to imagination and reverie, I hope? Good God, maybe the HR assholes are finally learning. Took them long enough, I tell you what. *I* sure as hell noticed the sky, and when I got here, sat in the same rickety ass office chair you're sitting in, my predecessor asked me what I thought about it. I thought he had to be some sort of psychic.

When you're in the car, as you inevitably are on your way to this unpopulated wasteland, you don't notice it. The sky's just a patch of blue at the top of the window. Your eyes don't wander to the widening sea above. They fail to notice how the trees have gradually given way to a harrowing expanse of emptiness. Distraction shields you from the realization that the sky you've known before was only the abridged version. When you get out of your car, when you finish gawking at the crumbling latrine of a store they've erected in order to provide an entrance to this godforsaken outpost, you see it: the impossible gash of blue that makes the world seem too small for all the shit that happens on its surface. Doesn't that vastness call to you? Isn't there vertigo right after that, the overwhelming sense that if you make a misstep, you'll float up into those cold, starry depths like a corpse dragged to the bottom of the ocean?

Right...you've already said you didn't notice. I forgot. *L'appel du vide,* by the way. It's French for "call of the void." That's what the *true* fear of heights its. My family took me to the Grand Canyon once when I was a kid. I refused to get out. I realize now that it wasn't a fear of falling that kept me huddled in the backseat of the family van. It was *a mistrust of my own will,* the inexplicable draw to the edge that I realized I was inclined to *obey.* Imagine that, if you can: annihilation resounding in your cells, and not because you've read too much Cioran as an adult, but because you were *born* that way! Imagine the Almighty fitting you with the hunger for oblivion just like he gave you speech and opposable thumbs. And it almost feels like love, kid. That's the strangest part.

...Ha ha, well, you can say that, kid. You have every right to *say* that none of this is relevant to your orientation. What do I know anyway? I've only been stuck here a few years. They told you I'm being transferred, right? Maybe it's because I'm crazy. Did you ever consider that?

So, it's business you want. Down to the brass tacks, am I right? Fine, kid. I'll humor you. Let me see...the facility can't be seen from the outside. It just looks like an abandoned grain silo to passersby. Fits right into the landscape. I'm sure you noticed how derelict the panhandle is, like someone bought the whole goddamned state in an auction and died heirless straightaway. And this *is* an abandoned grain silo as far as the occasional psycho who climbs to the top to deposit a body is concerned. The observation room and the living quarters above us are covered in a ton or so of grain, so even if you shine a powerful flashlight into the chamber, it looks the part...No, I'm not kidding about the bodies, kid, and don't get any heroic ideas. One outgoing call to state officials and you'll find out exactly how fast those kind, ever-so-helpful faces in HR can erase your ass. They stay in their lane, we stay in ours. Consider it firmly beyond your jurisdiction.

What else? Toilet's over there in the back of the locker room. Hayden and Dorris will be your partners for now. They're upstairs in rec, probably fucking. Generally, there's only one person here in observation. It's pointless to have everyone hunched over a desk all day, so you'll take shifts. I'll introduce you in a bit. They're easy enough to get along with, given their space. Seven on, seven off, if they haven't told you. It's not a bad gig. A couple years here and you'll have a tidy retirement.

...Ah, yes. There's always that, isn't there? You're looking at it, kid. Right there behind the glass. Feast your eyes.

...Damn, you are a sharp one, aren't you? You're right: nothing's there. Just a patch of dirt and stubby little mesquites. Ugly fuckers, aren't they? It wouldn't strain most people's imagination to describe this area as "treeless"—in truth, you're standing in one of the thickest forests in the nation. These knobbed little freaks are trees, same as any other.

Now, kid, I can tell you're disappointed. Who wants to spend exactly half their existence staring at a ten-by-ten patch of Texas dirt? I'd like to tell you there's more to it than that, but there really isn't. I just described your job in fairly honest terms. Oh, there's the usual distractions. Hayden and Dorris are on the tail end of their little fling. Fight all the time, so you have that to look forward to. You'll hear all about Hayden's obsession with video games, and he'll go into all sorts of abominable details about her addiction to multi-level marketing schemes, which, the way he tells it, is all she does on her off week. In time, when they get past this hump and call it quits, you'll have a fair shot at Dorris yourself, kid. You've got a decent enough appearance, and she's not bad on the eyes, I can tell you that. Otherwise, I recommend passing the time as slowly as possible. Cozy up to a good book. You got any intimidating reads you're itching to knock out lest you die a cultureless heathen? It's preferable if they're of the canonical variety. Joyce? Proust, maybe? You need something you can't burn through in a day.

Distract that big, gelatinous wad on your shoulders from the fact that you're spending your life watching a patch of stunted trees consume a steady diet of ultraviolet light.

...Shit, kid, save it. I'm not pulling anything over on you. Fact is, nothing's happened here since before my time. The disappearances go way back, sure, but they ended exactly three years ago. I shit you not when I tell you that my predecessor, as soon as he finished something approximating the spiel I'm giving you, walked out *into* that patch of sand—entry is forbidden, by the way, except in the mythic case of emergencies, and I'll give you the key the minute I'm—

...I'm telling you to be patient a second time now. Look, I don't *have* to sign off on your orientation. Part of my job right now is determining whether or not you're fit to operate in this little segment of nothingness. The decision is mine and mine alone, and I'm required to make this determination *before* I reveal just exactly what's behind the glass. We can't very well send people back to their old positions *after* we spill the beans on the nature of this highly confidential anomaly, can we? Now look, I personally don't give a shit. I'm gone either way. But I'll tell this at my pace or not at all, got it? Thanks.

Let's see, where to begin? Why not in 1885? It's the account my predecessor led with, and I don't see any reason to violate tradition. I'll even try to tell it like he did, hazarding little details from his research that lent the thing some flavor. To your memory, bud. I hope you've come closer to finding what you were looking for.

To begin with, you can imagine how empty this area was back then. This was ranch territory. A few cotton fields existed long before the soil was rendered useless by overharvesting, but this was before oil was a factor. The homesteads dotting the landscape were filled with tough individuals, families with the balls to face the elements and American Indians alone. Encounters with both, by the way, make for some pretty compelling horror, if you go back and read the firsthand accounts, and like I said, anyone living out here back then had to face these horrors alone. All these ghost towns you see scattered around here weren't there yet. Even Chasm, that town you passed some fifty miles out, had yet to become a twinkle in an oil man's calculating eye. Closest neighbors were a day's ride away, so even screaming for help as a Comanche warrior ran a sharp flint edge across your daughter's skull was as useless as begging mercy from God. Not that you can blame them, by the way: whites had done the same, so what did those old farmers expect?

Speaking of daughters, it's truly incredible that we know about William Hardbody's sixteen-year-old, Clarissa. I pity the poor asshole in research who had to read every journal from the area cover to cover, but somehow, they located an entry from the year in question detailing poor Clarissa's vanishing. It's the first that we know of, and fairly detailed.

Old William had heard something out in the red gloaming, and the dogs were going crazy. Now, in that time, it was unwise to hunt the source of a sound, even the animal variety, near nightfall. The Comanche were more than adept at luring members of the household into the plains for easy dispatch. William notes his well-founded misgivings, but he describes a recent coyote problem that had cost him a couple of calves over the past few months. It had been a rough year, and the coyotes, emboldened by starvation, were on the brink of inflicting hardship on the Hardbody house. He decided that saving the few remaining calves was worth the risk and recruited Clarissa, the eldest of seven girls, to wield a rifle in case the Comanche made a grab for William.

They were lucky, at first. The noise *was* coyotes, and by the time they arrived, the beasts were kept a distance from a calf by its mother. William got a few shots off before the coyotes retreated into the field. Then, confident in their safety, father and daughter approached the wounded calf.

That was right here, right where you're sitting perhaps. They walked over there to our little piece of heaven behind the glass—the calf and the agitated cow must've been just beyond it, across the room right about where that old desktop monitor is. Clarissa walked right between those mesquites—the trees themselves probably didn't exist back then, but we're certain the space hasn't moved—and vanished into thin air. William was obviously distraught. He saw it with his own eyes; one second she's there, the next, nothing. He scrambled around the dirt, knees in the grass, calling her name over and over again while the sun goes down. He never knew how lucky he was that he didn't pass through the exact space his daughter had during all that searching—I shudder to imagine how close he must've come. But for a time, it was him and that cow, both bawling in the dark until it finally occurred to him that he'd have to head home if he wanted to see the next sunrise. And maybe he didn't want to, but there were six more girls back at the house and a missus who would perish in the hideous spasms of hunger if he doesn't make it back and the winter proved harder than the summer and fall preceding it. There was no time for mourning: Clarissa became a journal entry lovingly evoked a dozen times over the ensuing years until waning into another faceless casualty of the frontier. A decade later, William's dead of consumption and that's the end of that.

...Well, we're certain it happened right here because it happened again. And again. Throughout the recorded history of this area, which, I admit, is largely scant until the past decade, people have vanished some right in plain sight of others, and a good many in the name of science. You see that bookshelf in the corner? The black hardbacks it holds are volumes in a set printed exclusively for this location. It lists and describes each disappearance chronologically, the earliest entry being Clarissa's and ending with my predecessor—they finally shipped the amended final volume two months ago. You can also find it all on this bad boy right here, along with other useful features, such as the ability to group cases by keywords and themes. For your first week, I recommend filtering by "rescue attempt," "multiple disappearances," and "theory." You've got a lot of time though, so don't rush it.

...Yes, in the name of science is what I said. Look, kid, don't tell me that you're naive enough to believe that the first priority in these situations is anything *but* determining the anomaly's viability for weaponization? This requires human testing in every case. Imagine it: the ability to make armies of troops, potentially even large vehicles, buildings, *nations,* vanish into thin air? What government wouldn't want a piece of that?

But don't you worry, human testing was all during my predecessor's time. I haven't seen a single soul pass through those two mesquites in person. I've watched the feed, sure—you will too, eventually—but you won't see any more interest from upstairs. They can't weaponize or monetize it, so it's off to newer and better things. That's why low-level operators like you and me get stuck here nowadays instead of Nobel-wielding physicists like my predecessor. We're not paid to figure this out. The name of the game is watching and waiting. You're here, I'm afraid, because they already *own* you, and you've been determined to possess normal eyesight and the ability to pick up a direct line in the unlikely case that circumstances call for it.

...We're watching and waiting for victims to return, of course. God knows how many of them after all these years are still trying to get back, kid. Clarissa herself might still be passing back and forth across the threshold, or any one of the sixteen children from Sunnyside Baptist in Chasm who came out here to utilize the gracious loaning of the then-owner's property for the Big Easter Egg Hunt back in '98—that was the case, mind you, that would've burst into national news if not for the swift interception and silencing from our friends in corporate. Imagine them: Clarissa, all those kids, running back and forth between those mesquites, trying to reset whatever crease in the smooth functioning of time sent them back there, skipping across and back again like kids jumping rope on a playground—

...Yes, I did say time, didn't I? Well it's just a theory, my predecessor's, actually. I've made a few adjustments to it on my own over the years, but I'll keep those to myself. *He's* the famous physicist, not me. You can find his official reports in the hard drive, and if you put some effort into learning the terminology, you might even understand some of them. Mind you I said *some* of them. You've got to remember that what occurs in the invisible patch of space between those mesquites is unexplainable by the standards of modern science. I imagine some of the appended proofs he scratched out seemed little better than nonsense to even his most brilliant colleagues. If there's one thing practical-minded physicists dislike, it's loopy math. My predecessor told me that before he walked off to put his theories to the test.

You see, some of the human subjects were fitted with recording equipment...Yes, paid employees, all of them, at least on paper. The stipend they offer for this kind of thing is something to behold. Don't ask me what methods they utilized to seek those who were ready to die to ensure the financial security of their families. Our friends in HR could tell us, if they were inclined.

...Yes, I said "die," didn't I? It's the wrong word though. All the words are wrong. "Vanished," "erased," "lost," we don't have the right words to describe what happens to them. "Submerged" might be closest. You see, it became clear that those who were fitted with recording equipment survived the transferal. What's more, they're still in our world. After they cross over, most test subjects seem to think that nothing happened. They look around the room and everything appears normal. The mesquites they look back at are the same ones you and I see. "Maybe they've fixed it," the poor bastards surely think. For one absurd moment, they breathe easier with the hope that they can collect their checks, go back home, and continue their lives. But suddenly, they realize their colleagues are looking past them, as if they were no longer there. That's when the panic sets in. Sometimes, they try to rush the glass only to find that they can't move like they used to. I'm sure they try to scream. One subject named Catherine removed the camera from her helmet and mouthed the words "I'm falling" as she struggled to make it to the doorway while the people in the room—the ones left on our side, the "normal" world—started moving faster and faster until their bodies were impossible streaks of color on the feed.

Yes, Catherine Garner, a twenty-eight-year-old chronic alcoholic with more guilt than sustenance to pass on to her children, changed the name of the game by turning that camera on herself. Sound doesn't carry on the other side. They never could figure out why. Garner's moment of inspiration turned into scribbled notes on whiteboards, ASL, everything down to a prohibitively complex color system meant to maximize the amount of information communicable within the briefest window of time. Have you read the *Glass Bead Game,* kid? Imagine the Ludi Magister at work, and you have an idea of the intricacy I'm talking about.

The biggest problem was the decay of the electronics. Recording equipment wouldn't last more than a few minutes, and transmissions couldn't seem to "cross over" with any regularity. Sometimes, it took months to receive just a few minutes of feed. Often, it never connected at all, the images lost somewhere in the ethereal flux of time that separates us from them. Even the color coders had trouble conveying anything across such an inconsistent environment. And therein lies the loss of interest, kid. You can't use what you can't control. You can't control what you don't understand.

...Hold your horses, kid. I see the spark in you now, and I like it. There may be hope for you yet, but I can only answer one question at a time. No, they're not dead, as I've stated, and where they go is...complicated. What they *did* find out is merely a hint of the answer, I'm certain. The only person to claim it made any kind of sense was my predecessor, and just you try to make sense of *his* work.

The subjects are shifted ever so slightly into the past. Just a flash of a moment, really—nothing you'd think would carry any implications whatsoever. We're talking goddamn yoctoseconds here, kid. That's less time than it takes you to formulate a thought. Less time than it takes you to feel pain. That's less than a step, less than a nudge on the space-time continuum. It's nothing, really, but it's all it takes.

The worst of it is, once you fall behind, you keep falling. I don't know if you've noticed, kid, but there's enough evidence out there for God's cruel streak to make a Gnostic blush. I consider this little feature of creation a damning piece.

Turns out, the present isn't what you think it is—we're not nestled on a continuum between comfy little bookends of the past and the future. This moment is all there is. Blink, and the space you occupied within that tiny spark of darkness is in free fall. You got any kids, kid?...No? Well, imagine one. A son, we'll say. When you look at this being, this joy-of-life, you see him on the living room carpet, bent over a mess of Hot Wheels, oblivious to his surroundings due to the illusion that the present is a stable point on a plane. Your son rolls his steel cars away from him with a similar confidence in the earth—the carpet, he's already learned, and the wood, concrete, and dirt beneath it won't swallow his toy in a horrifying lapse of continuity. The Earth is always there, a seamless sphere, and we tend to imagine time and space in similar terms. Our gut reaction against nothingness makes us see things this way. As they used to say, "nature abhors a void." By nature, they really meant "we."

That's the *appearance,* the "way of opinion," as wise old Parmenides once put it. The "way of truth" is much different. Imagine your rhetorical offspring again, but this time dangling helplessly over a limitless swath of decay. Below him, figures you can only glimpse in outlines writhe in the darkness, figures twisted and malformed beyond imagination, and beneath them, an impossible darkness. The only thing that separates the boy from the wastelands below is a thin golden thread he clutches between two fingers. That thread is the present, and what I've painted you is a fairly accurate account of things, kid. Stepping through those mesquite trees is letting go of the thread. Hence Catherine's words, "I'm falling."

You see this little box on the corner of my screen? That's what it looks like most of the time, just a blank, unused space on your monitor. Truth is, that spot's been reserved. Every once in a great while it will leap to life, brimming with sights you'd best not think about too much. Take my word for it. It leads the imagination to consider things that aren't in the interest of your health.

I call them rogue transmissions. It's widely considered an epiphenomenon at this point, so you don't have to worry about them if you choose not to. All they're good for is storing in some offsite database, which is exactly what's done with them. The only reason we have access to the feed is in the case of the statistically impossible situation wherein a subject makes intentional contact with us to convey a viable exit procedure. This, of course, has never happened.

Somehow, a rare glimpse manages to get through, just a momentary burst of video outside the far more stable seconds that pass before the initial transmission loses consistency. Those moments are the unseemly guests who reserve that little void-shaped window. I've seen a few of them myself. Once, I was halfway into a chicken salad sandwich when that window flickered with a pale lavender light. The screen revealed a serial number that I traced to Subject 334, a man named James who went in a few years back. He was walking in this big, empty space lit with an underwater glow. For a moment, the camera tilts down to his watch, which now displays what appears to be a random series of numbers. Stranger, James' wrist and the watch are no longer separate. They're melded together, the watch having grown bulbous new faces and reams of wire running from the casing into the subject's flesh. And his flesh...well, the end of James' arm was a mess of fingers, more than one could count in the brief instant of the video feed.

...I'm serious, kid. And that's a mild one, honestly. When the present passes, what's left is a hollow version of the world. That s where Catherine went after her coworkers vanished. That's where they *all* go. A landscape of vague memories, echoes of the shining moment of life that races by, never to return. They can still see the silo, the inside of this room, hell, even the gas station and the forest of mesquites in between. But it's all drained of color, light traded for darkness with a slight, lavender glow Angles are more angular but somehow less distinct. I've seen the gas station loom against the empty sky like an enormous, inanimate spider.

The mutations seem to come later. I remember how my predecessor described it when I was wearing a face of disbelief much like your own: The present holds things in shape. It's a spotlight that freezes form, an observer on the quantum level constantly collapsing waves of potentialities. Outside of this condensed beam of meaning-making lies chaos.

...The craziest thing I've seen? You're not getting some sort of kick out of this, are you? This isn't a fucking horror story, kid. This is reality, which is, so long as you don't think about it too hard, completely different. I admit that there is a lure, a *l'appel du vide*, but it's not in the grotesque details. You'll have time to review the feed yourself. You'll have weeks to see what Chasm looks like emptied of the present, its dilapidated structures stretching to dimensions repellant to the mind. Maybe you'll see the children, still hunting Easter eggs with their bulbous, glowing multitude of eyes and surplus of limbs. Look hard enough, and you'll find a series of clips assembled into a time-lapsed observation of Subject 8444, a man named Douglas who seemed to get stuck somehow, phased halfway inside a wall while the disintegration occurred. It's impossible to tell who is filming, since the identification numbers are distorted, but the observer must've watched Douglas grow with impossible patience, remaining utterly immobile until what was left of his colleague was a cancerous mass of cells and duplicated physical features towering to nauseating heights.

No, the ugly details do not call to me, kid. If that's where you find your kicks, you've got plenty of material, I promise. What I see—and what my predecessor saw—is *beyond* all that, further still down the ladder. The *real* "way of truth," you could say.

Think about it: all the horrors down there are part of *this*. This moment—the moment you and I inhabit, right now—is the purest intensity of being. *Being itself* includes it all, this light, the purple hell beyond, the long-lost humans towering like leviathans throughout the night land, *all of it*. It's real, kid. I've seen glimpses of it inside that little square.

At some point in this little occupational venture of yours, you'll wind your way to the inevitable conclusions. If the golden thread of the present alters the nature of being, then *what is it?* We're dealing with something entirely *outside* of being, an external element of a different substance than the undifferentiated sea it drags its finger through. How else can we conceptualize its trajectory across the surface of being? A pool of water can't cause a ripple, kid. Something *else* has to do it; the wind, a leaf. And something so utterly outside, from our limited perspective, must be a lot like Thomas Aquinas' "unmoved mover": God. The present is the gaze of God. That's the little detail my predecessor had some difficulty working out in his proofs. Nevertheless, he swore it was in his notes, scribbled in plain numbers for those with the willingness to see.

So think about what we've done, kid. Each crossing of that threshold is a violation of God's will. We've strayed from God's path, and yes, I mean that quite literally.

But oh, *the beyond!* Just *imagine* it, kid! What is the thrill of heights, the call of the void, but the suggestion, half whispered, to stray from the path! The devil's prerogative, the romantic suicide, it's all just the urge to jump, kid, nothing more. And what heights call to me now. How far does it go? When the disintegration is complete, when you've reached the furthest distance from God's cold, prescriptive light, what then? You wouldn't peg me for sentimental, I bet, but I've told you the leap has been built into me. I've been engineered to peer over the terrible ledge into nothingness. And if there's any of that in you, kid, you'll hear it too, before it's all over.

But that's enough of all that. Pay me no mind. All my time here's warped my perspective. Now let's take you to meet the others. While they show you the ropes upstairs, I have some final business to attend to down here. Welcome aboard. I hope you'll one day recall me as a worthy predecessor.

a prisoner's guide to stargazing

THE STARS REALLY are something here. That thick band of light's the Milky Way, a sprawling arm of the spiral of stars that serves as Earth's home. It seems close enough to touch. It's hard to imagine that Earth is some 165 *quadrillion miles* away from the supermassive black hole at the center of the Milky Way. Wild, huh?

When I was a kid, I paid close attention to the stars. Every chance I got, I turned to the night sky, watching the great shimmering swath of celestial bodies burn across a distance that light can't travel in a dozen human lifetimes. It's easy to think of the sky as a static backdrop, empty and cold compared to the bustle of the world below. It isn't though. It's bursting with movement, particularly now that the stratosphere is cluttered with satellites zipping across the sky like tiny silver gnats. The longer you watch the sky, the richer it grows. You simply can't absorb with a glance. It demands patience and something a lot like a child's sense of wonder, the kind that most adults leave behind. Not everyone, mind you, but most.

When Jamie and I went on our honeymoon to the coast, we were out on a pier one night, drinking from a cheap bottle of wine and dodging the silverfish as they scuttled past our feet. A meteor flashed overhead, so bright the water mirrored the blaze.

"What was that?" she asked, looking up from her glass.

"Shooting star," I said, drawing an arm around her shoulder and pulling her close.

"Really?"

"Yes."

"I've never seen one before."

I laughed since I didn't believe her. As the years wore on, I noticed she neglected the sky, her gaze always captivated by occurrences at the terrestrial level: phone, job, the house, kids, neighbors. I believe her now. I wonder what she would think of *this* sky. I wonder how she would handle it. The thought of her suffering so intensely makes me sick.

Are you getting any of this? I don't want to entertain the possibility that I'm speaking to myself. Don't you want to know how perfect your choice was? Do you see how *fitting*, given my natural proclivities?

I've seen the northern lights even though I've always lived in Texas. I watched Hale-Bopp pass in '95 from the backyard of my parents' double-wide. I remember how difficult it was to keep my father's binoculars steady. I don't know how long I chased glimpses of that great, icy tail in the viewfinder before giving up. I've seen meteoroids explode like fireworks in the lower atmosphere. One roared so low it sounded like a jet. When it finally disintegrated, the whole night seemed to catch flame. I've witnessed things I haven't told a soul, like the glowing green ball that receded to the horizon one night and vanished with a great pale flash.

I'd say it's a shame that all the best stuff happens when you're alone, but if I'm being honest, I'm glad it's that way.

In childhood, stargazing was an escape from my father. Maybe that's why I've made a point to include my son. There's something unsettling about how much of parenthood is a long attempt to undo the inadequacies of your own childhood. I see that, now that I've had all this time to reflect. When I'd take him out to the empty baseball field with the cheap plastic telescope, I was trying to right a wrong that wasn't mine, cure a pain that wasn't yet his. "The sky's there for *everyone*," I'd tell him, "just hanging up there in all its glory. If you miss out, it's only because you weren't looking."

To his credit, my son would humor me. He'd look through the viewfinder at the slightly brighter version of Polaris, nod through my failed attempts to snag Saturn's rings. Something like real joy snuck into his smile when we'd catch the thick contours of shadows around the moon's craters. We are fundamentally different, nevertheless. Unlike my son, unlike Jaime, I enjoy the quiet.

Quiet—there's lots of that here. More than I'd prefer, in fact. One thing I've noticed is that, deep down, people can't stand the quiet. Something in the stillness unsettles them. It poses a challenge and the things that rise to meet it are the very things people want most to hide. What they're hiding varies, a divorce's accumulation of indignities, the fear of failure so central to maintaining a "professional" life, the maddening futility of material possessions. It's *this* aspect of my imprisonment, the silence, that would crack people like Jaime. *This* is why it's better me than her—*for the love of Christ, please let it be me and not her.* For Jaime, the pain of silence would be worse than its physical counterpart, and that's bad enough.

I noticed the pain around the same time I noticed something wrong with the sky. It was dull then, throbbing against the back of my hands, shooting through my neck, burning behind my eyes. As it grew, I came to appreciate how rich and complete it is—a perfect achievement so long as it was designed to colonize every corner of the mind. I'm not trying to romanticize my suffering. The intensity is something I'm unable to forget for even a moment. If you're recording this—*Why would you not record this? Surely you wouldn't leave your subject unobserved*—rewind it far enough, and I'm certain you'll discover I've filled more than my share of long hours with screams. Eventually, I dissolved into this too, almost more completely than I dissolved into the faulty sky.

There's a threshold that must be crossed, since pain's function is to bring awareness to the body. Pain, in small doses, is a marker of physical and experiential boundaries: *this* is where the surface of your hand meets the tubing that runs into the machine you can't see; *that* is what happens when your muscles are immobilized far longer than they should be; *there* is where a sharp edge has ground into your orbital bones. At a certain point, however, the experience of pain blooms into vast and colorless vistas. In my mind, it's like a silky body of water, quartz white and limitless. The electrical currents pulsing along my nerves no longer indicate locality but set me alight with a weightless aura that can't help but permeate this black swath of space drifting impossibly before me. And in this connection between the sunken womb of the night and the screaming hurt that forms my amniotic sac, I've come around to the old chick n' egg problem: *Is pain something I project onto this proxy universe, or is it the underlying substance of all existence to which I've been tuned?*

Sometimes I can't help but wish my son were here. Sometimes I'm fooled into thinking I'm experiencing the essence of what we've been looking for together with that cheap, beginner's telescope. Sometimes I imagine that I've found an unobstructed view of *the real*, extracted like a gem from the bedrock of ephemeral distractions. For all its misery, I find myself pretending that he'd appreciate this somehow, after a period of adjustment. A cosmic father and son moment, how *wholesome.*

This is the kind of sickness you've forced me to. If you're out there, I hope you're proud.

I fall into this trap of sentimentality every time I remember I'm from somewhere else, a planet called Earth inhabited by beings resembling myself. I call these my "moments of clarity," although that's another joke. Context isn't clarity, not when it entails questions like *Where am I? How did I get here? Where is my family? How long have I been away?* The pure awareness of the pain and the sky is much simpler, an unbroken surface over which existence simply glides. Beyond the loss of loved ones and beyond the physical pain, the immensity of it is overwhelming. One mind simply isn't enough to encompass all I've been chosen to witness. It's unbearable, particularly now that they've started sending *Her,* but I don't want to talk about Her right now, since I'm never certain whether my thoughts introduce Her into being or if it's the other way around.

"Chosen." What's left of the human in me can't resist shoehorning some sort of agency into this. The human also can't help but appreciate the irony of the fact that I've gotten my lifelong wish. How many times during my

idle stargazing did I fantasize leaving humanity behind, which is a truly human fantasy, born from the human revulsion against all things human? I'd sit there, beer in hand, smelling the smoke from the grill, nodding absently as someone from work lamented the crimes of their department supervisor or bragged about their European vacation. All the while I'd peer over their shoulder, my gaze close enough to meeting theirs to convince them I was paying attention, and stare at the stars. I wanted *so terribly* to leave it all behind. And somehow, I *did*, although I don't remember the specifics. I couldn't tell you when I switched from being human to whatever fragmented and partial thing I am now, but I certainly got my wish. There's no denying *that.*

Here's another one of those impossible questions that arises: *Where is the pain coming from?* There's no way of uncovering the answer, no way of knowing anything at all. I am only a being that sees and feels, no longer one that manipulates his surroundings with extensions of flesh. I *swear* I once could, I *know* I held my son's hand on the way to that baseball field at night. I *know* that I extended a physical hand to his and I felt his cool soft palm in mine. I'm *certain* that I touched Jaime that evening when we finally made it back to the seaside hotel a little drunk. It was the evening after she had tried feeding the seagulls. I remember the indefinite panic that forced her to stop as they swarmed around her in growing numbers. For a brief moment, we could feel their beating wings, a cold breeze behind a wall of feathers. Later, that body beneath *mine* was *hers.* I *refuse* to entertain any alternatives, no matter how far you've burrowed into me. You can take everything but the mind, my friends. *Cogito ergo sum* and all that bullshit.

When I first awoke to this hell, I thought I must've fallen into a sinkhole and broken my spine. It would've explained the fact that I was unable to move, the clarity of the sky (I remember reading somewhere that the stars are much clearer at the bottom of a well), and eventually, the searing pain. All that was left was to wait for rescue or death. After some time passed, I saw that my hypothesis needed revision. I wasn't hungry or thirsty, and the night was unending. There is no wind and no sound to indicate the proximity of a living ecosystem. Nothing crosses the sky, no meteoroids or commercial airliners or insects or birds. Worst of all, as I watched the progress of the stars, I saw the sky reset.

Back when I still held onto the conceit of a firm ontological division between "reality" and "illusion," I thought it was a hallucination. As on Earth, the sky rotated steadily around Polaris, but at some point, it would revert to a fixed starting position. Again, the normal rotation would resume, but after reaching the end point, the sky would snap back into place. I thought that perhaps I kept dozing off for an unlikely span of time, and this led to the realization that I no longer sleep, that I can't even close my eyes. It's like a recording of the Earth's sky is projected into my mind, only it's incomplete, like whoever made the film ran up against their budget.

And why *wouldn't* they leave it incomplete? It's but another human conceit to assume that whatever put me in this place would go out of its way to render my pseudo-reality convincing. Why *not* use a slapped-together mockery of the night sky? It's not like I can protest, although that's what I'm presuming to do by saying all this, isn't it? The most unbearable aspect of this whole ordeal is its blatant artificiality. Despite the extended periods of forgetfulness—relative moments of ease wherein I dissolve in this crystalline expanse—I am denied the full escape I would undoubtedly enjoy if only this sky, alien or terrestrial, were *real*. I can't get it out of my head, this careless fakery. *One revolution* is all it would take. All that stands between the awareness of my internment and freedom is *one full revolution* of the night sky.

Despite my protests, I can't deny the terrifying possibility that I've been left with this repetitive diversion and forgotten. What if I've been tossed this slapdash sky and, of all things, *Her,* as "toys" during this state of total passivity? What if my screams—my truly inconceivable plateaus of agony— what if the words I'm uttering now, what if it's all unheard, unrecorded? What if they intended to leave me in relative ease and remain completely unaware of their mistakes, the result of some corrupted data upload? What if I'm left to suffer like this forever?

I might as well get around to Her, since She's really what shocked my consciousness into recognizing details I had missed before. It's *She* who snaps me back into place when I find myself wishing for my wife—*Jasmine? Julie? What is her name?*—and my child—*What did I call them back on Earth? Everything becomes indistinct when She approaches. She always takes something with her.*

My first encounter with Her loosened something inside of me. I'm not sure if it was the pain or the terror, but a memory dislodged from whatever method of erasure they—in their typically rushed, halfhearted way— attempted to employ. I remember stars—*real* ones, I'm sure, since they were wholly alien—behind a glossy, translucent surface, like glass but rippling and shifting like layers of water and oil. Any attempt to look at my own body was restricted entirely by structures I couldn't see. Incredibly, I could blink, at least before the soft, mechanical humming began and my skull vibrated with the sawing. Soon after, everything went black. I remember the smell and taste of blood, the searing, impossible pain as something was inserted into the space hollowed out behind my eyes. I can't say for certain what it was, but I felt every tiny adjustment since each one sent tidal waves of white-hot agony roiling through my brain. From then on, I have only seen this sky, familiar and brilliant and unapologetically false. I remember this all thanks to Her.

Hello? Are you getting all this, or am I just talking to myself? If your goal was to make this existence bearable to me—and I can only hope against hope that this is the case—then you've made a serious mistake. It would be better to experience nothing at all. When you inserted the machinery, you could've killed me with a slight mismeasurement—wouldn't it be easier for us *both* if things went that way? Why should this hell continue if it doesn't do either of us any good? I *refuse* to entertain the possibility that you *intend* for things to go on like this. No sentient creature could do this to another *on purpose*.

Good God, She's coming now. Every time I even *think* about Her, She's there, and how could I possibly purge Her from my mind? I know only one thing for certain about my captors: they do not reproduce sexually. Their understanding of procreation is so horrifyingly far from human, so impossibly beyond *biological*, that it truly outstrips all bandwidths of understanding. Is this supposed to be some kind of joke? My mind goes white as She materializes beyond the black glassy surface of the threshold. I can never tell if the shimmering ripples signaling her emergence are truly *lights* or some order of darkness beyond my visual capacity. The lights blind me, blind my mind, blind my senses to all but Her horrific arousal from the void.

How I wish I could erase Her, construct a description of Her that relegates Her to the harmless realm of language. Like the sky, She's a mockery, seemingly tossed together as an infantile diversion for my limitless internment. My God, how they anthropomorphized her, how they indicated the realm of human relations without going *near* far enough to breach the illimitable expanse between them and us, leaving only the abject remainder—the texture, the horrible wetness, the vertiginous extremes of sensation—distinct from the formal constraints that distinguish life in the individual sense from Life in the abstract.

Life. Maybe *that* is the joke, that something can be so far from living while embodying Life's impulses at their most horrifically exaggerated. Nothing She does to me can be unthought, unfelt, or unremembered. She's writhing to the surface from an impossible depth like a great, cosmic parasite. That any living creature could've *designed* this *for me* is itself a thought beyond thought. Imagine this as their attempt at a pin-up girl, designed to keep me warm in the dark. And the possibility that they modeled her on my wife—*What is her name? What is her name!*—is too horrible to contemplate.

Do you hear? It's all gone horribly wrong! End it now before She's here again, before it's all too late. But there is no ending, of course. I am but a nodule of pure receptivity, consciousness locked inside some cosmic being's shitty science fair project forgotten in the back of a closet. I can only hope that my suffering serves some pragmatic end, no matter how alien and terrible. But something tells me I'm no longer even a passing thought.

At some point, the pain-filled stillness will return. This is a certainty. While it's not a consolation by any means, there's at least a pattern. I can focus on the stars—fake though they are—while She emerges, concentrate on some distant segment of clusters before Her horrific surface eclipses them all.

The stars really are something here.

our endeavors

AT 6,544 FEET above sea level, the subject (male, early thirties) exits the driver's side of the vehicle and makes his way around to the back. Other vehicles pull into spaces behind his parked Toyota as he struggles with the door. The latch never worked quite right, so a little extra muscle is required to pop it open. The stuck door is a quirk the subject secretly appreciates since he can't bring himself to fully trust the child lock. While the subject is preoccupied, the following people exit the other cars: subject's girlfriend, her mother, and a family friend whom the subject acutely detests. They blink into the blazing sunlight and cluster together in the middle of the dusty parking area.

The subject extracts a child from the back seat (male, a toddler) and sets him on the ground. The child shields his face from the light and begins to cry. The subject gathers the boy up in his arms, rolling his eyes and flashing a smile to the girlfriend. The subject's girlfriend (also the child's mother) grins and shrugs. The acutely despised family friend attempts to intervene, speaking incoherent syllables the subject believes the child is too old to require. He angles himself slightly away from the woman and begins walking to the trailhead.

Note: at this juncture, no one, including the subject, is particularly inclined to walk the trail. It's been a long day, and everyone is hungry. It's an acute annoyance to the subject and his girlfriend (unconscious in the case of the family friend) that the girlfriend's mother provided a detailed itinerary for this outing, including a precise sequence of events punctuated midway by lunch at a specific Mexican restaurant near the outskirts of town (some fifteen minutes east of the park, its proximity all the more tantalizing to the group, including the mother). No member of the party, however, is willing to suggest a deviation from the itinerary. The subject wants his girlfriend's mother to come to regret her micromanagement on her own and has devoted himself to the itinerary to the point of sardonic enthusiasm. The girlfriend, suspecting the subject's dedication to the itinerary to be insincere but hoping it nonetheless makes a positive impression on her mother, in no way wants to ruin the moment. The mother, at this point, has begun to think of the itinerary less as an obstacle of her own devising and more of one insisted upon by her daughter's boyfriend. It's almost certain that this projection has occurred due to the boyfriend's convincing show of enthusiasm, which the mother has evidently taken at face value, therefore reversing, we're amused to note, the original intent of the boyfriend. The female family friend, by all accounts, has noticed none of this and remains indifferent to the itinerary, if not altogether unaware of its existence.

After a brief series of inconsequential exchanges, they reach the trail, which begins directly outside of the parking lot. This path traverses a thick knot of trees, which limits the view, a characteristic the boyfriend secretly appreciates, since the park's sheer cliffs and seemingly limitless stretches of distant valleys tend to make his palms sweat. It seems plausible that this fear originates with certain recurring dreams that punctuated the subject's childhood, most involving skyscrapers swaying wildly in the wind, or a jeep veering from the road into a void at the center of a valley (always the same valley). There is no reason to suspect that any of the subject's companions share his phobia. Only the girlfriend is aware of it, and it's touching to watch her reassuringly squeeze his shoulder every time a gap in the trees reveals the abrupt heights of the trail.

It is necessary to note that the day is beautiful. The sun shines brilliantly; the song of birds thread the canopy of limbs; rabbits and squirrels scuttle through the brush. It's an ideal seventy-five degrees. Only the family friend thinks it's hot and does not refrain from loudly voicing her complaints.

What happens over the next ten minutes is largely inconsequential. Not much is said—the group, to varying degrees, is now enjoying the excursion, "drinking it all in," as the girlfriend's mother says as she stops to admire the pale blue cliff faces on the horizon through a gap in the trees. The subject alone struggles with rising anxiety, most readily attributed to the surrounding landscape. There is also, however, a puzzling and unexpected concern for the wellbeing of the boy, which should be noted as another instance of the confounding human capacity to transcend the strictly causal flow of events. The importance of precognition has been related elsewhere *ad nauseam*—there is no need to reiterate here the vast consequences of this anomaly in human perception.

As they approach the peak of the trail—which also happens to be the site of the event to which this narrative accumulates—the family friend's audible and redundant complaints have begun to frustrate all parties. The child's mother tacitly suggests that lunch might improve everyone's mood, and the child's mother's mother, much to everyone's surprise, agrees. The subject, however, having committed to his role as the arbitrary itinerary's advocate, insists upon reaching the peak before turning back, despite being the most willing to quickly put as much distance between the park and himself as possible. Unaware of the irony, and with growing irritation, the group finally passes the wind-blasted sign reading "observation point."

The observation point is in a state of long neglect. The green paint on the small shack housing rest facilities is in a state of disintegration approaching total erasure. Several boards are torn away from the wall, exposing glimpses of rusted pipes that most visitors assume have stopped pumping water.

The tall, wire fence separating viewers from the vertical drop into a valley is completely intact, much to the subject's relief He puts the boy down and takes his girlfriend's hands, which are not sweaty like his, but reassuringly cool. Her mother walks up to the fence and laces her fingers through the openings in the wire as the family friend fusses over the toddler. The girlfriend rolls her eyes secretly to the subject, who cracks a smile despite the fearful throbbing of his heart.

Unexpectedly, the toddler dashes for the fence. "No, no, no, no," cautions the family friend, who stretches her arms out to herd him away from danger. "It's okay, he can't get through the fence," says the mother, still staring out into the open splay of misty blue atmosphere obscuring the hills and trees far below in the valley. The boy, redirected from the fence by the woman's hands, turns toward an enormous wooden fence post jutting at a slightly skewed angle from the dirt. An inexplicable rush of dread suddenly overcomes the subject, who breaks suddenly from his girlfriend's hands and runs at the boy. He screams "stop" just before the toddler slips into a hole at the base of the wooden post. Loose sand rushes into the gap, and the family friend covers her mouth with both hands.

As expected, the subject screams. He dives onto his hands and knees, reaching into the gap for his son's hand, a tuft of hair, anything. When the cascading sand stills, the subject sees that the hole is vastly deeper than the concrete base supporting the wooden post. It stretches on, a narrow blackness of unfathomable depths. He calls the boy's name and waits for anything—a cry or a whimper—to rise from the dark.

When he turns, his face is already streaked with tears. The boy's mother is next to him, shouting orders to authorities over her cell phone.

‡‡

Over the course of our endeavors, we have noted that grief is a bloom of many brilliant colors. Alcoholism, in the case of a child's death, is to be expected in parents, even among those with no predilection to addiction. Depression is unavoidable. A newfound proclivity to physical and emotional abuse among couples has often been noted, generally accumulating in divorce or separation.

The subject and his girlfriend sample all of these, settling finally on a return, in the girlfriend's case, to her mother's house, from which the family friend has been permanently banished following a bitter encounter with the girlfriend's mother. The subject is left alone in the apartment where he had watched his new family blossom.

The particulars of this period of time do not concern us. They are but steps, infinite in number and insignificantly minute. Following the completion of the first stage, the conclusion to this endeavor is inevitable. We need not remain fixated on the trajectory.

It does bear affirming as a point of pride in the efficiency of our endeavors that authorities were unable to find the boy. The exact depth of the hole remains indeterminate. Efforts are still being made to plunge its secrets with cameras attached to lengthy cables. It is, of course, impossible that such measures will amount to more than a glimpse at best of the vastness of the world beneath. In the meantime, the observation point has been officially closed for extensive remodeling.

We leave that all behind now. We must turn to what's important.

The subject is alone on the couch, deeply enveloped in ideations of suicide as he watches dust motes drift listlessly across the multi-leveled planes of light allotted by the spaces in the window blinds. Light has acquired a sick hue, a jaundiced tint, and its contact with the subject's flesh results in a sensation of near physical revulsion. He imagines leaping from these little platforms of light, a hundred miniature versions of himself dripping from their ethereal stages like puppets fleeing their strings. It can't be helped, of course. Throughout our endeavors, the subject's urge to die strikes us as perhaps the most relatable aspect of all.

It is entirely normal for time to stretch like a vast and gleaming blade with the sharp edge nestled against the subject's throat. He's evacuated the thoughts of his boy, the round, babyish face, the curious, happy eyes, and nothing is left to occupy the passage of hours. Failing to do so entails the inevitable imaginings of the boy, broken from head to toe and alone on the sandy floor of a perfectly dark chasm. A constant barrage of this imagery isn't conducive for the subject's sanity, and the truth of the situation would hardly do much better. Whatever disdain the thought of living arouses, he clings, as do they all, ever the more desperately to control of the mind.

But while they romanticize emptiness like a faraway paradise, they quickly find that nothingness is more terrible than the flashes from the nightmares that fill their consciousness.

He has turned to porn now, spending at least six hours a day online, straying ever further from what he once considered a "normal" sexual proclivity. Occasionally, he'll attempt to masturbate, and on even rarer occasions, he'll reach a strained and painful orgasm that leaves him feeling worse than before. For the most part, his enterprise is spiritless and half-hearted. Anhedonia is the subject's new state of equilibrium, the inevitable result of an overtaxed mind.

And soon, the moment comes. We wait patiently as he buys the gun and carries it from the pawn shop to the house in a paper sack. He smells the gun oil, noting with amusement that it smells much like any other oil and why shouldn't it? The gun is just a tool, he thinks, a precise and specialized instrument for dispatching beings who get in the way of living.

In a moment of pitiable elation, the subject swings the weapon around his apartment, aiming at the four walls separating his dwelling from those adjacent. He pretends to fire. "Boom, boom, boom," he says under his breath, imagining what death would look like from the outside, what patterns the brain would articulate against the crisp blue walls, what a face deprived of its central support looks like when it swallows itself. A face, he concludes, like his boy's—a dead one, turned to meat thanks to a careless decision to follow an arbitrary itinerary. And this thought, the horrible, unthinkable thought that always plagues him from the monstrous shadows limning the circumference of his consciousness, is what does it.

The subject collapses to the floor, back against the wall, barrel pressed firmly under his chin, unaware of the fact that the current angle would simply blow his face off without killing him. It is at this point that we find the plight of the subject most lamentable. With oblivion a mere click away— no more difficult than pressing play on a video—the mad urge to live rushes up and stops him. Here he hovers over a vast realm of limitless possibility only to find that the agony he despises is more of a comfort than the unknown. It is a moment of remarkable weakness duplicated *ad infinitum* across the globe: the realization that living, at its deepest impulse, is sheer routine.

This realization is our cue. Only at this point do we dare intervene again.

Absently, he picks up his phone, ashamed of his weakness. We ensure that his social media accounts alert him to trending content, among which is a video clip from a recent football game. Desperate for distraction, he clicks play.

‡‡

Sporting events have never aroused much excitement in the subject and he quickly loses interest in the clip, the content of which is inconsequential to our endeavor. It is the ad we want him to see. It appears, and after a span of fifteen seconds, it is over.

If asked, the subject would find himself utterly unable to recount what company the ad was calculated to benefit, or even the nature of services or products the company solicits. Instead, there's a nagging desire to remove himself from his humiliation, beginning with the gun in his hand that confirmed his cowardice, which he tosses carelessly aside. There was a number onscreen he wishes to call, and he tries to think back to any distinguishing characteristics of the ad. It is a testament to the mastery of our endeavor that he is unable to do so. Wasn't there a man onscreen, he asks himself? What syllables were uttered, low and nearly inaudible, to inspire this sudden need to act?

It is a certain point of pride, this creation of ours, the distilled essence of that which lures humanity ever past its confines. That it looks so much like our home is a point of irony not lost to us. If only they understood, they would come willingly. We do not, however, deny that an elaborate and varied art of seduction is necessary to the process. It is their *wanting* that slakes the hunger.

The subject restarts the video, seeking the ad that is no ad, that emptiness enveloped in a formal structure. It plays again and vanishes just as quickly. The number, however, is clear. He captures this. As he dials, I extend my hand to the phone.

‡‡

"I'm here to talk about your missing person," I say as he blinks in the sour sunlight.

"Yes...uh...right. Come on in," he says, recalling what little he is able from our conversation the day before. I note with satisfaction how eager they are to listen at this point. How *desperate* they are to believe. How *utterly* without chance of failure our endeavor remains. It makes me warm inside, and an involuntary erection presses hard against my black slacks.

"Excuse the mess," the subject says, tossing an empty plastic bag over the gun still resting in the corner of the room.

"Of course." I smile again as I make myself comfortable on an empty kitchen chair. I prepare myself for his misgivings, which do not take long in surfacing.

"Look," he says, running a hand through his unwashed hair, "I know this is probably crazy. In truth, I haven't been well, and I'm getting ideas in my head that...well...I don't understand why they won't leave."

"Ideas about your missing person?"

He nods and looks away, embarrassed, as they generally are, by the conclusions they've been led to.

I mentioned the name of the park. "If I understand correctly from our conversation yesterday, that's where he was lost."

The subject simply nods once more, burying his face in his hands.

I smile again, but it's wasted on him. I lean close. "That's what caught my ear, you know. That's why I told you I'd come here. I don't do that for just anyone."

He looks up at me then, a gleam in his eyes somewhere between expectant and disbelieving. "What do you mean?" he asks with urgency that wasn't there before.

"I think you're in precisely the state of mind to see exactly what I mean."

‡‡

At 6,544 feet above sea level, the subject exits the driver's side of the vehicle and makes his way around to the back. The parking lot behind him is empty, and wisps of dust dance around him as he struggles with the back door. The stuck door is a quirk the subject despises since it dredges up past events he'd rather not contemplate. When it finally opens, he lifts a backpack from the rear seat and slips it on. I then emerge from the passenger's side of the vehicle, careful to close my door gently. I turn to face the wind as I drape my own bag over my shoulders.

"This whole land," I say over the warm breeze, "is porous, honeycombed with interminable passages that wind thousands of feet down." Then I lie. "Back when I worked natural gas, it was my job to be aware of these things."

The subject comes up next to me and stares into the trees. Neither of us face the path leading up to the defunct observation station.

"Then why haven't they searched those?" he asks, not looking at me.

I offer a deep sigh before I turn to him—I intend it to convey a certain world-weariness I do not feel, a disgust with mankind I am able to feign but never embody. When I am close to them, it rips open an insatiable excitement that spills into every vein. I feel the subject's outrage, let it simmer in the gentle and still air before speaking.

"The phenomena is...not as well-known as you might think. This place," I gesture to the trees surrounding us, "is like a dream already. An artist couldn't imagine a more sublime scenery. To imagine it tainted with an internal darkness is difficult for those without imagination."

"But the officials, the firefighters—"

"Human." I shrug. "Certainly they gave it their best."

With that, I walk into a trailhead branching down into the valleys. A brilliant cardinal passes in front of me, and I wait until I hear the subject's footsteps behind me before I begin speaking again.

"To hate this world is the rational state of things. You have been offered evidence of its cruelty, and you have judged it correctly. In this way, you have been given a beautiful, beautiful gift, my friend." I wait for the subject to respond. When he doesn't, I go on. "It may not seem beautiful, but you have been wrested from the restless delusion of living, the constant need to perform your puppetry. You have been dismissed from the wan light of the stage into the weighted underground of shadows. It is what all of us want, truly: to leave, to walk away from the things that keep us spinning our frail, paper threads above the oceanic roiling of time."

I wait again. Our footfalls free small stones to tumble down the pathway. The silence is profound—beneath it, I sense the writhing will of the hive, its hunger.

"You're wrong," he finally says. "It's exactly those things I want: the distractions, the performances, just *normal life*. A life with my son, my family—their absence is a gaping, ragged-edged hole in my soul."

I try to keep the smile from appearing, but the pulses below the earth send thrills of electric frenzy through my borrowed body.

I step from the path into grass that reaches my knees. The subject follows and we wind through the trees. At a clearing, I point up to a hole in the sheer face of stone. He follows my finger to the entryway, gazing for a long moment through the cottonwood seeds dancing lazily in the light.

Contents of our backpacks: two hand-cranked camping lanterns, three hundred feet of rope, two 8 descender large bent-ear belaying devices, two climbing harnesses, one military grade first aid kit, one dozen industrial grade glow sticks, five MREs (assorted flavors), two zero bags, a dozen heavy-duty carabiners, two camel packs filled with water, the recently purchased pistol...

We will need almost none of this.

It takes little over half an hour to climb up to the hole. "Thousands of miles of cave systems lie just beyond this entrance," I explain, "most of it entirely unexplored. I must caution that getting your hopes up might be useless. He could be anywhere, and it is unlikely, as you're aware, that he survived the fall. The question is if the descent is better than returning to your life. Can you have a greater purpose at this juncture? Time stretches before you, vast, glacial, empty."

He needs very little encouragement. The subject's eyes burn with a new coldness. Maybe he sees what lies beyond, the network of fungal growth smeared black like dried blood against the rock. Perhaps he recognizes the hive, senses its amorous hunger. My cock rises once more as he struggles against the stone face, but the lust isn't related to my current physical inhabitance. Not once has he commented on the unnatural blackness of my eyes or the lavender hues dancing rhythmically within their irises. There's pain now as the stalks exert pressure from within my skull, but the pain is glorious, transcendent, a luscious overflowing. Perhaps he sees this, but it is not necessary. All that is required is hunger. The subject must open like a wound to the mind beyond.

I am close behind when he squeezes through the small opening into the dark. Our endeavor is complete. It is worth wondering if he sees the boy dimly in the shadows, his small eyes newly matching mine. I fall onto the stone floor as my own flowering begins, tendrils breaking through the sockets of my eyes like white sheets of lightning. The spores fill the air, and his panicked breathing only embeds them further into his lungs where they will grow roots down to the bone, swim like eager spermatozoa through his veins to impregnate his brain. Soon, he and I are no longer distinct. Soon, we are enfolded again into the timeless mass threading like blood through the park.

We are sated, for now.

laberinto

COPD'S WHAT YOU tell them, if they ask. That's chronic obstructive pulmonary disease, the smoker's doom. It makes no difference that I quit some forty years ago. Getting around is something of a difficulty, to understate it. It only takes two steps to get winded. Push past that, and you start seeing things that aren't there. It's rough business. More than sufficient to keep even the most stubborn specimens down.

Now, it ain't the *real* reason. That's just what you tell *them*. You know I've been part of the landscape in Chasm past my share of years. Over there in the Supper for All, I've worn a crevice on the counter where they keep the coffee and creamer in little plastic cups always just beyond their expiration dates. You know the place—I've seen you lurking, hauling that boy around while he filches a candy bar right out from under good old Jerome's nose. Heart of gold, that fellow, and don't you imagine that he doesn't see what happens within the walls of his establishment. He lets it slide either out of kindness or because he's got something of a past himself. Could be that the two elements are not entirely distinct.

Now, you see? I couldn't say this to what you might call *the old cronies*. Things are simplified for them, all the ragged edges lopped off like a good bit of leather. Crime is crime, white is white, and black is black. *That's* why you tell them COPD, if they see you with me and start asking questions (and they will, they see and question everything in this town). They wouldn't understand the things I'm here to explain. You know them, don't you? You recognize them instantly: Judges, preachers, ranchers, big fish in this dried-out septic tank, the kind of people who grew up in Chasm with their straight and narrows all but furrowed into the hard, Texas dirt. To them, I'm the face of law and order, a benign, approachable anthropomorphism of justice. I'm what keeps this little town humming in harmony to the music of God's angels from one day to the next. *They* think I'm doing a service, as if all those amiable conversations in the Supper for All were direly purchased by hard hours on the beat. You and I know it's just that nothing happens here.

Now, that's not entirely true, is it? That's why I'm darkening your threshold, why you're in mourning after all these months. Why you positively reek of liquor, why you swayed a bit when you invited me in.

Now don't you worry. I don't blame you one bit. The kind of *nothing* that happens here has a way of inspiring dissolution and decay. This town drags a quiet ruin behind it like a corpse tied to a cart.

You're not going to like what you hear. Let's just acknowledge that from the beginning. I'm an old man now, Christine, retired, dying, and in constant pain. You can take your anger out on me all you want, if there's anger left—there's nothing you could throw at me that life forgot already, but I do recommend hearing me all the way out. What happened back then might shed some light on your current situation, it might not—at least you'll know, when I'm through, that things could've been much, much worse. Just keep what I'm about to say between the two of us. The only thing that spreading this would accomplish is convincing the whole town that you and I are crazier than they already believe us to be.

Now let's see. You wouldn't happen to know Raul Montenegro, up on the corner of Market Street across from the abandoned Seven Seals of the Apocalypse? Chasm's social existence—at least as far as the old timers are concerned—emanates primarily from three central hubs: the Supper for All, El Bracero, and Raul Montenegro's garage. The first two are familiar to everyone, but Raul's garage is a shade less palatable. He's got this big Dodge on concrete blocks, and folks come around day and night to shoot the shit, crack a beer, or participate in activities they'd generally try to keep to a minimum around me, if you catch my drift. Raul's always outside working on that damn truck. His house is hardly more than a storage space for parts, but his enthusiasm for conversation exerts a gravitational force on a good portion of Chasm's idle and indigent. He's the best damn handyman around, so they bring along their busted microwaves, treadmills, bikes, and other mechanical appliances for him to tinker with. Nine times out of ten, he does the job for a song and a six-pack.

Well, I always saw it as my civic duty to make an occasional appearance at Raul's. A lot of the cronies at the Supper for All would've looked down their noses at me for that, but they don't understand that the office of sheriff is a *presence*. They liked to think I belonged to *them*, that my job was to *protect* them from folks like Raul. I didn't disabuse them—let them go on thinking that my patrol car at Raul's meant trouble, when really I was just gabbing, working as hard there as anywhere else to establish an aura of approachability around the Chasm Sheriff's Department.

It was at Raul's where I first heard of Maria's problem. It was me, Raul, and a good old boy named Harry all huddled under the hood of Harry's new something or another. I know nothing about cars myself, although I'm good at pretending to. Since it was a chore to nod and grunt at all the right moments, I wasn't displeased when a boy from a couple of streets down, Miguel, interrupted with his *Buenos dias*.

Miguel flicked a joint into the gutter as soon as he saw me, and I pretended not to notice. Raul cursed the kid under his breath. Harry descended into the junk at the back of the garage to fish out another round of Corona Extras, and Raul asked, "What is it this time, pendejo?" as if he expected trouble. The kid began a confused description of an infestation at his aunt's place. He mentioned rodents, birds, and something about God, mingling the presentation with awkward pauses and fevered glances to the sky. Raul got real frustrated with the kid, told him to lay off the *drogas*, although I personally attributed Miguel's confusion to innate simplicity rather than chemicals.

Now, Miguel, tough twenty-something that he is, didn't take kindly to Raul's chiding, and for a minute, things looked like they were getting ugly. The neighbors gathered quickly, so I intervened, making a show of asking the boy to take me to his aunt's house so I could assess the problem myself. That's how you build a reputation in a town like this—always act when Chasm's eyes are on you. I was congratulated for avoiding a bloodbath for weeks to come, as if Raul and Miguel were *cholos* on the brink of a turf war.

You cater to the ignorance of certain folks and you're sure to get your picture in the town hall, as I have, and my predecessor, and the good old boy before him. Now I know it isn't right to pander to prejudices, but the right thing isn't always the easiest, Christine. Sometimes, it feels damn near impossible. You can see it all laid out before you, a path you *know* you're supposed to follow, but comfort and familiarity are dead weights and they can press you down into the groove you've been running your whole life, transforming simple solutions into insurmountable difficulties. I suppose I've passed up one too many opportunities to do the right thing, and I tell you, if routine was the dead weight before, guilt is just as bad if not worse. That's why I'm here now, I reckon. That's why I'm here to share anything I can to help you with your own problem.

Miguel wasn't too keen on riding in the patrol car, and I didn't want to press the issue. Plenty of folks were watching—neighbors of Miguel's, if not family, I couldn't be too sure—and I was eager to spare the kid as much embarrassment as possible. I crawled into his ratty old pickup and we headed out of the neighborhood, past the concrete waste of the Seven Seals and toward the outskirts. I tried to ignore the smell of weed and made disapproving noises that I hoped the kid was keen enough to pick up on. I don't think it worked.

After a while, he started talking, and at first, I thought he was telling me about a dream. He described a bird—a hawk that, as he told it, covers the ground with a shadow as big as a cloud. When it would approach, everything would go dark. Then he'd look up and see it, wingspan a good twenty meters across, maybe more. He'd stand there and watch it drift closer over the empty plains. Then he'd run and the bird would chase him right into the closest line of brush. He said he felt the swoop of its talons sucking his clothes as it veered back up into the sky.

I asked Miguel to repeat what he said next. I couldn't make heads or tails of it, which shouldn't have surprised me, given the yarn he'd already spun. He said that once, as a kid, after the hawk had zoomed past him and Miguel turned to watch it climb back into the sky, he saw that its feathers were brilliant gold and its head was a bare skull. In its sun-bleached beak sagged the partial remains of a calf.

I tell you, I didn't think Miguel was all there at the time. To calm him down I told him about the roadrunner I kept seeing in my yard back then, just a stupid little story about how I could never snap a photo if it. When I finished, Miguel looked at me and the strangest grin spread across his face. I'll never forget that smile, like a canvas pulled too tightly across a skull. It set my skin crawling. I began to think I had made a mistake letting the kid take me way out into the plains in his own truck.

To my relief, we pulled into Maria's not long after that. I recognized the place immediately—you can still see it, in fact, that run-down little farmhouse way up where Cactus Spiral bends east to merge with 287. It looks about the same as it did then, so I was surprised to discover that it was inhabited.

I knew the good old boy who owned the property, Mitch Barlow. He had been a deacon over at the Open Gate of the Second Coming until hard liquor began to make all but owning property too much of a hassle. Worse, he'd already had trouble with varmints before.

A family from Mexico had rented one of his mobile homes and complained of possums. Mitch was a tight-fisted son of a bitch who wouldn't lift a finger unless circumstances forced his hand. Getting nowhere with him, the family vented their grievances to some neighbors, who offered the use of some old rodenticide they had sitting in the garage. They brought over a few plastic containers, and the father covered the clearance space beneath his home with lead-colored tablets. The only problem was, the tablets were aluminum phosphide, and when they switched on the sprinkler and the water ran under the house, it created phosphine gas. Few days later the mailman noticed the smell of six corpses rotting away in old Mitch's rental property.

Not that Mitch was held accountable in the slightest—I don't even recall an official inspection of the property—but Maria's rodents were sure to evoke the tragedy. I shook my head, already anticipating unpleasantness with Mitch as Miguel led me around back. When we stopped, we both stood there, staring, and Miguel muttered "Fucking raccoons," under his breath.

I knew straightaway it wasn't any raccoon.

It was a fibrous material curled up neatly in the grass. Sure, it was shaped like spoor, but there was simply too much of it. It looked like hair, perfectly vibrant and black. There wasn't an animal I knew that could make that. At least not in the panhandle.

"Hogs maybe," I said, and asked Miguel if he had noticed any wallows nearby, but the boy was already lost again, staring into the big merciless sun as if searching for the wings of his giant golden hawk. I nudged the pile with my foot and the segment that met the toe of my boot withered as if it were hollow, insubstantial. I don't know when Maria emerged from the ruined house, and I didn't see her until she was right next to us, pointing to the strange knot of hair on the ground and saying "El laberinto, el laberinto" over and over. I looked at Miguel and he shrugged. "She's saying 'the maze,'" he said, without bothering to explain why.

If I was certain then that Miguel and Maria shared some hereditary mental affliction, it didn't stop me from being smitten by her dark wary eyes and delicate figure. It wasn't often that I was struck by people in that way— my own sexual decline began early, and I'd long traded the pleasures of the body for the joy of discourse. Still, I found myself smiling at the young woman, and part of me was embarrassed at how that must've looked. It was the first time in years I'd felt outright ridiculous.

I played my part and dialed Mitch, making a show of having his cell number. "Howdy, Gordon," he said with some surprise, which turned to irritation when I asked him to meet me at Maria's. "Caught your ear about those damned piles, I guess. God have mercy." As luck would have it, Mitch was in the area to check on an AC unit and made it before things had a chance to get too uncomfortable. Mitch glowered at Miguel when he got out of his new Dodge and pumped my fist with spirit that bordered on rage.

"Look, Mitch," I said, pulling him out of earshot of the woman and the boy and looking him square in the eye, "due diligence is all I'm asking. Let's see if we can't come up with a solution that makes everyone happy."

He gave me a tight smile and walked over to the pile between Miguel and Maria. Mitch shrugged. "I don't know what I'm supposed to do about a lump of hair."

"It ain't hair," I said and nudged it with my foot. Once more, a small area of it imploded.

"Well, it ain't spoor neither, that's for sure. Maybe it's some sort of burned synthetic, like plastic or Styrofoam or something." He turned to Maria. "Any of y'all been burning packaging out here?"

I figured then that Mitch had a point. I looked at Maria, her eyes soft but unflinching in the face of Mitch's question.

"Would it hurt to lay out some poison just in case?"

Mitch shrugged again, a vile sneer snapping across his flushed and furrowed features. "Whatever you say, Sheriff."

‡‡

Thank you, Christine. That was mighty kind of you. I'm in no position to turn down a good beer. Retirement ain't all it's cracked up to be. No, ma'am.

It's lonely, to tell the truth. By the time you've stared at your walls long enough to memorize every niche and tear in the paper, you can bet an absence has eaten its way into your existence, one you're more than happy to fill with a beer, even if the event it occasions is of the unpleasant variety.

As you've already figured, the little pile of black stuff wasn't hair. Mitch *did* lay the rodenticide out, truth be told. I came around and saw for myself a few days later. Those little blue tablets are essentially human-grade therapeutic doses of the same stuff that lands me in the lab every week for my INR. Never can get my levels right, no matter what I do. You see these bruises? It's from the blood thinners. Imagine what it would do to the internal organs of a rat or a possum.

I figured it was the end of the rodent story and didn't think anything about it for weeks. I never did see Miguel again, although I looked, dropping by Raul's a little more often on the off chance the kid would come over and provide an excuse to check in on Maria. I didn't harbor any *real* hope of seeing her, and I wouldn't have known what to say to her if I did. It was silly, really, a man my age acting that way.

At about the same time I decided it was best to forget her entirely, she walked right into the Supper for All. I was just telling the district attorney about some cows that had gotten loose from Chasm's northernmost ranch and ended up blocking a train when I saw her at the counter, ordering a sack of potato wedges. I muttered, "Excuse me," and left the DA hanging, mid-sentence and slack jawed. That's the state of mind she put me in.

I greeted her as naturally as I could, feeling the blood gather in my forehead. I just about wanted to die on the spot. I was overcome by the need to get the hell out of the Supper for All. All at once, it felt too crowded, filled to capacity with the DA's staring eyes and the circle of gossiping mouths I had so diligently cultivated over the long eventless years. I grabbed a soda from the fridge next to the register and handed it to Jerome, who gave me this sly, knowing look, since he was fully aware that I never drink sodas.

We made it to the sidewalk and all Maria's responses were truncated, all *biens* and English monosyllables and I realized that she hardly understood what I was saying. Like an idiot I babbled away, too accustomed to yammering through every situation to know what else to do with myself. Desperate to strike up some semblance of conversation, I remembered the little pile of hair and tried to conjure the word she used to describe it. I recalled only that it was something strange, a word that felt wrong but oddly fitting. *Puzzle? Mystery? Madness? Maze?*

"El laberinto?" I said as it came to me, lifting the final phonemes into a question even though I lacked the grammar to ask it in full Spanish sentences. The word startled her, and for a moment I was afraid she was going to run away. Instead, she turned a searching look to me, and her lips curled in a rare, subtle smile, revealing a dimple on one side you'd never catch otherwise. She nodded, and I gestured to my patrol car. "I'll follow you," I said. This she understood.

On the way out, I started thinking about Dotty Lancaster, this sweet little thing from my childhood who was found right out near Maria's place. Some ranch hand had spotted her wrapped in bedsheets and propped against the barbed wire that used to run along the road for miles. Her eyes had been removed, and when they shifted her bloated little corpse, clouds of flies erupted from her emptied sockets, right into the faces of the responding officers. Turns out, one of the damned things laid eggs in old Jim Coswell's eye. That's why he wore a patch. By the time they found the maggots, it was too late to save anything.

I didn't learn that until late in my career—it was one of those stories the churchgoing public consider too lurid to repeat, and all but the cronies Coswell's age and older had forgotten it. I can't imagine why it came back to me then unless it was the sun. It was devilishly hot, the wind pumping off the plains like waves from an oven left wide open, and the sunlight seemed all wrong, like it was distorted by great invisible prisms way up there in the endless depth of the sky. Something in the way the sickened light hung languid in the air made me think of death and decay. When we pulled into Maria's, the sensation only deepened.

I don't know what I expected, you understand. I wanted her, but had she taken me directly to her bedroom, I don't know what would come of it. In a way, the idea of sex with her damn near terrified me. Old age complicates things. I know this is a lot of detail, but you need to hear the truth. I'm not sure what part of this story will prove helpful to you, so I'm giving you all of it, including the unmentionables. I hope you'll pardon me, Christine.

I was almost relieved when Maria avoided the little house entirely. She grabbed my hand—I'm sure my blood pressure jumped a few points in the damned fool state of excitement I was in—and took me around back. I was smiling like a jackass, even though something that looked like a blue northern had formed on the horizon. The sick sunlight skidded across it like a tongue of flame against the rim of a black mirror. Rusted car parts were scattered everywhere in the fence alongside the remains of a busted pump jack, all too old and sunken into the dirt to belong to her. I followed her all the way to the foot of a big, lonesome oak, where she dropped my hand. Still, I stood there smiling at her, trying to think of something to say in Spanish that would lacerate her silence and soothe my discomfort. Instead, she just pointed at the tree.

For a moment, I couldn't figure out what I was looking at. Somehow, the tree was draped from its highest branch all the way down to the dirt with that black, hairlike substance. Now that rattled me. A small pile of the stuff on the ground was one thing, but seeing enough to bury a tree was altogether beyond my abilities of comprehension. I kept my composure well enough, since unexpected situations have always had a strange way of calming me—it's one reason I've always been a good officer, I suppose. I was back in my element, distracted from my attraction to Maria.

I slowly began circling the looming mass, trying to understand it. It should've become increasingly comprehensible. It should've yielded *something.* That's how impossible situations work: you meet them with a certain clear-headedness and soon their impossibility begins to dissolve. You notice elements you missed before. What seemed impossible a moment ago unfurls with perfect clarity when contemplated from the correct angle. That's what I'd tell addicts after I busted them, since addiction is nothing but an attempt to master the impossible: no matter how hopeless a situation seems, it gets better the moment you look at it the right way.

The mass covering the tree was different. More I circled the damned thing, the harder I looked, the stranger it became. It didn't seem like hair anymore—the smaller strands had clumped together, forming black vines as thick as my wrist. The pattern they made was complex, running perfectly parallel from the ground to the top of the tree. It was like a work of modern sculpture, but without *agency.* It ain't easy to explain, Christine, but the clump was too perfect to be random and not perfect enough to be artificial. It was stuck somewhere in between, like it had grown out of the ground based on an inherent design locked inside of it, coded like DNA.

I snuck a glance over at Maria, and it's like I was no longer there. She stared at the tree with a strange edge of menace. I sucked air through my teeth and tried to sooth the jagged throb of my heart before stepping closer.

It was difficult to look at. My eyes couldn't find a place to rest, and the more my vision swam across that black mass, the more a headache blossomed somewhere behind my eyes.

I circled again and again, not daring to touch it, probing the surface for something—*a way in,* I realized. As soon as I thought it, I found it, a man-sized hole toward the back. It seemed to suck the air down into it, and I couldn't see anything inside, just a perfect, empty blackness that somehow felt infinite. I was overcome with vertigo then, that strange feeling that something other than myself was willing my body toward the ledge. I stood firmly in place but bent closer to the opening. My ears began to ring, and the sucking of air grew into a low moan as it passed over the lip of the maw.

I wasn't aware of Maria's hands looped in my belt and tugging. I didn't hear her screaming or feel her small fist unlatch in desperation to pound my back. I would become aware of this only after I tore my eyes away from what appeared in the hole. Or I should say *up there,* since the interior of the mass had taken on impossible dimensions, and through the opening I saw a pale, lavender sun hanging in a strange, incomprehensible sky.

Things were less distinct after she managed to pull me away from the entrance. I couldn't understand her words, but I understood the panic in her voice. She took me inside where I slumped onto the living room couch.

There was no light. The scarce edges that caught sunlight through the blinds contrasted blindingly against the dark. Everything seemed distant and false, like a painting, and I immediately fell into a thick and vivid sleep.

I dreamed I was in a forest. Black bands of tree trunks stretched far up into the purple sky. When I followed their ascent, I saw that there was no canopy of leaves. They weren't trees at all, but great obsidian columns. The forest floor was covered with grass like the plains, except there was no wind, and the sun that beat down on everything was the dull, nightside twin I had seen inside the mass. It was like the unhinged world of a fairy tale, only more sharp and real than anything I'd ever experienced before.

I wanted to wake up. I knew I was dreaming, but I couldn't snap out of it. I've never been a vivid dreamer, and the sensation of the ground beneath my feet, the sudden sharp smell of blood, the syrupy resistance of my limbs, was nearly too much to bear. I think I prayed to God, Christine, right then and there. I hadn't done that in years, at least not in earnest, and there I was praying before I even saw what was just beyond the hill I was mounting against my will.

A mewling filled the forest, a terrible, unforgettable sound I can still hear if I don't work to turn my thoughts away. It was the cry of a baby, but impossibly magnified, loud enough to leave the columns resonating a dissonant harmony like a chorus of tuning forks. It was a teeth-shattering, maddening sound, so close to musical yet desperately shy. I would've rather died than continue forward, but I couldn't stop myself. I couldn't stop myself, Christine, and no matter how hard I prayed, God did nothing, just sat back and watched as I beheld the great, fleshy mass, quivering with pain.

I could only tell it was a calf by the immaturity of its features. Otherwise it was far too large, and I couldn't say whether it was Angus or longhorn, since it was all muscle and blood. Huge sections of its abdomen had been carved away by something enormous. It lay on its side, viscera pooling in the nest of its hooves gleaming dead blue in the surreal sun.

My heartbeat was like gunshots echoing in my head. It turned to me, sightless eyes gleaming white in the half light. It wailed again, the sound of a human infant. The sound of helpless agony.

I saw the source of its pain. Masses of small, yellow insects churned against the calf's exposed musculature. I screamed and waved my hands, trying to chase them away.

As I rushed toward the giant calf in the shallow valley, the yellow things erupted in an angry cloud. I saw them clearly then, tiny golden hawks with fleshless heads, the sound of their chewing audible in the silence between the calf's all-too-human screaming.

And then the columns expanded, connecting with others to form walls. Soon, I could see nothing at all.

‡‡

I don't mind telling you, I've never been more afraid in all my life. Not only did I fear the reality of the black substance, but the possibility of its unreality disturbed me deeper still.

I woke up a full day later. Maria helped me find the bathroom in the perpetual dimness of her house. I realized at some point she didn't have electricity. Her walls were covered with paintings—brilliant flowers and landscapes that would've been serene had they a little light to shine under. I think they were hers, but I wasn't in the condition to chew over the little nothings on which I wasted so many words over the course of my life.

I did my long-delayed business and immediately asked to see the tree out back. Most of the stuff had blown away by then. Only sparse strands still lingered on some of the higher branches which, at first glance, could pass for tangles of moss.

It was shortly after that when the cattle mutilations around Tule Creek began. I can't say that I slept easy in the interim. I could hear that calf mewling somewhere in the back of my mind when things got too quiet, so I threw myself into the cattle cases, even if they evoked that terrible dream in their own way. At least these were dead. Dissected and scattered across the banks of the creek, but mercifully dead and silent. Small blessing.

They were Judge Forrester's stock, and he was more than eager to get his hands dirty. He had all kinds of theories. He'd stand there and rattle them off while I bent over the corpses with rubber gloves, picking up each piece and examining it like I hoped to find something. He said it was a satanic ritual. Said it was a UFO hoax. Said it was a Mexican drug lord trying to get back at him for a sentence. All the while I nodded solemnly, hoping it would last forever, this waste of time, this redirection of the mind into the solid, tangible, absurd world we share. Finding nothing, Forrester gave me some names and I said I'd take them in for questioning. I have sins to answer for, Christine, even if there ain't no God to confess them to.

Somewhere in the middle of it all, Miguel disappeared. One of his cousins found a shoe out in the fields behind El Bracero, where the kids would sometimes go to smoke pot, fight, or fuck. It sent a coldness down my spine, but I couldn't bring myself to pay Maria a visit, not even to offer condolences. I handed the case off to a deputy and tried to forget about it. The cattle mutilations were costing Forrester money, and he expected all resources to remain at his disposal until we found someone to lock up.

I'm not sure I would've returned to Maria's at all had I not found another mass.

Forrester was with me again, agitated to the point of fury at the latest wave of mutilations and screaming for justice, pounding the butt of his shotgun against the ground with every syllable of every name he added to his list of folks to investigate. I saw it slumped up against a mound of hay, black and throbbing with an aura of menace that might have simply been my imagination.

"Shut up, Forrester," I told him, and he stared at me like I'd lost my mind. My hand was on my pistol. "Don't you go near the mound, if you want what's good for you."

"Well, what the hell is it?" he asked. When I couldn't give him an answer, he gave me a half smile and stepped toward it.

"We ought to call for backup," I said, but he didn't listen. Kept walking like it was all some big joke.

This is the beginning of the end, Christine. I've never been more humiliated in all the years of my profession, but I don't regret what I did.

As soon as I heard the horrific mewling, my arm worked on its own, like a spring. Before the judge could turn around, I'd put a half-dozen rounds into that mound. A dark dust like graphite filled the air as the mass dissolved behind Forrester's back. When I lifted my gaze, his eyes were wild with fear.

I didn't wait for him to say anything. I holstered the weapon and marched straight for the car.

Maria's wasn't too far, but the ride seemed to last forever. The sun looked wrong, broken and distorted behind cosmic shards of glass I couldn't see. The wind died entirely, and the heat bore down on everything like a heavy layer of boiling molasses. I thought of old Jim Coswell's eye again. More, I *saw* it, this time swelling with life, bursting as thousands of wet, golden hawks buzzed like yellow-jackets past my face. I swerved nearly into a ditch.

Maria wasn't there. Her house was empty, filled with pretty paintings starved of light. I didn't find the mass either, *el laberinto*, the maze. I carried part of *that* inside me, in my lungs, from the dust my bullets had stirred, or from getting too close to the tree out back. Old Forrester came down with lung cancer shortly after my own diagnosis of COPD. Those closest to him claim dementia followed shortly, that his decline was worsened by visions. It's hard to write it off as a coincidence.

That's what worries me about your situation, Christine. I've heard what they said about your boy, before he went missing. With shaking heads they repeated his wild stories about the great bird that would dip from the sky, breaking the glass of windows with its beak, fishing for flesh like a sparrow digging seeds from a feeder. They admonished you—not outright, they're too polite for that, but with shared whispers—for his fear, how he'd speak to any adult who would listen, for his mental health, not even conceiving the possibility of *drogas*, thanks to his color. They talked and talked and talked until they whipped up their whirlwind that forced a draft into my living room, which, like yours, like Maria's, is covered with those lines.

You see it, don't you? You see *el laberinto,* its purple sun frozen behind the endless rows of black columns that aren't columns, the maze that lies outside of God's laser beam of grace. There are things far worse than my calf and Miguel's golden hawk, you know. I sure hope you haven't wandered far. I hope you haven't taken a part of it with you, because it never leaves once you do, Christine. It's a good thing Forrester told the commissioner about my "breakdown" and that they asked me in no unclear terms to retire, since it wasn't long before I began to see it everywhere, resting just beyond this side of the light like a dream dreamt by matter itself, a shadow cast by existence. Like you, I began to map it out. Only it won't do any good, Christine.

I hate to say it, but you won't find your boy. He's part of it now, sunk down into the corroded bedrock, like the calf, like old Forrester, like Maria. Pretty soon, like me. I can't help but wonder if it's Chasm's destiny, a quiet end to a quiet existence, this sinking into the horror we've kept at bay with our refusal to see past the rim of the sky. If there's a way out, it's with wings, and the price of flying is burning.

But I can already see it, the lavender sun. It's in your eyes, like a reflection, already boiling your corneas a foggy white.

the puppet king:
a monologue

"AND WHAT IF you should look at yourself—the most everyday object there is—and feel at a loss to attach a quality and a meaning to what is being seen or what is seeing it. What now indeed." –Thomas Ligotti

A lecture hall.

The audience, perfectly silent, occupies less than a quarter of the vast auditorium.

THE SPEAKER, well-dressed in a suit and tie, enters from stage right carrying a single sheet of paper. He is extremely thin but nearly groomed, a mild-looking individual whom no one would suspect anything of besides an inclination toward excessive reading. The stage is half-lit and crossed by shadows. In the insufficient light, it is difficult to make out details of THE SPEAKER's facial features. He approaches the lectern and surveys the audience. Like him, they are half-hidden in shadows. He places his paper squarely before him, and without introduction, begins to read in a mild, monotorous voice.

SPEAKER: The coming of the Puppet King is a theory of madness. In this, it's far from original, aligned closer to ancient traditions (the roots of which can often be traced to the puppet stage) than to the contemporary efforts of professional philosophers. But the doctrine of the Puppet King does not exclude unoriginality. It is a pulp philosophy, more at home on the streets—the degraded realm of the puppet play—than in academic institutions. It refuses to conceal its debts. It embraces them, rather, as a condition of being. There is, after all, no escaping the circular machinery of the puppet stage. To be a puppet is to mime a preconceived place in the world, to sing for one's supper. Every puppet act is a ghost of a ghost, "an echo of an echo of an echo," as Trent Reznor sings in a song imminently relevant to the work at hand, or as Marcel Schwob wrote long before the fixation on the sign came into fashion, "the world is but signs, and signs of signs."[1]

[THE SPEAKER pauses to retrieve a small device from his jacket. He lifts it to his mouth and places it in his throat. When he speaks again, his voice is shrill and metallic.]

Ladies and Gentlemen, pray how you do?
If you all happy, me all happy too.
Stop and hear my merry little play;
If me make you laugh, me need not make you pay.[2]

[The strange voice fails to seduce a reaction from the audience. Smiling mildly, THE SPEAKER returns the device to his pocket. When he continues, he speaks once again in a colorless monotone.]

Thus begins a Punch and Judy show. Why shouldn't it suit us? It's no crowd of children Punch's weird shriek summons this evening, but a gathering of the *pupamaniacs:* Thomas Ligotti, Heinrich von Kleist, Marcel Schwob, and all writers of their turbulent ilk. There are few who would feel the thrill of "happiness" at the announcement of this austere gathering, but those who do know already why we are here. This modest heralding of the Puppet King is redundant in that it is an initiation for the initiates, a prophecy over which prophets have already exhausted their fervor. Like all things, the coming of the Puppet King is a play of itself, a puppet playing puppet.

Let us begin with Schwob, a true *pupamaniac* with his fiction of masks and his manic insistence that the world is layer upon layer of superficialities. In "The Terrestrial Fire," one of Schwob's characteristically brilliant apocalyptic tales written well over a century ago, he says this of the state of mankind as it approaches its collective death rattle:

The final thrust of faith which had swept the world was unable to save it. New prophets had arisen in vain. The mysteries of the will were expounded to no end; it was no longer a question of controlling it, but rather its quantity seemed to diminish. The energy of all living things dissipated. It had been gathered in one supreme effort toward a future religion, and the effort had failed. All withdrew into a very gentle selfishness.[3]

Well? Let me be frank. It is difficult to avoid seeing Schwob's prescient passage reflected in the anxious efforts to keep traditional tenets of faith firmly embedded in the fabric of the law. Nor is it invisible in the rise of the

---

[1] Marcel Schwob, preface to *The King in the Golden Mask* (Wakefiled Press, 2017), 8.
[2] John Payne Collier "The Tragical Comedy, or Comical Tragedy of Punch and Judy," *New England Review* 21, no. 4 (2000): 192.
[3] *The King in the Golden Mask*, 37.

various and amorphous "spiritualities" loosely associated with the "New Age" movement and constructed with fragments from the history of established religions. How weary the world has grown of its own creativity! It is not impossible to imagine that advancements in faith have shared with the arts a postmodern sterility, a Jamesonian primacy of pastiche that manically redeploys the past in an ever-desperate mimicry of the new. Perhaps more startling is Schwob's "very gentle selfishness," where "[e]very passion was tolerated,"[4] an apparent precursor of the nonsensical fear of "The Future Liberals Want." The true "gentle selfishness" is less a regression into some imagined state of decadent morality than pure capitalist excess. Capitalism, as we know, has always rewarded selfishness, and its fruits are more withdrawn from the public gaze than ever. The more visceral wants of late capitalism, intensified by their withdrawal from life—sex, society, charity, tribalism, violence—are serviced almost exclusively online. As we move into the Deleuzian society of control, the ugly necessity of gratifying our desires "outside," like some barbarian horde, has passed. It is all, as the cliché goes, at our fingers, and with them we masturbate freely in the security of the home.

[A small gasp escapes the audience. THE SPEAKER smiles softly and raises his hand, signaling an unseen OPERATOR enthroned in the shadows gathered at the back of the lecture hall. The lights dim. For a moment all is quiet. Then, a beam of light bursts through the heavy air, projecting the words "EMPIRICAL SOLITUDE" in large black letters on a screen behind THE SPEAKER. THE SPEAKER nods slightly and continues]

There is already a dimension of play here. At home, we play at sex, play at politics, play at violence, play at charity, play at social engagement, all by the "once-removed" of online mediation.

We know this human-playing-human is close to what Schwob had in mind with "gentle selfishness," since "The Terrestrial Fire," like nearly all Schwob's work short stories, centers around the impossibility of existential authenticity.[5] In Schwob's vivid and imaginative tale, the Earth allies with the cosmos in an apparent attempt to purge the planet of life. The sun expands and volcanos erupt; the sky bursts into flame as the sun sears the atmosphere. The puppet-people collapse onto the ground, too beaten to resist incineration. All but two of them perish.

---

[4] Ibid.

[5] We can forgive THE SPEAKER for neglecting a thoroughly defensible definition of "authenticity" here, particularly since the existentialists themselves have failed in that respect. If authenticity is no more substantial than a mirage, we shouldn't wonder at the lumbering, inadequate contraptions the philosophers of modernism have been forced to construct to support it. If we bemoan the absence of a similar edifice here, it's due to the habit rather than the necessity of bearing such a useless load.

The two who emerge are a boy and girl, "hardly beyond the confines of childhood," sharing, innocently, "the affection of a brother and sister."[6] Hand in hand, they make their way through the ruined waste of civilization. In the heat of destruction, they come across a boat. With it, they flee the wall of fire the sun now drags along its course. Eventually, they find themselves adrift in the endless dead ocean. Here, Schwob's gift of hallucinogenic scenery is at full force. As a tower of steam begins to swallow the young couple, "[l]ife embraced them; suddenly, they were living more quickly; adolescence seized them in the burning of the world."[7] We cannot imagine that the children's age has supernaturally advanced. Their sudden maturity is surely the child of shared disaster, the eminence of death and the dim consciousness of the promises their bodies will never fulfill. In the end, the girl turns to the boy, naked. "Let's fall in love," she says.[8]

It's the desperation of the play of the premature couple that gives the story its ultimate power. It isn't quite innocence, given the face of the sheer destruction they've witnessed, nor does Schwob allow for innocence in the explicit introduction of an artificial "adolescence" that "seizes" them. Their "love," Schwob suggests, is more sincere than the "gentle selfishness" of the recently annihilated, but it is nevertheless a play. "Let's fall in love"—as if it's a scene in a movie! Rather than a sudden burst of truly sexual desire— their age and situation preclude that—their love is the conscious acting of a script written inside them for a future play they will not live to embody. Their future denied, they have decided to act love out, however prematurely. They are little humans playing human, but unlike their gently selfish parents, they play their parts consciously. In the self-conscious resignation of the illusion of humanity, the reign of the Puppet King is at hand.

Our "gentle selfishness" is that life has become more thing-like. We are less like the seductive illusions of autonomy we create than puppets playing at them. In the occupational sphere (which accounts for the majority of our public existence), the drive toward mechanical efficiency—the initial thingification of the human at the heart of the industrial revolution—has given way to a loosely defined attitude of "customer service." Work, uncomfortable with the uncanny face it necessarily presented the consumer, now demands a further artificiality, a self-conscious play at humanity—*Greet them with a smile! Show them that you are genuinely happy to be of service!* It is no longer enough to play the part of the worker—now you must play the worker while playing the human. Give lie to the bald fact that you are not here of your own free will. The workplace of the future will be designed to mime the comfort of your living room.

In politics as well, we are humans playing human, halfheartedly miming a political presence already diluted by a simple either/or duality of

---

[6] Ibid, 39.
[7] Ibid, 41.
[8] Ibid, 42.

party alliance. Where are our stakes? Is there any true sense that political change is possible? Do we not dimly suspect that our culturally approved options have subtly excluded any real access to radical alternatives? Is our weary, inanimate politics of half-felt but vociferous convictions the result of simple satiety? Is it the case that the old grievances against capitalism have been sufficiently addressed? Or does our puppet theater operate under the shadow of a political presence that we have forgotten how to fully inhabit?

Above all, the thingification of the cosmos has sealed the thinghood of humanity. The Hermetic correspondence between the macrocosm and microcosm, so easily dismissed in the purely quantitative discourse of the sciences, is a powerful concept that we ignore at great risk. If philosophy has neatly divided the human and the natural with its blind anthropocentrism (a division sharply criticized by Object Oriented Ontology, or, as it is popularly known, "OOO"), it hasn't weakened the intuitive sense that we share the substance of the cosmos no matter the mode in which we appear. The microcosm—never the macrocosm, ever secure in its unchanging indifference—is what is at risk when H.P. Lovecraft famously wrote that "[t]he most merciful thing in the world [...] is the inability of the human mind to correlate all its contents."[9] It's science's revelation of an indifferent, mechanistic cosmos that provokes Lovecraft's horror, and it's the same sense of cosmic dread he seeks to cultivate in his fiction. How, indeed, could such a revelation be terrible if it were not reflected in our own existence? Or, as Jason Bahbak Mohaghegh writes in a provocative mirroring of this terror, "is the dread of the universe not the same as the dread of the machine writ large?"[10]

[THE SPEAKER pauses to signal THE OPERATOR again. After a moment, the slide behind him changes, reading "EXISTENTIAL SOLITUDE" in the same large font. As he continues his monologue, THE SPEAKER's voice begins to exhibit signs of decay. An occasional, quiet creaking is audible, like gears under strain. He bites off the ends of some words with a snap, as if his jaw is victim of an infrequent but involuntary spasm. His tone, no longer monotonous, is enthralled, sardonic.]

The reflection of the mechanical universe in the vacancy of the puppet's soul brings us precisely to Thomas Ligotti's troubled doorstep. If Lovecraft sublimated horror's fixation on violence against the body into a violence against the mind, Ligotti's work furthers the process of rarefication with what might be called ontological violence, a violence against being. His best stories pursue this violence with monomaniacal fervor, climaxing in a dark transcendence of the metaphorical mirror in a literal recognition of the microcosm *as* the macrocosm. Ligotti's maniacs—for his strongest characters

---

[9] H. P. Lovecraft, "The Call of Cthulhu," in *The Cthulhu Mythos Megapack* (Wildside Press, 2012), loc. 7070.

[10] Jason Bahbak Mohaghegh, *Omnicide: Mania, Fatality, and the Future-in-Delirium* (Urbanomic Media Ltd. & Sequence Press, 2019), loc. 477.

are all maniacs—repeatedly find themselves drawn to some haunting feature in their lives or community. Either individually or as part of a collective effort, the protagonist resolves to satisfy his obsession with the otherworldly feature *at all costs*. Under investigation, the mechanical, hollow, or puppet-like nature of the thing is revealed, only to be equated to a hitherto defining aspect of the character himself. It's not that the hollow machines in Ligotti's tales swallow the protagonist, but that the hollow core of the protagonist swallows the machine—it's as if something in their puppet humanity actively seeks atonement with the puppet hollowness of the void.

There are plenty of stories in Ligotti's oeuvre to support this observation. Here, we will examine four of them. In "The Bungalow House," a man who spends his listless days eating in a threadbare art gallery that doubles as the headquarters of some obscure, backdoor industry listens to *The Bungalow Tapes*, a prerecorded meditation on the titular (fictional?) locale. With an increasing obsessiveness, Ligotti's protagonist tries to gather more work by the same artist, only to discover that *he* is the artist, uncannily projecting his creations from a split self locked away in the vacuous underworld that lies outside of consciousness. In the end, the attainment of his manic object—the original manuscripts of the recorded audio—fails to bring him relief, tormenting him instead with a doubled emptiness.

In "The Town Manager," we are again called to observe an obscure but desperate curiosity edge itself into oblivion. The residents of a ruined, nightmare town are in constant wonder before the inscrutability of an increasingly invisible series of town managers. It's clear that a supreme uselessness pervades the community, which has already seen and forgotten its heyday, inhabiting the "post-apocalyptic" tense of Samuel Beckett's work, a time "after the end." The story opens with the arrival of a new town manager who, like his predecessors, pushes the town's designs further toward functionless absurdity. Briefly transformed into "Funny Town," the buildings and alleyways are expanded into maddening labyrinths scattered with "attractions" that the townspeople are now forced to tend. Ligotti's protagonist uncritically embraces his new employment as a broth vendor and, briefly, the town enjoys a fresh wave of commerce attracted by the novelty of the place. Still, the tourist trade was never expected to last for long, and the time comes for a new town manager. Who should be selected if not our own, now-disenchanted protagonist?

Our third example, "Dream of a Manakin," returns us explicitly to the realm of *pupamania* (although we have never truly left it, just as Ligotti's stories are always imbued with the terrors of living thinghood). In this epistolary tale, a psychoanalyst writes to a colleague concerning a patient who complained of startlingly realistic dreams haunted by the malicious presence of mannequins. As the story progresses, it becomes clear that the recipient of the letter is a *pupamaniac* in the grips of a metaphysical obsession that posits an all-devouring, uncanny self in charge of the lesser selves hidden behind the guise of the unified subject. A familiarity with *The Conspiracy Against the Human Race*, Ligotti's own book-length meditations on nihilism and the uncanny, is helpful here, since much of the obscure theory underlying "Dream of a Manakin" is clearly articulated in the former. In short, his female colleague's *pupamania* infects the protagonist by his (accidental?) encounter with the shared analysand, and the story climaxes in a literal thingification, a startling atonement with the nothingness of the mannequin as reflected in the dissolute nature of subjectivity.

[THE SPEAKER, in an apparent effort to subdue his agitation, suddenly grips the lectern. His gaze flickers blindly across the hall. A cold paralysis seizes his features. The ridge of shadows cast across his face intensifies in a pained grimace. Quickly, he centers on the darkness gathered at the back of the hall. After a moment, he finds what he needs there—an unseen signal, some unknown reassurance from the depths—and he regains control, shuffling the notes before him with a slight tremor. The audience doesn't react. He continues.]

But let us briefly pause this worship of Ligotti, whose ideas are both central to and must be transcended for the purposes of the present work. Before we move on to our last and most vital example from his dazzling oeuvre, it's necessary to explain the relevance of *mania* to the coming of the Puppet King. Why have I brought a vaguely clinical discourse carrying overtones of psychosis to bear on a subject that decidedly emphasizes our proximity to thinghood? Could any area of study be more alien to "mental health"? The denizens of the puppet kingdom are already aware of "mental health," even though it's partially the regulatory function of the DSM itself that ratifies their melancholy citizenship. While puppets play human by adjusting their act to fit the confines of normalcy, the Puppet King has long recognized itself as an object in play and fills the same motion with a trickster's multifaceted energy. In this, the Puppet King makes mental health, along with the madness his royal existence entails, an art.

But the Puppet King is no *pupamaniac* himself. In his magnificent book, *Omnicide*, Jason Bahbak Mohaghegh employs a hermeneutics of mania to literary works from the Middle East. What results is "nothing less than a catalogue of insane reinventions of subjectivity in an always already insane world, transpiring under the guidance of the self-misguided: namely, those who claim alternative titles, missions, lineages, and stakes in creation."[11] Already we see that mania operates well outside of the puppet play of the everyday sort. It is simultaneously a refusal to play human combined with the adoption of an alternative role. Within the throes of this acute madness we find "[t]he mesmerizing costume that perception must wear in order to overthrow the regime of an inherited existence (individual fiction versus

---

[11] Ibid., loc, 244.

universal fiction)."[12] It is with this fiction that *pupamaniac* radically externalizes the puppet stage, the only method that frees reality as an object for characterization. Nevertheless, it is a dangerous step outside, tantamount to the destruction of reality (omnicide). The singular vision of the *pupamaniac*, like all maniacs, is subject to the process whereby "[t]he arrival of a minor fixation (a luring of the fascinated gaze toward some object, image, sensation, or whim) increasingly expands and mutates into a lethal articulation."[13] This is why Ligotti acknowledges the dangers of his own ruminations, candidly pointing out that "the worst possible thing we could know—worse than knowing of our descent from a mass of microorganisms— is that we are nobodies not somebodies, puppets not people."[14]

Mad they may be, and seductive to those who have already begun to suspect their surroundings of a curious emptiness, we cannot deny the nightmare logic of the *pupamaniacs*. It is impossible to approach the Puppet King without them. I bring the maniac sharply into focus here to prepare us for our final reading of Ligotti. You have been prepared, now let us act. The realm of the manic, as Mohaghegh articulates it, "is the performative engagement of the neo-magical, though devoid of its former affiliations: the prophetic without transcendence (for no higher power must intervene), the miraculous without belief (for no great leap of faith is required), the sacred without law (for no dogmatic structure can tame its ecstatic arc). Just the leanest mixtures of anomaly, revelation, and disaster."[15] It is, then, a vision without the supporting structure of tradition, a radically individual metaphysics that refuses to maintain appearances. This is why the *pupamaniac* is at home in the ontological violence of dreams.

In this terrible spirit of imaginative fermentation, a sea-change sharpened into nightmarish vigor by the delirium of creation, we turn now to "Dr. Locrian's Asylum." Ligotti's protagonist, Mr. Crane, shares another of the communal obsessions that populate Ligotti's work. At the edge of the town lies the ruins of the titular asylum, whose appearance and troubled history haunts the adjoining citizens. Faces peek through the building's opaque windows, recalling to each citizen some half-forgotten glimpse of the institution's bizarre interior. Like the Red Tower in "The Red Tower," the emptiness inside Dr. Locrian's asylum remains productive even though it has surpassed its functional capability. Instead of resting in the stasis of discarded things, it actively decays the town—or at least the consciousness of its citizens—with the persistence of a steady gaze that can be felt but not seen.

---

[12] Ibid., loc, 251.

[13] Ibid., loc, 280.

[14] Thomas Ligotti, *The Conspiracy Against the Human Race*, (Hippocampus Press, 2010), 109.

[15] *Omnicide: Mania, Fatality, and the Future-in-Delirium*, loc., 272.

Eventually, the citizens decide to eradicate the asylum. Soon, Mr. Locrian, the grandson of the institution's founder, visits Mr. Crane to pick up an order of books. Mr. Locrian then tells Crane of his grandfather, a man who did not seek to heal the patients under his care but used horrifying means to exacerbate their illnesses to the furthest extremes. In a whispered tirade against those who questioned his methods, he laments that "[they] did not look into the eyes of those beings, the eyes that reflected the lifeless beauty of the silent, staring universe itself."[16] The elder Mr. Locrian had sought—and apparently found—a relentless plateau of madness that surpassed the object of mania, that negated *all objects*, an instance of violence against the very notion of being itself. By the end of the tale, the ghostly inmates of the asylum have repopulated the town, hiding behind windows of abandoned buildings and tapping against the floors of apartments in the dark, unwilling victims to the old doctor's negative ecstasies. But while Ligotti's characters dissolve in the miasma of supernatural invasion, we must note here a boon, however terrible, gleaned from facing the extremes of uncanniness: "The result was something as pathetic as a puppet and as exalted as the stars, something at once dead and never dying, a thing utterly without destiny and thus imperishable, forever consigned to that abysmal vacuity which is the essence of all that is immortal."[17] All hail the Puppet King!

[THE SPEAKER signals THE OPERATOR and the slide changes once more. Now it reads "ONTOLOGICAL SOLITUDE." By this time, THE SPEAKER's voice has altered radically. The popping of gears is constantly audible and strange, metallic harmonies shimmer on the edge of his voice. As speech becomes more and more of a physical strain, an increasingly desperate vigor carries it further, as if THE SPEAKER found in the pain of his articulations a source of limitless pleasure.]

Just as Punch escapes death by fooling his executioner into suicide, just as he murders the Devil who has come to take his soul, the Puppet King, summoned by madness, will lift us above the omnicidal violence we have employed to summon him. Although Ligotti's work thrives in the dim light of the uncanny, there is more to the puppet than mere emptiness. There is another side of our inanimate selves, a vast hunger appropriate to our emptiness that drives the Puppet King further into the play of existence. He thrives in an intimacy with life that can only be obtained by thingification, for becoming inanimate is an equalizing force that erases the tired distinction of subject and object, man and nature, being and thinghood. As an energetic agent of difference, the Puppet King is a trickster, like Carlo Collodi's Pinocchio (let's ignore the neutered Disney retelling): it plays the human only too well, with all the usual (and often magnified) faults and

---

[16] Thomas Ligotti, "Dr. Locrian's Asylum," in *Songs of a Dead Dreamer and Grimscribe,* (Penguin Books, 2015), 194.

[17] Ibid., 196.

graces, an object of divine light and abysmal darkness contrasting brilliantly the cold gray of those puppets who haven't the courage to realize they aren't human. The Puppet King isn't human—he is more.

Heinrich von Kleist, a *pupamaniac* of a different, more aerial comportment than our previous companions, writes in "On the Marionette Theater" of the comparative grace of the puppet and human dancer. Framed as a conversation between the narrator and a dancer friend, the former expresses some dismay at the latter's enjoyment of the low art of the marionette theater. Astonishingly, the dancer tells the narrator that "a dancer who wanted to improve themselves could learn from the marionettes."[18] What ensues is a fascinating argument based on the puppet's superior lack of a "soul." As any public performer knows, the dancer's consciousness is his own greatest enemy. It is consciousness that erupts a movement of grace with a paroxysm of doubt; it chokes a musician's memory with intrusive distractions. Consciousness withdraws exactly when the amateur calls upon it in speech and persists stubbornly when the more experienced speaker wisely seeks to banish it. Consciousness is Ligotti's true enemy, the thing that perceives the puppet in the human and can't reconcile the challenge to its own authority. The puppet itself, mercifully unfettered by such things, is closer to a god than man.

Kleist concludes his dialogue as follows: "when knowledge has gone through infinity, it comes to grace again; so that simultaneously, in the human body's form, grace shines purest either in bare emptiness or in infinite awareness, i.e., in the form of a god."[19] There is no way back to a state of innocence from knowledge. All that is left is the way forward, a conscious embodiment of our thinghood, a playing of our role with the mad fervor of a vessel awaiting the invasion of a strange god.

We must accept our role as Puppet Kings. We cannot turn back the clock. We have read the "fiction" of Ligotti, Schwob, and Kleist. We have heard the cold, cosmic wind moaning through the cracks in our facade. To continue glancing over our shoulders for the blind, star-filled eyes of the machine is to tease the lock on the door to oblivion. Let us throw open the door entirely! We crumble before the void only to be reborn in "infinite awareness," new mouths for the voracious hunger of cosmic emptiness ready to feast on all we have been hitherto denied.

The Puppet King continues the play of humanity knowing that all its science, politics, religion, and philosophy is mere artifice, a fiction miming life—hasn't philosophy acknowledged as much with its indispensable *noumenon?*—and therefore best approached as play. Yes, the Puppet King is a terrible, joyous thing, creating with enthusiasm and destroying with glee,

---

[18] Heinrich von Kleist, "On the Marionette Theatre," in *On the Marionette Theatre and On the Assembly of Thought While Talking: Two Essays by Heinrich von Kleist*, (2019), loc. 9.
[19] Ibid., loc. 111.

laughing at the scripted role before it while fulfilling it with fanatic vigor. That is the divinity of the Puppet King, this intermingling of joy with horror, this endless hunger—a true desiring-machine of appetite out of which the fabric of the cosmos emanates.

At the end of *Don Quixote,* perhaps the greatest puppet play in all of literature, Sancho Panza, Quixote's loyal companion, urges the Knight of the Sorrowful Countenance to take up the role of puppet once more. "Don't die, Señor," he pleads, "your grace should take my advice and live for many years, because the greatest madness a man can commit in this life is to let himself die, just like that, without anybody killing him or any other hands ending his life except those of melancholy. Look, don't be lazy, but get up from that bed and let's go to the countryside dressed as shepherds, just like we arranged: maybe behind some bush we'll find Señora Doña Dulcinea disenchanted, as pretty as you please."[20] All hail the coming of the Puppet King!

[As he screams this last line, THE SPEAKER collapses. His body convulses violently in the bare light of the projector. The clamor of his wooden frame echoes throughout the vast auditorium. The puppet audience recoils in horror. After a few moments, he falls still. All is silent. Lights dim.

Hesitantly, a few members of the puppet audience gather their belongings, glancing at each other for reassurance. Others join them, and they are suddenly emboldened. One of the puppets mutters something and those close enough to hear it laugh. They are at ease now, as if the whole affair was a joke. THE SPEAKER, willfully forgotten, is left behind onstage. One by one, they shuffle out of the lecture hall and into the night.

Out on the sidewalk, one of them points to the sky. They all stop. It's you they see, reader, looming enormously against the star-choked emptiness, a featureless silhouette above their tiny, inanimate world. They look away, taking forced, measured steps to their abodes, trying to forget the impossible thing they've witnessed. If they would've dared look longer, they would've traced the faint outline of your strings, disappearing far above you in the deep, vertiginous black.]

---

[20] Miguel de Cervantes, *Don Quixote,* (Harper Collins, 2009), 937.

Bibliography

Cervantes, Miguel de. *Don Quixote*. Translated by Edith Grossman. Harper Collins, 2009.

Collier, John Payne. "The Tragical Comedy, or Comical Tragedy of Punch and Judy." In *New England Review* 21, no. 4 (2000): 191-215. Middlebury College Publications.

Kleist, Heinrich von. "On the Marionette Theatre." In *On the Marionette Theatre and On the Assembly of Thought While Talking: Two Essays by Heinrich von Kleist*. Translated by Andrew Jansen. 2019.

Ligotti, Thomas. "Dr. Locrian's Asylum." In *Songs of a Dead Dreamer and Grimscribe*. Penguin Books, 2015.

Ligotti, Thomas. *The Conspiracy Against the Human Race*. Hippocampus Press, 2010.

Lovecraft, H. P. "The Call of Cthulhu." In *The Cthulhu Mythos Megapack*. Wildside Press, 2012.

Mohagheg, Jason Bahbak. *Omnicide: Mania, Fatality, and the Future-in-Delirium*. Urbanomic Media Ltd. & Sequence Press, 2019.

Schwob, Marcel. *The King in the Golden Mask*. Translated by Kit Schulter. Wakefield Press, 2017.

publication history

"The Toy Shop" original to this volume

"Sister" first published in *At the Rim of Daylight*, a Patreon-exclusive chapbook, Silent Motorist Media, 2021)

"Devourer" original to this volume

"The Rubber Man" original to this volume

"Endemic" original to this volume

"ABDN-1" original to this volume

"m.Other" first published in *Esoteric Sausage and Other Malformations* by NihilismRevised, 2018

"She" first published in *Mannequin: Tales of Wood Made Flesh* by Silent Motorist Media, 2019

"The Enucleator" original to this volume

"The Golden Thread" original to this volume

"A Prisoner's Guide to Stargazing" original to this volume

"Our Endeavors" original to this volume

"Laberinto" original to this volume

"The Puppet King" first published in a limited edition of five promotional, Kickstarter-exclusive chapbooks, Silent Motorist Media, 2020

acknowledgments

FIRST, THANK YOU, reader, for purchasing and reading this book of mine. I hope it brought you something—if not happiness, then the strange, lingering pleasure derived by the vague recollection of a nightmare will do. Thanks to Scarlett Algee for providing these stories a home, and Sam L. Edwards for the kind introduction. Thank you to Matthew Henshaw for the endless encouragement and support. Every subscriber over at Silent Motorist Media's Patreon page deserves a hearty wave as well (honestly you are the ones who keep this machine running). And Vincenzo Bilof, I can't thank you enough for being this collection's biggest supporter from the beginning—I often recall your encouragement as I lumber ahead. Jo Kaplan, your enthusiasm truly pushed me across a speed bump of insecurity surrounding this project—thank you for that. I'll never forget your response to this book, Justin Isis (I literally have the whole thing saved in a docx file). Also, Brian Evenson, not only for writing the books you write, but for your friendship and advice (in writing and reading alike). Philip Fracassi, Matthew M. Bartlett, and Jon Padgett—I consider myself lucky to know you all. Scott Dwyer, B.R. Yeager (hope all is well with you, friend), and Rebecca Gransden: you as well. There are also the many writers I admire from a distance (Ligotti, Cisco, Shipley), some of whom I've even had the opportunity to work with in some capacity (Campbell, Files, Langan)... the list goes on. They're no small part the reason I've been able to make bring this book into the world.

There are undoubtedly many who should be mentioned here but aren't. The list of generous souls who have contributed in some way to my ability to remain sane despite the insane compulsion to produce books grows daily.

Above all, thanks to Chelsea and the kids for the love and support through all this. I'm sure it isn't always as easy as you make it look. I'm lucky as hell to have you.

about the author

JUSTIN A. BURNETT is the author of *The Puppet King and Other Atonements*. He's also the Executive Editor of Silent Motorist Media, a weird fiction press responsible for the publication of the anthologies *Mannequin: Tales of Wood Made Flesh*, which was named best horror anthology of 2019 by Rue Morgue magazine, *The Nightside Codex*, and *Hymns of Abomination*, a tribute to the work of Matthew M. Bartlett. He currently lives in Austin, Texas, with his wife and children.